THE WOMEN OF BAKER STREET

Michelle Birkby has always loved crime stories, and read her first Sherlock Holmes book when she was thirteen. She was given a beautiful collection of all the short stories and has been hooked with the wonderful, gas-lit, atmospheric world of crime and adventure ever since. A few years ago Michelle was re-reading *The Empty House* and a blurred figure in the background suddenly came into focus. It became clear to her that Mrs Hudson was much more than a housekeeper to 221b and she'd always been fascinated by Mary Watson's character. So she set about giving the women of Baker Street a voice and adventures of their own . . . *The Women of Baker Street* is the second book in the series, following *The House at Baker Street*.

Also by Michellé Birkby

The House at Baker Street

THE
WOMEN
OF
BAKER
STREET

MICHELLE BIRKBY

PAN BOOKS

First published 2017 by Pan Books
an imprint of Pan Macmillan
20 New Wharf Road, London N1 9RR
Associated companies throughout the world
www.panmacmillan.com

ISBN 978-1-5098-0973-8

Pan Macmillan does not have any control over, or any responsibility for,
any author or third-party websites referred to in or on this book.

1 3 5 7 9 8 6 4 2

A CIP catalogue record for this book is available from the British Library.

Typeset in Adobe Caslon Pro by Palimpsest Book Production Ltd, Falkirk, Stirlingshire
Printed and bound by CPI Group (UK) Ltd, Croydon, CR0 4YY

Visit www.panmacmillan.com/www.picador.com to read more about all
our books and to buy them. You will also find features, author interviews
and news of any author events, and you can sign up for e-newsletters
so that you're always first to hear about our new releases.

To Shyama. For all the book talks.

THE WOMEN OF BAKER STREET

HOSPITAL WARD LAYOUT

PUBLIC WARD

CORRIDOR

SISTER'S DESK

Sarah Malone		
Martha Hudson	STOVE	Flo Bryson
Miranda Logan	DESK	Emma Fordyce
Betty Soland		Eleanor Langham

TOILET	CLOAKROOM
TOILET	
BATHROOM	STOREROOM & GAS RING

PROLOGUE

I am lying so still. My body is a leaden weight that I cannot move, my eyes fluttering open and closed, open and closed over and over again. I am hardly aware if I'm awake or not, dying or living. Perhaps closer to dying. I can feel death creeping up on me, waiting for that one moment of weakness.

Stupid, stupid! Don't be so melodramatic. Don't be a silly old woman. What would Mr Holmes think? And yet . . . I can see Him. Death, I mean. He's there, right there, creeping between the beds, choosing one of us. He doesn't look like his pictures. There's no scythe, or robe. He barely exists, just a patch of shadow in the pale moonlight, but he is there.

As he passes me, I know enough, even in my drug-induced stupor, to close my eyes and feign a peaceful sleep. He passes by, and once I feel he is gone, I open them again.

I'm safe. I've passed whatever test he had for me. Now he is examining the others. I feel I ought to call out, warn them, wake them, but I can't move. My limbs feel weighted down, my body feels part of the bed, my voice won't come.

I can't stop him. I can only watch.

The shadow crosses to another bed; another woman is

breathing heavily, fast asleep. It only takes him a moment. The shadow moves on top of her, and in less than a few minutes, she is silent.

At night, in pain, drugged, I dreamed I saw Death come. In daylight, well and awake, I know I saw a murder.

But who will believe me? After all, people die in hospital all the time.

AN UNEXPECTED WEAKNESS

My name is Mrs Martha Hudson. I am landlady, house-keeper and goodness knows what else to the Great Detective, Sherlock Holmes, at his home (well, my home, he is my tenant), 221b Baker Street. It is 30 October 1889, and he has only recently returned from his adventure in Dartmoor. He has been quiet, insular almost, since his return, keeping to his rooms. His friend, Dr John Watson, took his wife Mary Watson – my closest friend – away on holiday for two weeks to Edinburgh as soon as he returned from Dartmoor. Billy, the page-boy at 221b, has gone with them, to try to expand his horizons beyond London, and so I have been blessedly, wonderfully alone and silent for almost two weeks.

I need the peace.

Months earlier, Mary and I had tracked down a man who had been blackmailing women, not for money, but power. He had gone mad, and progressed to bloody murder, and we found him. And when we found him – well, I tried not to think about that. I still cannot decide if it was my fault.

When I was around other people I couldn't push the image of that night from my mind. Someone would say something and back it would all come to me, flooding my

3

mind with memories I didn't want. Just an innocent phrase, even a word would trigger such disturbing recollections, and I would have to stop myself from crying out, all too aware I could give myself away. But alone I could push the thoughts away, I could hide them in the back of my mind, I could just not think about it. When I was alone, I could choose my own thoughts. No one would remind me.

To distract myself I have been baking: my favourite pastime. Today was my last chance, as the Watsons were due back. Cooking is my greatest skill, and I have just delivered my latest batch of cakes to Rebecca Fey, the owner of the grocery ten minutes down my street. I had welcomed her to the neighbourhood with a homemade cake (it pays to be on good terms with the local grocer) and she had, after tasting it, told me that many people would pay good money for a homemade cake they hadn't had to make them- selves, and asked could I supply more.

I didn't need the money, but I do enjoy the work. Still, Rebecca had noted I was a little tired, and I was glad to be home.

I was tired, I admit. I usually don't run 221b by myself, but the latest daily help had to be sacked after I caught her reading Mr Holmes' notes. The women I hire to help me turn out to be working for criminals, or newspapers, or even the police! It's very difficult to find someone trustworthy these days. Still, I was strong; I could manage until I found someone reliable.

At least, I told myself I was strong. I had not been

altogether well lately, though I was not going to give in to my temporary weakness.

I let myself in through the front door of 221b, and heard Mr Holmes come out of his rooms on the first floor.

'It's only me,' I called. 'Dr Watson isn't back yet.'

He grunted and went back in.

'I'm sure he'll come round as soon as the train gets in!' I shouted after him, amused at Mr Holmes trying so hard to look as if he wasn't waiting for his friend.

That was when I found myself grasping the stair post, waves of pain shooting through my body, horrific, tearing pain that took my breath away and made my knees buckle. I hung on, panting, waiting for it to stop. It had to stop, it always stopped. It had never been so bad before, though. Above me, I heard Mr Holmes leave his rooms. Why now? What if he saw me? I didn't want him seeing me in this state. I just had to get down the steps to my kitchen, it would be all right, everything would be all right, as long as I could get to my kitchen.

And that was when it all went dark, and I collapsed in a heap at Mr Holmes' feet.

It all happened so fast after that. I felt Mr Holmes gently raise me up and heard him question me. I heard the Watsons come through the door, and knew John had sent Billy to fetch a cab, but all I could focus on was the pain shooting through my stomach, and then, to my eternal embarrassment, I passed out again.

John actually carried me to the cab! And then to St Bartholomew's Hospital, and even through to the small ward. He had doctor's privileges there, and he had me admitted right away.

I had been ill for a little while, just pain in my stomach that came and went after meals. Indigestion, I thought, possibly some sort of stomach infection. Nothing to worry about, or make a fuss about – how I hated making a fuss! But now, here I was, in hospital, and they were talking about surgery. I was afraid, but I didn't tell them, and I didn't murmur when they put me to sleep for my operation.

I woke up still hazy from the morphine and anaesthetic.

It was dark by then. I was lying in a narrow, iron-framed bed. There were two green fabric screens, one on either side of my bed, so all I could see was the bed directly opposite me, and the corners of two others on either side of it. In the very dim lamp light, I could discern another woman sleeping in the bed across from mine. I lay still, looking around me as much as I could. I was aware other people were in the room though I could not see them: I could hear breathing, and snoring, and someone shifting in bed and the pages of a book being turned. I could hear soft footsteps, and a murmur.

I didn't like being here. I didn't like sleeping in a room with strangers. I am uncomfortable being helpless at any time, let alone in a strange place, and I missed my warm and cosy bed. I tried to move, but my limbs felt so heavy I just lay still. I could not think straight. The whiteness of the sheets floated in the darkness. Noises that made no sense came and went. This sharp-smelling world was strange to me, and my head spun and ached. Somehow, in this odd new place, I was not surprised when I realized there was a shadow in the corner, just beyond the edge of the screens, so much darker than the rest of the room. I watched, uncaring, as the shadow crossed the foot of my bed. It was a vaguely human shape, but I was so befuddled it could have taken the form of a giant hound and I would not have cared. The shadow crossed to the bed diagonally opposite me. It leaned over the bed, and I finally drifted into a fitful sleep.

The next morning I discovered the woman in that bed had died. The shadow, I was certain, was nothing more than a bad dream, caused by drugs and darkness, all on the morning of Halloween.

That was the start of my second case.

THE VIEW
FROM MY BED

I woke slowly the next morning, as the thin grey daylight flooded into the room. I could see now I was in a small side ward. The green fabric screens on either side of me had been pulled back, hanging from the frame at the top of the bed. I could see the room had white-painted walls, and high, large windows. The floor was wooden and highly polished and the heels of the nurses clicked on it as they walked up and down the ward. There was a wooden door at the far right end of the ward, and another door, open to the corridor outside, to my left, directly in front of the Sister's desk. Within the centre of the room, dividing the two rows of beds, was a stove and another desk. It was warm in the ward, but the windows were open and I could feel a cold breeze across my face. It must have been early, as most of the patients were still asleep, hunched under brilliantly white sheets and heavy grey blankets. The woman to my left, however, was wide awake, and I could hear her restlessly clutching at her sheets and murmuring. A nurse was trying to soothe her, and I could hear what I assumed to be the other nurses, and a woman I supposed to be the Ward Sister, gathered at the top end of the ward, having a low conversation.

Beside my bed was a locker, and wooden chair, and such a welcome sight: Mary Watson, my best and perhaps only friend.

Her head was slumped in sleep, her hat fallen on the floor and her golden curls askew.

'Mary,' I whispered. She woke immediately, sitting bolt upright in her chair.

'How do you feel?' she asked. I took a moment to think whilst I assessed myself. I was unsure of where I was and what was happening, my head felt oddly empty, my body stiff and my throat sore. I was aware of an odd, tight sensation in my stomach.

'Like I ought to be in pain, but I'm not.'

'That's the morphine,' Mary reassured me, sitting down gingerly on my bed, careful not to jolt me. 'John says you can't have it for very long though.'

'I've no wish to become addicted,' I assured her. 'I can take pain.' I thought of Mr Holmes and the dark haggard days when the needle barely left his arm and his eyes were full of oblivion.

'You won't,' Mary said. 'You won't be taking it long enough.'

'Mary,' I said, peering round the clean, bright room and at the women beginning to awake and the nurse casting a disapproving glance at Mary on my bed, 'where exactly am I?'

9

'Oh, right, sorry!' she said quickly. 'I suppose it all happened so fast. We arrived at Baker Street just as you collapsed, perfect timing. John took you to St Bartholomew's.'

'This doesn't look like St Bartholomew's,' I said dubiously. 'I thought it had those huge pavilion wards.'

'You're in one of the private side wards,' Mary confided, 'for special friends of the staff and supporters of St Barts. John pulled a few strings.'

'I see.' It didn't feel private, sharing a room with other women and countless nurses, but I supposed it was better than the main wards which could hold over a hundred.

'You had a stomach obstruction,' Mary told me, standing up and restlessly straightening my sheets. 'They operated immediately and cleared the blockage. Now you just have to heal.'

'How long do I have to stay?' I asked. I missed home already.

'I'm not sure,' Mary said, not looking at me, a sure sign she was lying. 'John will talk to you later. I'm really not supposed to be here at this hour, I just came to bring you a few things.'

I was too tired to press her. She picked up a carpet bag and put it on the end of my bed, taking the items out and storing them in the locker to my right.

'I've brought you some personal linen, and cutlery, because they don't supply it, and towels and soap and tea and sugar and a change of clothes.'

'Mary,' I interrupted, but she continued.

10

'I'll visit every day, but in visiting times, of course. I had to sweet talk the Matron into letting me be here when you woke up, but the Sister in charge isn't too happy.'

'Mary . . .'

'I'll bring you books and newspapers, of course, but you need to rest now.'

'Mary!'

She finally stopped talking and looked at me, her face flushed.

'An obstruction?' I asked.

She nodded.

'What kind of obstruction?'

She suddenly saw what I was trying to say.

'Not a tumour!' she said quickly. 'Not that! It was a twist in the bowel, I believe, but it's all sorted out now. You'll be fine.'

'I see,' I said softly. That was all it was, an obstruction? I had imagined all kinds of horrors inside my body. Foul suppurating tumours, black decaying flesh, sapping my strength, and yet it was just an obstruction! I lay back in my bed, berating myself for being a fool.

'You must have been in pain,' Mary said softly. I looked up at her, standing beside my bed, clutching the carpet bag tightly. 'John says it must have hurt. You must have lost weight. You surely knew something was wrong.'

'I didn't, not at first,' I told her. The truth was, I was afraid of whatever had been happening inside me. I didn't want

11

to admit something was going badly wrong. I didn't want to appear weak. 'I thought it would just go away.'

'Go away!' Mary snapped. The nurse shushed her, and she lowered her voice. 'You know this sort of thing doesn't just go away. Even if you couldn't or wouldn't see John, there are hundreds of doctors in London. Thousands! You could have died, Martha!' There were tears in her eyes, and she was shaking, her face as white as my bed sheet.

Oh, I had been so stupid. Mary's mother had died when she was young, her father died in India, her father's friend had died protecting her, and her husband and Mr Holmes came closer to death on a regular basis than any man should. I was supposed to be the safe one. I was supposed to be the one she could depend on to always be there.

'You weren't . . . punishing yourself, were you?' she asked softly, almost in a whisper.

'Punishment?' I asked. She inched closer to the bed, looking round to make sure no one heard.

'For what happened. A few months ago. You know . . .'

We had worked together, back then, she and I. But the ending was wholly mine.

'Is that what you did?' Mary insisted. 'Did you let the pain go on and get worse because you thought you deserved it?'

I didn't answer. I didn't know. I hadn't even thought about it until she mentioned it.

'Because you don't,' she insisted. 'You don't.'

'I'm sorry,' I said to her. 'I am truly sorry. Next time I have even the slightest illness, I will tell someone.'

'Well,' she said, mollified, 'see you do.' She bent down to kiss me. 'Don't worry about Sherlock and Billy,' she said. 'They're coming to stay with me for a while.'

'Is that wise?' I asked her, smiling a little, to show that solemn, heart-rending moment was gone.

'My cook loves John's detective stories,' she said, smiling back. 'She's giddy with joy to think Sherlock Holmes is in the house. He could burn down the kitchen and she'd still think it the most exciting thing to have ever happened to her.'

I laughed as I watched Mary leave the ward. Once she was gone, I looked around me.

Now that the curtains were drawn back, I could see the entire room. The ward had four beds on each side. I was second on the right from the entrance. Beside me, to my left, was the woman who muttered all night long. She lay on her back now, talking to herself still. She didn't sound happy. To my right was a rather exotic woman with long straight black hair, sitting upright in bed, staring out of the window as if she, like me, longed to be elsewhere. She didn't look ill. Beyond her was a woman in her mid-fifties, I'd guess, with fly-away hair, and a huge workbag on her bed. She was already knitting some nondescript garment in grey wool. Opposite her was a woman sitting in an upright chair by her bed. She had a large bandage on her chest, mostly hidden by her white linen nightgown. She sat and watched us all. Even from here I could see her eyes were blue, and piercing, and made me feel distinctly uncomfortable. She saw me looking, and nodded. I nodded back. To the left of her was a woman with very obviously dyed blonde hair, and a heart-shaped face with very fine bones. She looked to be in her eighties, and was smiling happily as she read a magazine. She looked vaguely familiar, but I couldn't place her. Beside her, opposite me, was another grey old lady, with brown round eyes. When I was little, I had a rag doll given to me. The eyes were boot buttons, and were flat and dark. I didn't like that doll, I felt it was always watching me. This woman's eyes reminded me irresistibly of the boot button eyes, flat and dark and staring, set in a doughy face, like a cake that had sagged in the middle. She smiled incessantly, at everyone and everything. And beside her, at the top of the ward – well, it was an empty bed now. But last night I had seen a woman die in that bed.

I was still staring at it when John appeared by my bed.

'I hear Mary was here,' he said to me.

'She was, it was very kind of her,' I said to him. I was slightly embarrassed at him seeing me like this, in a nightgown, vulnerable and helpless, but then he took my pulse with such a professional air that I felt silly to have felt embarrassed at all.

'Well, we caught you just in time,' he said. 'But there's no need to worry. You'll be fine now, after some convalescence.'

To tell the truth, it wasn't the illness that had bothered me. It was that I had given in so easily. I had always thought

14

that I would be one of those who would fight death with all my might. Even with my boy and my love waiting on the other side, there was much to keep me here. I found life sweet. And yet, when I had felt weak, I had not struggled. I had not fought. It just seemed easier to close my eyes and drift away. I had accepted my fate.

Perhaps that was what my dream was about. I stared over at the empty bed.

'What's wrong?' John asked.

'Someone died there last night,' I told him. He frowned at the other bed.

'Did they?' he asked.

'I think I saw it. I had a confusing dream.'

'The morphine and the anaesthetic,' he assured me. 'It's been known to produce odd dreams.'

'How long do I have to stay here?' I demanded. He looked surprised.

'Normally we give you six weeks to recover . . .'

'I can't stay here six weeks!'

'No, I don't suppose you can,' he said, amused. 'That would take you almost to Christmas.'

'Exactly. I have things to do.'

'Well, shall we say three to start with?' he compromised. 'It's not actually up to me, you know. I just got you in here; it's your surgeons you have to convince.'

'I'll convince them. What am I going to do here for three weeks, let alone six?'

He looked around at the ward, at the empty bed, at the other women.

'You're in a unique position,' he said softly. 'You have no calls on your time but to simply sit and observe. You can learn all there is to know about this ward, and these people, and no one will think it odd, or intrusive. I think Holmes would almost envy you.'

He leaned and kissed me on the forehead.

'Do what you do best, Mrs Hudson,' he said quietly to me, so no one could overhear. 'Listen, watch and learn.'

LISTENING, WATCHING AND LEARNING

No one spoke to me that morning, leaving me to recover from the previous day's ordeal. After my bandages were changed (I had an enormous but very neat cut down my stomach), I pleaded tiredness, and was left alone to sleep. Therefore I was content to lie there, and listen.

As you probably know by now, I like to eavesdrop. I like to sit in my kitchen and listen to Mr Holmes in his rooms through the air vent. I like to sit in a tea shop or on the omnibus and listen to people talk about themselves to each other, never dreaming I am listening. I know it's wrong, but it's something I have a talent for. I look the very picture of a quiet, ordinary woman, so absorbed in her own life she couldn't possibly be interested in yours. And yet, I find other people's lives irresistibly fascinating, so I listen.

It was quite a noisy ward, with the Sister, several nurses and cleaners in and out all day. The doctors and surgeons came in to discuss the cases in the ward that morning, and luckily, they talked loudly. I could hear everyone's name, and diagnosis, and therefore knew who was who before I spoke. (I pretended to be asleep when the surgeons came to discuss my case. Apparently my stomach obstruction was quite ordinary, and nothing in my case was worthy of note.)

The woman to my left was Sarah Malone. She was dying. She muttered all the time. I could not hear the words, but judging by the way she clasped and tore at her sheets, she had a great deal on her mind. She stared up at the ceiling as if she saw her doom there, muttering constantly to herself, though her words were never clear. But she wasn't the loudest person on the ward.

That was Betty Soland, in the next bed but one to my right. She had broken her leg falling down the stairs. She knitted or sewed or did some sort of work all the time. The bag on her bed seemed bottomless, and she was constantly pulling a new piece of work out of it, either in shades of grey or brown, or in the most virulent shades of pink or green. She had six children, all girls, between eight and twenty years old, and she talked at the top of her voice constantly, whether anyone was listening or not. By the end of the morning I knew all her children's names, their favourite toys, what schoolwork they were good at and every detail of her own medical treatment. I could not help but think that perhaps her girls were welcoming the silence at home.

Between Betty and me was the quietest person on the ward: Miranda Logan. She barely spoke to anyone. She sat in bed, in a magnificent red dressing gown, and read papers. Apparently she was there because of fatigue and anaemia – which puzzled the doctors as much as it did me. I snatched a quick glance at her as she spoke to them, and saw that she sat upright in her bed, looking strong and healthy, although she insisted she was very tired. Still, this was the special ward, for friends of friends of the hospital, and no one was about to question her too closely. The hospital needed donations. Her accent was – I was going to say odd, but she had no real accent. She spoke in perfectly correct English. However, she hesitated almost imperceptibly before she did so, as if she was remembering exactly how a word ought to be pronounced.

Opposite her was Emma Fordyce. She just seemed to be happy. She had fluffy blonde hair and a mischievous smile, and was basically suffering from old age. Actually, she seemed to be enjoying old age. That morning I discovered she had quite an interesting past, and loved to talk about it. She also had a ribald sense of humour, and occasionally slipped into distinct swearing – laughing as she did it. I liked Emma Fordyce. I resolved to get to know her. She mostly spoke to Florence Bryson, the woman with the brown boot-button eyes opposite me. She had a lung infection, which occurred regularly, so she had stayed on the ward often. Florence's bed was always covered in newspapers – not *The Times*, but the more scandalous gossip sheets. She was fascinated by crimes and detective stories and by gossip about everyone – she was always talking to Emma about her past. I resolved not to let her know I was Mr Holmes' housekeeper. She had already said she loved John's book, and knew every word of it, as well as following any mention of Mr Holmes in the papers. I doubted I would have a moment to myself if she knew who I was.

That left Eleanor Langham.

She had the bed to my far right, diagonally opposite, across from Betty. She rarely sat in the bed. She liked to sit in the chair beside it. She had heart problems and had recently had an operation, and I could see the dressing over the top edge of her plain linen nightgown. She didn't read. She talked, but not much. She just sat, and watched everything that went on. She watched us all. Now I, too, watched, but I watched to learn. I felt, even then, that Eleanor Langham watched to judge.

I did not like Eleanor Langham.

That was all my fellow patients. All that was left was the empty bed.

I still pretended to be heavily asleep, when in fact I was listening to a very interesting conversation indeed.

The Sister of the ward and a doctor stood by the empty bed discussing the previous night's death. They kept their voices low, and as far as they were concerned I couldn't hear a thing.

'I don't understand,' the doctor said. 'The treatment was working. There had been signs of improvement.'

'Sometimes people seem to be doing well, and then, all of a sudden, they're gone,' the Sister replied. She seemed to be far more pragmatic than the younger doctor. Perhaps she was more used to death. Perhaps she just gave up sooner.

He didn't understand how life could just slip away, like sand through fingers.

'But . . . it makes no sense,' he insisted.

'The post-mortem will tell us more,' the Sister soothed him. 'But these things do happen.'

'Well, they shouldn't,' he said irritably as he left.

I kept up my sleeping act until lunchtime. I was only allowed beef tea, but contrary to my suspicions, it was delicious. Then our visitors arrived.

First was a family of six girls, all quite pretty, but all very badly dressed. Their clothes sat wrong, the stitching pulled, the sleeves were too short, or too long, the skirts trailed along the ground unevenly. In short, they could only be the daughters of the inveterate clothes-maker Betty Soland. They lined up at the foot of her bed, where she held out the latest garment she was making for them. I heard the oldest girl sigh a little at the sight.

A tall, military-looking man in his seventies arrived next, and made straight for Eleanor Langham's bed. He kissed her gently and presented her with a posy of violets, which she accepted with a smile. Much as I disliked her (for no other reason than a snap judgement at first sight), he obviously deeply loved her. Opposite me, Emma Fordyce had a man in a suit sit down beside her. He didn't kiss her or touch her like a relative or friend would, so I guessed he was a business acquaintance of some kind. Now what would a woman like her want with a man like that?

21

Mary came rushing in a moment later, hat askew and jacket wrongly buttoned.

'I'm not late. Am I late?' she said breathlessly, recklessly sitting on my bed despite printed warnings on the walls that she should not do that.

'No, you're not,' I said, laughing at her. 'It's kind of you to come.'

'Kind, nothing,' she said cheerfully. 'I'm being nosy, I want to see what goes on in these private wards.'

'Nothing, so far. They all seem very ordinary.'

'Really?' she said, glancing sideways to Miranda Logan, who was managing to look dark and mysterious whilst reading *The Times*.

'Well, have you ever heard the name Emma Fordyce?' I asked in a whisper.

'It rings a bell,' Mary admitted, glancing over her shoulder to the woman I gestured to. 'I'll look her up. In the meantime, I brought you books, *Dr Jekyll and Mr Hyde*, and *Frankenstein*. And *The Times*.'

'That's a bit bloodthirsty, isn't it?' the nurse asked, as she went by.

'Well, that's the way the world is going, *The Times* can't be blamed,' Mary told her sweetly. The nurse tutted and walked away.

'I longed to read *Frankenstein* when I was young, but my mother didn't let me,' I confided.

'I remembered you told me that, and you enjoyed the play of *Jekyll and Hyde* last year. I thought you'd prefer these to

Miss Leman's tales, which I was informed were the very thing for a lady in hospital.'

'I agree with you,' I assured her. Mary looked around, watching the other visitors, but she seemed less curious than usual.

'What's wrong?' I asked. 'What's worrying you? Don't say my illness; I'm fine.'

'Nothing's wrong,' she insisted, trying to be light.

'Your jacket is buttoned incorrectly, your shoes don't match, and you lie abominably,' I told her. She smiled at me.

'Something Wiggins told me,' she said. 'Well, Wiggins told Billy, who told me. Nothing important. I think. Maybe. I'm not sure.'

Wiggins was a street boy, head of the Baker Street Irregulars. He ran around together with our page-boy Billy a lot, and I was sure they had a secret life of adventure they kept very well hidden from us.

'What?' I insisted.

'No, let me look at it a while. It's just impressions for now. I will tell you, I promise.'

I sat back in my bed, defeated. Mary might not be able to lie, but she could keep a secret. She saw my face, and relented a little. She held out *The Times* towards me, folded so I could see the classified advertisements on the front page.

'Look at that,' she said.

'"Waterfall for sale",' I read. 'It's odd, but . . .'

'No, that,' she said, pointing at the advertisement.

'"Required, the entire physical, intellectual and moral

training of a delicate weak boy, even one with physical defects",' I read. I put the paper down. 'This worries you? There are advertisements like this all the time. Someone has a new education system they wish to try out, and requires a subject.'

'A child,' Mary said under her voice. 'A weak boy! And he'll get one, too.'

'You think there's something wrong here?' I asked her.

'Not just here, but in an entire system that sees children sent here and there and everywhere, all over the place, abandoned to strangers by parents who should know better! Who looks after these children? Who ensures their welfare, who makes sure they are not dragged down into depravity, or worse?' she told me in a low, angry voice. 'Parents don't seem to care what happens to their children when they abandon them to the whims of strangers.'

'We care,' I said softly. So, whatever was worrying her, it was to do with children. I wondered what Wiggins had said. And, as always when I thought of Wiggins, my own dead boy appeared in my mind, always running ahead, always beyond my reach.

Mary saw my face, and was instantly contrite. She reached out to grasp my hand.

'You know I didn't mean you. I know you loved your son.'

'Yet I would probably have sent him away to school,' I told her.

'I know, I meant—' She was interrupted. Florence Bryson apparently liked to spend her time wandering up and down the ward, dropping in on other people's visitors, because now she loomed over the end of my bed.

'You have a son?' she said eagerly, grasping the rail at the bottom of my bed.

'I did,' I told her. 'He died, when he was very young.'

'I had a son too,' she confided, utterly ignoring Mary. 'He died also, when he was sixteen.'

'I am sorry for your loss,' I said formally, unsure how to respond.

'At least we have this blessing,' she said, leaning forward to touch my leg through the blanket. 'Our sons can never leave us. They are always with us, even if only in spirit.' She smiled beatifically and walked back to her bed.

'Well, that was slightly morbid,' Mary remarked.

'That's how some people cope with loss,' I said. It wasn't the path I had chosen. My son had gone, my husband had gone and I was alone, but I would live the life I had been given. 'How is Mr Holmes?' I asked, changing the subject.

'I've barely seen him,' Mary said, smiling. 'In fact, he's here now.'

'Here?' I questioned, alarmed he was going to appear in the doorway. It really would not be suitable for Mr Holmes to see me like this.

'He's not visiting,' Mary reassured me. 'He's in St Barts' labs, doing some noxious chemical experiment. He says I shouldn't expect him home until late.'

'Oh,' I said softly. I didn't know what else to say. I glanced towards the walls, as if I'd see him through them. I had always taken a certain comfort and strength from being in the same home as Sherlock Holmes and now, it seemed, I was still only separated from him by a few thin walls.

'Wiggins is keeping an eye on 221b,' Mary said, standing up. 'I am taking care of Sherlock and Billy. All you need do is get better.'

'Thank you,' I said to her, 'for looking after me.'

'Oh, I owe you,' Mary said lightly. 'Remember when I was first married? I was an excellent governess, but knew next to nothing about running a home. You came and taught me all your tricks.'

'Not all of them,' I said.

'Still, I owe you,' she said, turning away. Then she turned back, her face suddenly serious. 'And my life,' she said quietly. 'I owe you my life. You saved me, remember? So when you decide you deserve pain, or deserve to die, remember you saved my life.'

She left quickly, before I could argue. I sat there for a long time, staring after her, thinking about what she had said. It was only when I looked away that I saw Eleanor Langham sitting in her chair, watching me steadily.

THE OTHER PATIENTS

Now that I was officially awake, I sat up on the bed, looked round, and smiled in what I hoped was a welcoming way to the other patients. I didn't feel welcoming. I felt impatient and restless. I hate hospitals. People die in them. All I wanted was to get out of this sharply clean room and go home, to my kitchen and my soft bed and my solitude, but that wasn't going to happen soon. Therefore, I had to distract myself, and people are always interesting.

'Hello,' Florence Bryson said to me. She smiled sweetly. 'We weren't properly introduced. Welcome to the ward. I'm Flo.'

'Mrs Hudson,' I said, smiling back. I don't like to hand my first name out to all and sundry. Some distance must be maintained with strangers. But it seemed it was the right thing to say, because Flo's face lit up.

'Really? You're not *the* Mrs Hudson, are you?' she said brightly.

'Of course not, dear,' Betty Soland said, in an achingly patronizing way. She was knitting again, some shapeless garment in a sickly shade of green.

'Hudson is a very popular name,' Miranda Logan said.

She was sitting in her chair, reading a newspaper. She looked far too healthy – and too young – to be with us on the ward.

'I'm sorry, which Mrs Hudson do you mean?' I asked, feigning ignorance.

'Mr Holmes' housekeeper!' Flo cried out. 'Mr Sherlock Holmes, the Great Detective.'

'I'm sorry, I've never heard of him.' I shrugged, hoping that neither John nor Mary would cry out Sherlock's name across the room next time they visited. (I had no fear Mr Holmes himself would visit. He might be in the building, but he would never be so sentimental as to stand by my sick bed.) 'I am just a . . .' I started to say. Just a what? Who could I possibly be to justify a position in a private ward? 'Just a retired nanny. I used to look after a mill-owner's children, but now they're all grown up. They don't forget their old nanny though.' That should do it. Old nannies were looked after, everyone knew that, but no one had any interest in anyone who came from trade.

Flo lay back on her pillows, obviously disappointed.

'You've upset her,' Eleanor Langham said, her blue eyes gazing at me, as if she could detect me in the lie. I stared back, as innocently as I could. 'Flo likes to collect famous people. She thought she had a prize in you.'

'I'm sorry,' I said, smiling at Flo. She nodded at me, losing interest.

'Now all she has is Emma Fordyce,' Eleanor said, gesturing towards the woman in the bed between her and Flo, the elderly lady with the dyed blonde hair and sparkling brown eyes and a pink bed jacket. I had heard her singing to herself earlier, a ballad I had known as a child. She seemed only half aware of what was going on around her, but she also seemed happy, smiling and laughing to herself. Something about her fine-boned face did tug at a memory in me, but I couldn't tell what.

'She is famous?' I asked.

'When she was young,' Flo explained eagerly. Her bed was covered in her usual dubious gossip papers – as well as the *Illustrated Police News*, which was not suitable reading for a lady. (Of course I read it. That's how I know it wasn't suitable.) 'She was a great . . .' Her voice trailed off as she searched for the right word.

'Tart,' Betty supplied.

'Courtesan,' Miranda Logan corrected her, not looking up from her paper.

'Lover,' Flo said, glancing at Emma. Whatever Emma was, Flo obviously had a great deal of affection for her. I wondered if they had known each other before, or whether they had simply been in this ward together a very long time.

'I see,' I said. I'm not good at drawing people out with conversation. It is normally Mary who chatters, seemingly artlessly, persuading people to tell her all kinds of things, whilst I watch their face and hands, and other people's reactions. Left to my own devices, I had no idea how to get people to talk.

Flo, however, just talked with or without encouragement.

'She has some amazing stories, about kings and politicians and poets,' Flo confided.

'Stories or lies,' Eleanor said sharply. I really did not like this woman. 'When she can remember. She's quite batty now, I'm afraid.'

'Silly old cow,' the elderly lady Emma said suddenly. I stifled a laugh – Flo giggled.

'See what I mean?' Eleanor said sharply. 'She doesn't have the faintest idea what's going on.'

But I suspected from the gleam in Emma Fordyce's eyes that at that precise moment she was in a state of perfect clarity.

'I don't think we should be placed in a ward with such people,' Betty Soland said, sniffing. 'It's not respectable.'

'That's not what you said the other night when she was telling us about the King of Bohemia,' Flo said sharply. 'I saw your eyes gleaming; you were hanging on every detail.'

'The present king's father,' Emma said suddenly, sitting up and looking directly at me. Her voice was low and sweet. 'I was a blonde. I understand the current King of Bohemia prefers clever brunette opera singers.'

She smiled at me, a mischievous grin that was utterly enchanting. I could see more than a trace of the charms that could have ensnared princes. Her eyes were intelligent now, and bright. She must mean Irene Adler, of course – how had she guessed I knew her? She may have been losing her memory, but in her moments of lucidity she was obviously very sharp.

The woman in the bed to my left cried out, then was silent again. She hadn't joined in the conversation at all. She merely lay on her bed, staring at the ceiling, her face drawn. She looked like a picture of an early Christian martyr – not peaceful, but agonized.

'Sarah Malone,' Flo said, staring at her. 'She's dying.'

'She's taking her time about it,' Eleanor said harshly. 'See her hands? See how they move on the sheets? She's saying the rosary. She's a Catholic.' Her voice dripped with scorn.

'She doesn't have any beads,' I said.

'A good Catholic doesn't need the beads,' Miranda told me. 'The hands remember. The words come, the hands move, the mind supplies the beads.'

'She seems in pain,' I said to her. Miranda looked over at the thin grey woman, her white and brown hair scattered over the pillow.

'They give her morphine,' Flo told me, as if defending the nurses.

'It is not pain of the body,' Miranda told me. There it was again. Her voice, her accent, her grammar was all perfectly English, but there was a slight hesitation, as if she had to form her speech in her mind before she spoke.

I looked across at the empty bed.

'Who was she?' I asked. The others stirred. Perhaps it was not the done thing to ask about the dead. We were all too close to death ourselves.

Eventually, Eleanor answered. 'She was only here two days. She wasn't very ill.'

'She's dead,' Flo pointed out.

'It happens that way sometimes,' Betty said. 'Very suddenly.'

'Very suddenly,' Emma repeated softly. We were all silent, each with her own morbid thoughts.

But you never have time to be silent and still in a hospital. There is always something going on. I heard a rattle, and everyone brightened up as the tea trolley, pushed by a nervous young girl with squeaky shoes, entered.

I had questions. I tried to remember them for when Mary came round – it was so frustrating to not be at home! I could have gone to the library, or Mr Holmes' collection of newspapers in the garret. Or sent Billy up there, or wherever I needed him to go. I was worried I would have forgotten the questions by the time Mary came round again.

Who was Emma Fordyce, and what exactly had she done in her scandalous past?

Who was Sarah Malone, and why did she suffer so?

Emma Fordyce would be easy to research, due to her notorious past, but a woman called Sarah Malone would be far harder to track down. All I knew was that she was Catholic, and I deduced given that, and her name, she was probably Irish. All of us here were special patients, friends of the Friends of St Bartholomew's, or staff here. That meant someone had made an effort to place her here – maybe that would be a lead.

The last question wasn't one Mary could answer. I'd have to find an answer myself. I sat and sipped my tea and thought about it. Why, exactly, did Miranda Logan watch Emma Fordyce so hard? Because I had seen her. She read her newspapers, yet every time Emma moved, or spoke, Miranda looked up, and didn't take her eyes off her until Emma was quiet again. She paid no one else the same attention. In fact, she barely spoke to us. She had briefly shown a spark of interest in me, when the ward had discussed if I was '*the* Mrs Hudson' but that had faded. She occasionally looked at Sarah Malone, but given what Miranda Logan had said, I felt that was no more than a fellow feeling for another Catholic.

I felt sure that Miranda Logan was not ill. She claimed to be tired, but her eyes were bright, and she moved freely, almost impatiently around the ward. John had set me to watch and learn, and this was my first lesson. Miranda Logan was here to watch Emma Fordyce, whether for good or ill.

A LITTLE BIT
OF SCANDAL

Another restless night. It is impossible to sleep in a hospital. Someone is always groaning, someone else talking. There are always footsteps in the corridor outside, even up and down the ward. Sounds are magnified so the scratching of a pen on the page becomes an intolerable racket. Other people breathe and snore and toss and turn and keep you awake until you are trembling with rage at their noise. Sarah Malone muttered. Betty Soland knitted (she was apparently proud of her ability to do so in the dark), and it is amazing how loud knitting needles are at 3 a.m. Flo Bryson got up six times in the night to use the conveniences. By the time 6 a.m. arrived, and the first medicines were dispensed, I was more exhausted than I had been the previous evening. I also fully understood how people in crowded rooms could snap and kill each other. I spent a good hour that morning planning how to destroy Betty's knitting needles.

Therefore, I dozed all morning, only half aware of Emma telling Flo a series of scandalous stories that only got more so as Betty tutted. Flo was Emma's main audience, and she lapped up every word, punctuating every tale with oohs and aahs and expressions of shocked, but delighted, disbelief.

34

They were good stories. Emma had quite a past, and a gift for telling a tale. She told of politicians running hotfoot to her home after late-night sittings at the House, and gamblers ruining themselves for her, and peers of the realm setting her up in absolute luxury. Then she had run away from all that, and travelled, first through Europe and then Russia, adding kings and emperors to her conquests.

It sounded dazzling, at first. But then I thought of Irene Adler, also conquering kings, and giving it all up to marry a country solicitor for love. Emma never spoke of love. She spoke of passion, and lust, and greed, and desire, but never love. Now, at the end of it all, she seemed content, but still, she was alone.

But then again, she seemed perfectly happy. Very happy, in fact. She didn't seem to have missed love, in fact, she had done very well without it. I suppose love can be dangerous, especially for women. Especially women alone in the world.

Forgive me. Hospitals, I have discovered, make me introspective and maudlin. I shook the feeling away, and settled down to read *Frankenstein* until Mary came.

As soon as visiting hours started she was through the door, bearing cake. It was good to see her, to see someone I could talk to without having to check everything I said for clues to my identity, or revealing too much of what I was thinking, or even just plain rudeness.

'What awful clothes. Those poor girls,' Mary observed, glancing towards Betty's daughters, lined up at the foot of the bed.

'She makes them herself,' I told her.

'Can't someone stop her?'

'I have thought of throwing her workbag on the stove,' I admitted. 'Mary, have you found out about Emma Fordyce?'

'Yes, I looked her up in Sherlock's books,' Mary said eagerly, sitting close to me on the bed. 'He cut and pasted all of Patrick West's columns about her. You remember, that gossip columnist, the one who's been writing for years. West wrote about her a lot, she seems to have been some sort of muse for him. Apparently she was a great courtesan.'

'Well, that's the kindest word I've heard for it,' I remarked dryly.

'A long list of lovers, only the very best,' Mary said, glancing over her shoulder. Emma was still speaking eagerly to Flo in a very loud voice. Mary whispered, 'Kept all the secrets, though. And there were plenty of secrets. She was right there with all the influential men of her time. The Duke of Wellington, half the royal sons . . .'

'Was there a courtesan who didn't sleep with royalty, back then?'

'But she was supposed to have the truth about all those secret marriages and bastard children! But she never told, not a soul, though she was offered thousands by writers and lawyers and all kinds of people.'

'She's talking now,' I said, nodding towards her. 'I wonder if she's planning to tell her stories to anyone else.'

'Like an author? Someone to write all her stories down, finally? There are rumours that there is a bit of a bidding war for the rights to her memoirs. Do you remember when I was doing all that research into society scandals, back in April, in the newspapers?'

I nodded. Of course. That was when we were trying to track down the blackmail victims.

'I came across her name a few times. Oh, it was all fifty years ago, or more, but people still remember. She was right in the heart of things – her lovers were the most powerful men of her day. Battles were planned in her rooms – not just military ones. She'd have these glittering salons and invite all the great thinkers. She was right there when they devised parliamentary bills and poems and scandals – and she's kept quiet about everything!'

'Quite the grand courtesan, then,' I remarked.

'One of the greatest,' Mary agreed. 'And the only one who hasn't published.'

'Yet. Her visitors look like publishers. Or possibly lawyers.' I leaned over to whisper to Mary. 'That woman next to me, Miranda Logan,' I said, in the lowest of voices, 'she watched Emma all day, and she isn't ill. I wonder if she's here to stop Emma telling her life story?'

'Or protect her. I bet a lot of people would like to keep her quiet, even now.'

We smiled in joint mischief. We didn't really mean it. It was joking, just a game to play to keep my mind busy whilst I was in here. Emma's secrets were from so long ago I doubted anyone cared. Miranda Logan could be sicker than she looked, and here perfectly legitimately. It was all just a way to pass the time.

Sarah Malone, on the other hand, was a woman in true anguish. I turned to look at her. She was silent for once, still staring up at the ceiling.

'Who is she?' Mary asked, following my gaze.

'Sarah Malone, apparently,' I told her. 'She moans all night.'

'She's in pain?'

'Of the mind as much as the body, I think.' I turned back to Mary. 'Could you find out more about her?'

She grimaced. 'It's a common name,' she said.

'I know, I'm asking a lot.'

'There'll be a home address in the hospital administration files. That's a start.'

'Don't do anything illegal,' I insisted. She merely smiled, and asked me why I wanted to know.

Well, why? Because I was bored, and needed the distraction? Because I was used to living in a house of intrigue and mystery and needed it everywhere I went? Because I had nearly died, still could, and I wanted to assert my sense of being alive? Because wrapping myself in other people's pain stopped my own? Because she was in genuine pain, and I wanted to help?

'Because I'm nosy,' I said, and Mary smiled secretly. It was a vice she shared. 'Now, tell me what's bothering you.'

Mary's smile faded.

'It's nothing. I don't want to bother you . . .'

'You said you'd tell me,' I insisted. I was worried now.

'It was something more I heard from Wiggins, via Billy,' she said softly.

'What about? Are they all right?'

'Yes, yes, he's fine,' she insisted. 'But he's worried. There are boys disappearing . . . from the streets of London. It's been going on for years, and no one has noticed.'

MARY'S CASE

'What boys?' I asked.

'Billy wasn't breaking a confidence. I don't think Wiggins is quite comfortable telling me things yet, and this was his way round it.'

'He doesn't know you well enough,' I reassured her. I wasn't sure that was the answer. Wiggins had built some sort of fragile trust with Mary back in April, when we were hunting down the blackmailer. But Mary had been reckless, and put us both in danger, and I don't think Wiggins forgave her for that.

'Is it Wiggins' boys who are disappearing?' I asked. Wiggins ran the Baker Street Irregulars. He kept his rag-tag army of boys safe and fed, and in return, they carried out errands for Sherlock Holmes and me and various other people that I probably didn't want to know about.

'No, his boys are safe,' Mary told me. 'It's other boys, not just from the street, but all over London.'

'What do you mean?' I asked, sitting up in bed. The mild speculation about Emma suddenly seemed quite dull.

'Wiggins noticed a crossing sweeper who wasn't there one day,' Mary explained. 'A few days later, another boy, who had a home and a mother, disappeared. She was a drunk and may not have noticed him leave, but he never came back.'

'That's just two,' I pointed out.

'Yes, but no one knew where they went. No one. Not the police, not the workhouse, no one. Wiggins set his contacts looking for them, and they weren't anywhere to be found. It's unusual, two boys to just fall off the face of the Earth like that.'

It was unusual. Wiggins had an extensive list of contacts all over London, and skills refined by Mr Holmes himself. Wiggins could find anyone.

'Go on,' I told her. She glanced around to see if anyone was listening. Miranda Logan was chatting calmly to Betty's children, Flo and Emma were absorbed in a newspaper together, and Sarah Malone heard no one. Only Eleanor Langham sat silent, and surely she couldn't hear us from over there.

'So Wiggins did a little digging,' Mary continued. 'He asked for rumours and stories, things that people had no proof about, but just had a suspicion. He went all over London, Whitechapel, the Docks, even down to Mayfair.'

'He found something,' I said, judging by the light in Mary's eyes.

'He did,' she confirmed. 'Stories about boys disappearing, just snatched off the street. Some taken right from the workhouse door. Just poor boys.'

'No one's ever said anything; surely there'd be an outcry?' I objected.

'Well, they weren't all taken at once. And not from the same place. No one cares about poor boys, or street boys or runaways. There's all kinds of charities to save the street girls, but no one notices the boys. It's assumed they can look after themselves.'

'Maybe you should look at that advert in *The Times* again.'

'Oh, I did,' Mary said, dismissing it with a wave of her hand. 'It's just some madcap professor with advanced educational theories. He's quite wrong, but as it turns out, quite kind.'

'But still – how many boys have gone missing?'

Mary took a deep breath.

'I think – I may be wrong, maybe some of them really did run away – but I asked around and looked at some old parish records and old police reports and I think I've tracked down about twenty.'

'Twenty?' I cried out. Flo turned to look and Mary smiled at her winningly. Flo turned back to her scandal sheet.

'Oh, come on, Mary, that would raise some concerns, no matter the circumstances,' I objected. She nodded.

'I know, but it didn't all happen at once, it happened over a number of months. Well, years,' she said sheepishly.

'How many years?'

'Around ten . . .' she said slowly, aware that this was beginning to sound a tad unbelievable.

'Ten,' I said flatly, sitting back on my bed. Twenty boys disappear over ten years – no wonder no one noticed. In fact, I was surprised anyone said anything after all this time. It wasn't so high a number, not in London.

'You've been busy,' I remarked.

'It started when John was with the Baskervilles,' she admitted. 'I had to do something with my time.'

'You never told me,' I said suspiciously.

'I didn't think there'd be anything to tell. And honestly,' she said, smiling in what she hoped was a winning way, 'I wanted to present it all as a fait accompli and impress you.'

'Hmm,' I said, not at all convinced. Maybe Mary was a better liar than I gave her credit for. Or maybe, so consumed with worry over my own health, I just hadn't noticed.

'I've got as far as I can get now, though,' Mary said ruefully. 'I have all the information; I just don't know what to do with it.'

'Present it to Wiggins. Or Mr Holmes,' I said.

'I don't think I can. It's all just conjecture and rumour, and someone heard from someone else and so on. Even the cases with some sort of police record are years old. You know what Sherlock would say.'

'Data. I must have data!' I said, laughing, quoting Mr Holmes.

'Besides, Billy and Wiggins told me. I don't want to hand it over.'

Why her and not me? I felt a sudden stab of jealousy.

'Well, not to anyone but you,' Mary said, suddenly insightful. 'I'm sure Billy would have told you, but you were . . .'

'Preoccupied,' I finished for her. Worried by my pain, unsettled by Mr Holmes' absence and still worrying over the outcome of my last case, I had sent Billy to Mary's most days, wanting to be alone. No wonder he had confided in her.

'I must talk to him,' I said, meaning Billy, pinching the bridge of my nose.

'He understands,' Mary said. 'Especially if we do take this on.'

'Take what on?' I insisted. 'Unsubstantiated reports of missing boys? It's not much to go on.'

'No . . .' Mary said, musing, but I knew that look. I was sharper now, and watching her.

'What else?' I insisted.

'Nothing, really. Just a tale. A story. Something Wiggins' boys tell to frighten each other.'

'What?' I said again. 'What do they say, Mary?'

'Wiggins says it's silly but . . .'

'Mary!'

'The Pale Boys,' she said cryptically.

'Excuse me?'

So she told me the tale of the Pale Boys. Boys who came onto the street only at night. They never came into the light. They never went onto the main street. They had pale faces, and all black clothes, and they melted into the shadows. They walked in dark corners and deserted alleyways. They never grew old, and never ate or drank and if you saw them, you would die.

'Mary, it's a ghost story!' I cried. 'It's nothing but a horror story for children.'

She nudged my copy of *Frankenstein*.

'Even horror stories have some basis in fact.'

I looked down at the book. It was fiction, but the horrible science within had some basis in fact.

'Well played,' I murmured.

'Thank you,' Mary said, smiling.

'So the Irregulars think that the boys who disappeared became Pale Boys? Who never age, and never feed and kill those who see them? Some kind of vampires?'

'They didn't actually say vampires . . .' Mary objected. 'And Wiggins doesn't think so. It's just the younger boys who say that.'

'All right,' I said. Visiting time was ending. 'Just ignore the Pale Boys connection. It's just a ghost story. If I were you, I'd start with the most recent disappearances. Talk to the people in the shops near where the crossing sweeper was last seen. They'll be used to him, they'll know if he did something unusual.'

'I will,' Mary said, smiling happily.

'I still think you're making a fool of yourself, though,' I warned.

'Well, it passes the time,' Mary said, standing up. She looked round at Sarah Malone and Miranda Logan and Emma Fordyce. I understood. I, too, was grasping at hints and shadows to pass the time. Mary and I understood each other perfectly.

NIGHT TERRORS

I regret to say, in our ward, we barely noticed the day staff. They were bright and clean and efficient and they seemed to be not separate individuals, but part of the fixtures and fittings of the hospital. They bustled around in their blue and white striped dresses and brilliant white aprons and lace headdresses, followed by eager probationers in brown, and were so many that I never learnt their names.

It was different when night came. The staff changed over at six in the evening, and we were left with the Sister, and two nurses for the night. Then the room become more personal and intimate.

I like the night-time. I like how the world changes, becomes private and quiet. I like how logical impossibilities in the day become just possible by moonlight. I feel I can hide, and watch, in peace at night.

In the ward, the lights were turned down low in the evening. Later, only a single lamp on the Sister's desk would burn. That end of the room, closest to the door, was panelled in dark wood – I believe it had once been some kind of vestibule. In the dead of night, that part of the ward was full of shadows.

The great windows were left uncurtained. They were supposed to be open, according to Miss Nightingale's rules, but some of the patients were convinced the night air was poisonous, and were always complaining, and asking that they be closed. The hospital became quieter, but never silent. There was always the cry of someone in pain, or someone alone and suffering, always the sound of footsteps, and low voices.

Our Sister was called Ruth Bey. She never actually told anyone her name; I found it out later. She was a small woman, with smooth dark hair, and she never smiled, or looked at peace. She sat at the desk at the end of the room by the door, the one with the lamp, and wrote in her logbook all night. She rarely came to the patients, and when she did, she was silent and efficient.

It was odd for a Sister to be there at night. They lived on the wards, in a separate suite of rooms, so were always available if needed, but most stayed on the wards during the day. However, Sister Bey (the only Sister not to be given the name of her ward, as if it was important she be known) slept during the day, and stayed on the ward, at her desk, all night.

There were two night nurses, one for each side of the ward. The nurse on my side was always Nora Taylor. She was tall and slim and with a gentle smile, and a soft voice and strong hands. She had a sweet mouth, but also had an air of 'do not touch'. She looked very efficient in her blue and white uniform, with a gold medal pinned neatly to it (a medal awarded to the top three probationers). I would come to know her very well, even count her as a friend, but on this second night in hospital she was just another stranger. The other nurse for tonight (although that nurse often changed) was Nurse Barry, also slim and tall, with a mass of golden curls like Mary, only hers were neatly confined beneath her cap, and never worked loose.

I turned back to reading, *Jekyll and Hyde* this time. I had seen the play the previous year, accompanied by Mary. I had been most impressed by the lead actor, and the way he had transformed from Jekyll to Hyde. Later, when I returned home, I had mentioned this to Mr Holmes and how unsettling it was, and he had pooh-poohed it.

'Just lights and a clever actor,' he said. 'No more than that. Nothing to be afraid of.'

Then, a week ago, once he had returned from Dartmoor, Mr Holmes had appeared at my kitchen door one night and said:

'You were right. Lights and mirrors and transformations, while still just tricks, can be terrifying, at the right moment.' And he was gone.

Then he had given me this book, via Mary. There was a message, I knew. We all had a Hyde. I looked around the room at the sleepy, harmless, middle-aged and elderly ladies around me. We were nothing to be afraid of. And yet, I had done things, dark things, dangerous things, things I had never known I was capable of. There were acts I was proud of, and yet, at least one act I was ashamed of. It lay on my conscience and I could no longer deny that I, too, had a darkness inside me.

If I could do that, what could they do?

That was when Nurse Taylor came to introduce herself.

'I'm Nurse Taylor, I shall be looking after you at night,' she told me, softly, as she straightened my sheets. 'Don't be afraid to ask for anything, and call me if you need to. I shall hear you. Are you in pain?'

'I am, but it's bearable,' I told her. The pain was a sign I was healing, and I couldn't bear the fuzziness the drugs gave me. 'Are you a Nightingale nurse?'

'I am,' she told me, pleasantly trained. 'My sister and I are both Nightingale nurses. How did you know?'

Mr Holmes could have told her in detail what had led to that conclusion, but all I knew was that she had an indefinable air of competence and duty that I had only seen in Nightingale nurses.

'The way you walk, I think,' I told her. She was pleased but puzzled and, straightening up, glanced at the book in my hand.

'Won't that give you nightmares?'

I smiled, and shook my head. Oh, I had nightmares all right, that left me fighting my way back to wakefulness, panting and terrified and soaked in sweat, but they weren't caused by books.

They came again that night. I dreamed of my son, standing in a summer meadow, calling to me, waving me onwards. Behind him, in shadow, stood his father, my husband, my love. They were waiting for me, they wanted me to come to them, and I wanted to join them. I wanted to run through that tall grass in the sunshine and join them – but something held me back. Someone. Someone had hold of my arm. They grasped me tightly, hurting me, squeezing me and no matter how I twisted and turned I could not break free. I looked down at the hand, and saw it was charred and blackened. I could smell the stench of burnt flesh. I knew if I turned I would see a face, the skin burnt away, the bones and tendons and muscles laid bare, his mouth forever in a silent scream, and I knew I could never get away. He was dragging me down with him, to where he burnt.

I woke sweating and panting again. I was not surprised. This was only a variation of the same nightmare I had been having for months. Relieved to be awake, I looked around the ward.

I wasn't the only one awake that night. I could hear St Paul's clock striking three in the distance, and in the bed beside me, Sarah Malone was calling out, screaming incomprehensibly. I could hear Nurse Taylor try to soothe her.

The screen was pulled between our beds, but as she moved round, Nurse Taylor's skirt caught the screen and drew it back. In the light of the lamp on the desk I could see it all, Sarah Malone twisting and writhing in her bed, in the grip of some horrific pain. Nurse Taylor was trying to hold her down, and Ruth Bey watched from her desk, eyes wide.

I could hear one clear word coming from Sarah.

'Confess,' she repeated over and over again.

'Where's the Catholic priest?' Nurse Taylor asked Sister Bey. The other nurse came running in, and rushed to the bedside to help hold down Sarah.

'There's been an accident at the docks; he's gone down there. He won't be back in time.'

'Surely there's another priest?' Nurse Taylor asked.

'Not at this time of night,' Sister Bey replied. I heard someone mutter about heathenish practices, and realized it was Betty. We all lay still in our beds, but we were all awake, all watching Sarah Malone struggle and scream her way out of life.

'I can help,' Miranda Logan said, sitting up. 'I am a Catholic, too.'

'You understand?' Nurse Taylor said, as Sarah cried out again.

'She cannot die unshriven,' Miranda agreed, getting out of bed and pulling on her dressing gown.

'You're not a priest,' Eleanor pointed out. 'It won't count. Isn't that how you Catholics work?'

'God won't mind,' Miranda said, as she walked to Sarah's bed.

I will never forget that sight. In the dim light Miranda walked past the end of my bed, wrapped in a red gown that trailed behind her, her dark hair loose down her back, her head held high. She looked imperious, regal even, a medieval queen.

She waved the nurses away, and took Sarah's hand. The nurses stood in the shadow, and watched.

'I am of your faith,' Miranda said clearly. 'The old faith. You are dying.'

Sarah, still now, looked up at Miranda and nodded.

'You wish to confess?'

Sarah nodded again.

'There is no priest, but I can hear your confession. I will keep your secret and absolve you in the name of the Father, Son and Holy Ghost. Will you accept me?'

Sarah nodded, and pulled Miranda down to her. Miranda sat on the bed and bent her ear to Sarah's mouth. Sarah whispered urgently, her voice fast and harsh. I could not hear a word, though I tried. She did not speak for long. The clock was striking the quarter as she finished, and then she lay back, exhausted.

'And do you regret these sins?' Miranda asked. Sarah nodded again. She looked peaceful now, more so than she had done since I had arrived in this room. 'Then we will pray,' Miranda told her and, taking Sarah's hand between her own, they prayed.

They spoke in Latin. I was from an old Scottish Presbyterian family that distrusted Catholics, wary of their easy forgiveness and elaborate trappings. Yet I lay there and listened to this prayer that had been spoken for hundreds of years, men and women placing faith in old words that could never be understood, and I felt something peaceful and magical in it.

The prayer said, Sarah Malone sighed once, and finally

fell still. Miss Logan said the blessing, crossed herself, and stood.

'She is dead,' Miranda announced. The nurses hurried forward to take care of the body. The Sister made a note in both of her logbooks.

Miranda Logan looked at me. 'She is safe now,' she said, calmly.

'She seemed desperate to confess,' I said to her. 'Surely her sins can't have been that bad?'

'Her sins were great,' Miranda said, as she walked back to her bed.

My third night in the hospital. My second death.

A CASE FOR
MRS HUDSON

I awoke to find the bed next to me empty, golden sunlight filling the room, and Dr Watson standing at the foot of my bed, reading my notes. It was very early, and the night staff were still on the ward, everyone else asleep.

'Good morning,' I mumbled. Dr Watson looked up and smiled.

'You're doing well,' he said, putting down my notes. He came and sat on my bed. 'I hear there was a death last night,' he said in a low voice, nodding towards Sarah's bed.

'That poor woman,' I said softly. 'She was in agony.'

'In mind or body?' he asked.

'Both. But I think her mind was soothed when she confessed just before she died.'

'I see,' he said thoughtfully. 'She had a tumour; her death was expected. She had been ill a very long time.'

Something about his tone puzzled me. Why should it be important that she was expected to die?

'You know you're not supposed to sit on the bed, Dr Watson,' Nurse Nora Taylor said firmly, but with a smile as she came to join us.

'Sorry!' he said, quickly jumping up.

'I forgive you. I'm off duty. I'm just about to go home. Sister Bey has already gone to her rooms,' she told him, and they both looked at me.

Well, it was obvious that they knew each other. She knew he was Dr Watson – and therefore she knew exactly who I was: Sherlock Holmes' housekeeper.

'You know who I am,' I said quietly, anxious not to disturb the others.

'I won't tell a soul,' she said. 'In fact, I'd rather they didn't know who you are either.' She nodded towards the rest of the ward.

'I'm not a simpleton. What's going on?' I demanded. They exchanged a look. 'Now!'

'Nurse Taylor came to me a while ago, worried about this ward,' John told me. 'As you know, it's a private ward, very small, for the exclusive use of Friends and benefactors of the hospital.'

'I know. You arranged for me to be here,' I said.

'Yes, well, this ward . . .' John tried to say, but he wasn't sure how to explain himself. He seemed rather sheepish.

'It's odd,' Nora Taylor said, in her brisk way. 'There's a strange atmosphere here, like nothing is ever quite right.'

'It's a hospital. We're all ill: nothing is right,' I told her dryly.

'I know, and I am used to that. But there is a constant sense of expectation in this ward, almost of dread.'

She seemed, under that prim blue and white uniform, to be somewhat of a romantic, of the Gothic sort.

'What do the other nurses think?' I asked.

'There is a different nurse with me each night,' she confided. 'The others don't like it here either. As for the Sister . . .' Her voice trailed away. It must be difficult to betray someone you have been taught to revere as the voice of all sense.

'Tell me,' I said quietly.

'She never talks to patients,' Nora said, even quieter, so I could barely hear her. 'Never walks round the ward. She never takes time off. And she writes in her logbook all the time.'

'She's supposed to keep a logbook, surely?' I asked.

'Yes, the official one,' Nora told me. 'But she has a second logbook she keeps herself. No one has ever seen inside it; she takes it home every morning.'

That was odd, I agreed. And there was the fact that she only ever seemed to be here at night. I asked Nora about this.

'I did ask the Sister once why she wasn't here during the day,' Nora said. 'She said the ward was busy during the day, and she wasn't needed. But at night-time, she said, things happen, and she needed to be there to see. That's all she would say.'

It had occurred to me that John was making more of Nora's worries than he really felt, giving me something to occupy my mind so I wouldn't be worried about my illness, or my home, or Mr Holmes, but Nora had something else to say.

'There have been some deaths . . .' she said, hesitating.

'I hate to press the point, but again, this is a hospital,' John said, smiling to take the sting out of his words.

'I am aware of that,' she said primly. 'I am aware people die, even die unexpectedly. But there seems to be a higher than usual proportion of unexpected deaths in this ward: people who weren't expected to die.'

'Like that woman the first night I was here,' I said softly.

She nodded. 'I try to watch all the time, but often I am called to help in other wards. However, Sister Bey rarely leaves her post. I cannot be certain anything is wrong beyond my own feelings . . .'

'So this is your idea, John?' I asked. 'I fell ill, and you saw an opportunity to place me here, in this ward where nothing is right and people die unexpectedly, in the night?'

'Ah,' he said, suddenly aware that what he had done might not have seemed like the best choice, presented like that. 'I didn't mean for you to be in danger; I just wanted you to observe, from the point of view of a patient. You know, someone who's here all the time and talks to the others. I am aware of Nurse Taylor's suspicions, and I don't mean to dismiss them, I am merely questioning everything, just as Holmes would. I don't actually believe any of the deaths were unnatural, otherwise I'd never have put you here . . .' His voice trailed off as he realized Nora was looking at him, shocked. 'Maybe I should move you to another ward . . .'

'Don't you dare!' I said quickly. I might have been angry

at first, but now I could feel something inside me stirring. Something I'd not felt since Mary and I hunted down the blackmailer, an excitement, a fascination, a sense of being truly, fully alive. 'I'm staying right here, and watching and listening to everything,' I insisted.

Nora looked at John, then at me, and seemed to make up her mind. She nodded, said she would see me that evening, and left.

'Sorry,' John said, sitting back down on my bed. 'I didn't really think.'

'I'm happy to help,' I reassured him. 'It will do me good.'

'Right,' he said, still not sure what he had done. Of course, he had no idea what had happened back then. He knew Mary had been hurt, and we had been investigating something together, but she had refused to tell him any more. 'The most important thing is that you get well, though, so don't—'

I interrupted him. 'Do you suspect one of the staff?' I asked quickly. 'The patients change all the time, surely.'

'I don't suspect anyone!' he snapped. 'I'm still not convinced anything is wrong here. I'm doing this out of respect for Nurse Taylor, who incidentally would make a fine doctor. Anyway, yes, patients come and go, but some patients have a recurring illness, and so are in and out of here. They get ill, come into hospital, get better, go home, do whatever they were doing to get ill in the first place again, and end up in hospital again.'

'Who comes in and out of this ward?'

'Florence Bryson, Eleanor Langham and Betty Soland. Sarah Malone was here often too.'

Well, that was somewhere to start – though as far as I was concerned, Emma Fordyce and Miranda Logan were the interesting ones on this ward. I disliked Eleanor Langham intensely, but I found no mystery about her as I did about Emma and Miranda. She was just a nasty woman. There might be nothing in John's mystery, but there was certainly a story with those two.

'The day staff are coming in,' he said, standing up. 'I should go, before someone sees me and puts two and two together.'

'I'll be all right,' I reassured him. 'I'm not helpless, Nora is here in the evening, Mary visits every day. And I hear Sherlock is somewhere in the building. I can always call for him,' I joked. As if I would call for help from Mr Holmes! It would be an inexcusable lack of control to show such weakness in front of him.

'Not at the moment,' John said. 'Lestrade's dragged him off to that Richmond case again.'

'The house in Richmond?' I felt suddenly sick. John couldn't know what had happened there, what I had done there.

'Just a case Lestrade won't let go,' he said, suddenly looking closely at me. 'A house that burnt down, a man died. Lestrade is convinced it wasn't accidental. He's been looking into the owner. He keeps popping up, trying to convince Holmes to look into it too.'

'I didn't know,' I said, suddenly weak. 'Inspector Lestrade hasn't visited 221b.'

'No, he likes to accost Holmes in the street; it's very annoying. Holmes keeps telling him there's nothing he can do, but you know what Lestrade is like.'

'Like a terrier hunting a rat. He never lets go,' I murmured. This time the rat wasn't a thief, or a murderer. Well, not the kind of person he normally hunted. This time the person he hunted was just an ordinary woman, keeping a horrific secret, thousands of secrets I had sworn would never be told. This time Lestrade's prey was right under his nose.

'Is there anything you want to tell me? You and Mary?' John asked, peering at me. I looked up at him. He knew something. He wasn't a genius like Mr Holmes, but he was clever. He must have seen how my face turned white and my hand shook.

'Not yet,' I whispered. He nodded, just once, put on his hat and left.

I sat back. If Lestrade was out there, hunting me, maybe I was safer in here in the hospital ward – even where people who were meant to live, died.

SECRETS AND LIES

And so the days passed, melting into one another. Sitting in hospital all day is very boring. Oh, it's busy enough, with nurses and doctors and visitors rushing back and forth all day, but they never stopped and talked – or if they did, it was in low voices I could never hear. There is a lot of activity, medicine rounds and wound dressings and doctor's visits, but it's the same routine, day in, day out. Always the same faces and the same tasks all within the same four walls. I was soon bored beyond comprehension. There were books, but even I could not read all day.

Besides, there was John's task. I was there to observe. What, though, could I see?

I did not like Eleanor Langham. There was no reason for this, at least not at first, just an instinctive, deep-rooted, instant aversion. She watched, too, and talked. She chatted to the nurses all day about their homes and families and pets. I found her intrusive and irritating – especially when I caught her passing stories about one nurse on to another. She was stirring the pot, to see what rose to the surface. When the two nurses argued, I saw Eleanor smile. She liked the conflict she caused.

On this day, a week after I had arrived, Flo and Emma had their heads together over a newspaper, reading bits of it out to each other.

'I'm not sure I should read this,' Flo said. 'It's an account of the Phoebe Hogg murder and it's very bloody.'

'That's the best part!' Emma insisted. 'I do like a bit of blood. Lots of blood. It's not a good story unless there's lots of blood.'

Florence winced a little.

'Perhaps I should read a good detective story,' Flo went on. 'The one about that nice Mr Holmes.'

Involuntarily, I snorted. Nice? Eleanor glanced sharply at me, but I ignored her.

'I've always found Mr Holmes to be rather attractive, in those drawings,' Flo said, rather forlornly. 'I wonder what he's like in real life?' John had only published one book at this time, but another was on its way, and John was preparing the short stories for the *Strand*. Not to mention Sherlock's name was turning up more and more in the police reports. People were becoming very curious about him.

Well, he's not nice, I wanted to say. He's bad-tempered and careless and demanding. Too thin – and a drug addict! He has a terribly bad opinion about women. He never gives a thought to anyone but himself! And he likes to play tricks and games . . .

And yet, he was the most fascinating man I'd ever met. I would, if ever asked, sacrifice a great deal for him. I felt proud that I was his housekeeper.

Perhaps I could understand, a little, the light in Flo and Emma's eyes when they spoke of him. Just occasionally, he could be devastatingly charming. Not that I was ever fooled, but Emma Fordyce would have been enchanted. And Flo would have melted . . .

I caught myself smiling at the image, as Eleanor Langham continued to watch me, and I schooled my face to remain still.

'I like stories about royalty,' Emma said wistfully. 'They remind me of myself.'

Out of the corner of my eye, I saw Miranda Logan pause in her writing.

'You seduced a king?' Flo asked breathlessly. Emma laughed.

'Several kings. Kings are easy.'

'I knew a woman once . . .' I started to say. 'She seduced a prince,' I finished, remembering not to say Irene's name. Although no one knew she knew Mr Holmes.

But my discretion was in vain. 'Irene Adler,' Emma said immediately, her face glowing with reminiscence. 'Do you mean her? She still writes to me,' she said, nodding gently at me, enough to say Irene had mentioned me, but Emma wouldn't tell. 'I knew her when she was a little girl, in France. Oh, I know she says she was born in New Jersey, and maybe she was. But I knew a skinny, awkward girl with the voice of an angel living on the streets of Paris. I would pay her to sing for me, and with her voice, and my charms, no man could resist me.'

'She learnt a lot from you,' I said.

'There was a lot to learn. If you have to make your living seducing people – and no singer can live on their voice alone – make sure you only seduce the very best. You see, dukes and earls are never quite sure of their place. They need comfort and support, but done very delicately,' Emma explained. Flo's eyes widened to the point they almost popped out. 'But kings,' Emma continued, confidingly, 'are in charge of everyone. They know exactly how powerful they are. What they really want is someone to take charge of them. To say no before finally saying yes. It's very simple, you see.'

Betty had stopped sewing and now she flung her work down on her bed.

'I don't think we want to hear details of your disgusting, Godless life!' Betty snapped.

'I do,' I murmured. This was the most fun I'd had since coming here.

'You're nothing but a Jezebel, worse!' Betty spat, shaking with anger. 'A vile, foul creature that should never have been placed in a ward with decent people! You should be in the stocks rather than in a comfortable bed!'

'I may be a Jezebel, but at least I don't make the worst clothes ever worn by a woman!' Emma said back, grinning. She wasn't in the least upset by the stream of invective. 'Honestly, if you want to speak about "vile", what was that green woollen dress your oldest girl was wearing the other day? You do realize dresses are supposed to fit, not hang there like an empty sack?'

Betty really was remarkably angry. It was astonishing to see.

'You shouldn't be here, polluting my girls!'

Ah, of course, her girls, who visited every day, and might be tempted from the path of pure righteousness by this vision of sin, fun and fashionable clothes.

'Let he who is without sin . . .' Miranda murmured, though she still had her head down, seeming to be concentrating on the letter she was writing.

'Sin!' Betty practically screamed. 'Don't you talk to me about sin, you . . . you . . . Catholic!'

To her mind that was almost as big a sin as being a prostitute. Miranda merely looked at her with an expression of mild surprise for a second, then looked away. One of the nurses – who'd all been studiously ignoring the argument – hurried up to calm Betty, who was now extremely agitated.

'What's wrong with Catholics?' Flo asked, surprising everyone. Up until this point she'd been sitting back and thoroughly enjoying the argument.

'They lie and cheat and kill and say it's all right, because they can confess and be forgiven. No, I don't want that!' Betty said, as the nurse tried to get her to drink some medicine. 'They keep secrets!'

'Well, if you want to talk about secrets,' Eleanor Langham said, 'what about Mrs Hudson?'

My heart sank. I had wondered when Eleanor would enter the fray, and now it turned out I was her target.

'She claims not to know Sherlock Holmes, just to share

a name with his housekeeper. And yet, first thing this morning, in a most secretive way, before any of us were awake, she was visited by a man who the nurse addressed as Dr Watson!' Eleanor said triumphantly. 'Now isn't that stretching a coincidence? Mrs Hudson being visited by Dr Watson? And not openly where we all can see, but in secret.'

'It wasn't in secret,' I said. 'He was just early.'

'Is that true?' Flo asked breathlessly. 'Are you actually *the* Mrs Hudson? And he is the Dr Watson? From the story?'

'Of course not,' I told her, but she didn't believe me. She didn't seem able to make up her mind whether she was disappointed or excited.

'Why won't you tell us? Are you here to spy on us?' Eleanor demanded.

'Don't be ridiculous,' Miranda Logan snapped. 'Watson is a very common name. So is Hudson. There are probably a dozen Dr Watsons talking to a dozen Mrs Hudsons at this very moment. Are we to accuse them all of being characters in a story?'

'As I said, I was a nanny, not a housekeeper,' I said firmly. 'And yes, Dr Watson is an old family friend. We were quite amused when we read *A Study in Scarlet* and realized both of our names appeared in it! But I can assure you, neither of us knows Sherlock Holmes.'

I could only hope that Sherlock would not choose to visit me whilst I was in hospital. Mrs Hudson and Dr Watson were quite ordinary enough to be anyone, but Sherlock Holmes was utterly unmistakable.

But, for now, that seemed to take care of that. Flo sat back, obviously giving up, and Betty had taken her medicine and lay down quietly.

Miranda hadn't quite finished yet. 'As for secrets – Mrs Langham, didn't that nurse tell you of her engagement, and ask you to keep it secret? And didn't you then tell the Sister? Causing the nurse to be sacked? You know perfectly well a married, or even affianced, woman is not allowed to work here.'

Hot red colour flushed up Eleanor's cheeks. She had been caught. She shifted uncomfortably in her seat. The nurse by Betty's bed stiffened, and turned to look at Eleanor.

'It was my duty,' Eleanor insisted uncomfortably.

'It seems to be your duty to tell a lot of people a lot of things that were told you in confidence,' Miranda said calmly.

Who was this woman? She had taken control of the argument and the ward in moments. And yet I felt as soon as this crisis passed, she would subside again into her silence.

Eleanor Langham didn't speak. The colour had faded now and she had gone dead white. The nurse went over and straightened her bed sheets, making the point she would do her duty to this woman, horrible as she was. I suspected the nurses would be silent around Eleanor from now on.

Emma and Flo turned back to talking to each other in low undertones. Miranda looked at me once, nodded, and went back to writing her letter. The argument was over.

'I have a letter for you,' a nurse told me, handing me a long white envelope. I recognized the large, spidery handwriting: it was from Mr Holmes. What would he make of this place, this particular room, crossed with lines of hate and affection and secrets and contempt?

I know exactly what he would say. He would say it was ripe for murder.

SEEING, NOT OBSERVING

I tore open the letter. It was not the first time I had received a letter from him, but it was the first that was not simply a list of instructions.

Dear Mrs Hudson,

Mrs Watson has informed me that a letter from me to you would be gratefully received at this time, though I can't think why. However, she is usually right in such petty matters. Therefore, I wish you well, hope you recover soon etc etc, whatever the usual sentiments are in this situation.

Watson has told me something of the reason you were placed in that particular ward. Whilst I approve the action, I cannot approve the reason. 'A disturbing atmosphere', 'unexplained tensions' – these are not conducive to clear, rational thinking! I understand that as a woman you are prey to such fanciful notions, but you are one of the more intelligent of your gender, and I hope able to rise above supernatural imaginings.

Having said that, however, some of my recent experiences have altered my perception of such fancies.

Dartmoor is old, and dark, full of strange noises and shadows. It is littered with the remains of those who believed in a literal devil, and ghostly hounds and the dead rising from the grave. I can see that there, away from gaslight and people, it is easier to believe. Perhaps a certain atmosphere can lend verisimilitude to stories we would otherwise dismiss, and perhaps, conversely, a real danger we cannot see can express itself as something more nebulous.

Therefore, perhaps there is something in it. Perhaps the hound will turn out to be real after all, in one way or another. Both ghost and real hounds bite, after all! So observe. Learn. Watch. Inwardly digest. Take care to note what happens in the background. Remember the tricks of magicians who tempt you to look at one hand whilst they perform the trick with the other. Take care to look into each and every shadow whilst the light is pointed elsewhere.

Whilst I write, I must apologize. I did not notice your illness. I am aware I shut myself away somewhat on my return from Dartmoor. I must admit, you did an excellent job of hiding your condition. I, however, broke my own rule. I saw you, but did not observe. It is not a mistake I shall make again.

Your return, safe and well, will be gratefully appreciated – by myself as well as the Watsons, who I am sure must be heartily sick of my constant company by now, although they are politeness itself. I am aware

that I am a difficult companion, and a worse house-guest.
Your ability to accept my failings and foibles without fuss
or anger is greatly appreciated, I assure you.

 Yours, as ever,
 Sherlock Holmes

P.S. I have just heard from Mrs Watson that you are
aware that Lestrade is bothering me about that death in
April he wished investigated. I should tell you that I
have been to Richmond. I have seen the house. I have
done some research. I am putting the sparse facts together.
Alone: Mrs Watson, Billy and Wiggins have been
stubbornly, and loyally, silent.

 I believe I know what you did. I believe I would have
done the same. Have no fear: Lestrade will never know.
You have my word.

 Holmes.

I don't know why, but I felt a little tearful after reading the
letter. I ought to have destroyed it, in case someone found
it, and let out that not only was I the Mrs Hudson, but I
was there to spy – yet I could not bear to. Instead, I folded
it neatly and tucked it into the spine of my copy of *Dr Jekyll
and Mr Hyde*.

I had another visit from Mary that day. She looked tired,
with dark smudges under her eyes. She flopped down into
the chair by my bed.

'I was out all night,' she told me. 'Wiggins and I were looking for the Pale Boys.'

'Any luck?'

'No,' she said, as she yawned. 'He says it's just a fairy tale, and I think he's right. Still, it's the only lead I have.'

'So far,' I reassured her. She shrugged, demoralized.

'I haven't tracked down anyone who saw the boys go. I haven't even tracked down anyone who cares!' she said fiercely. 'Well, that's not true. There was that story of the boy stolen from a garden, do you remember that? Well, no, why should you. It was something Wiggins mentioned, he'd heard it from a friend, who picked it up from a ballad-singer, and then he'd talked to a boy who knew the police constable who was on duty at the time. A boy, around ten, who just disappeared from his garden one day. Nothing was ever seen of him again. It was quite the wonder at the time.'

I nodded.

'That was about ten years ago. The parents went frantic trying to find him, but they both died, and when they were gone, no one carried on looking. The other boys had no parents, or parents who cared. They were too poor to look after a child. Or they think their boy has run away to a better life, and who I am to disabuse them?'

'So people do care,' I said. She looked up.

'I was exaggerating,' she admitted. 'All right, people care. One or two, but not enough to do anything. Not to actually find them. It's very frustrating.' She sighed, and ran her fingers through her hair, dislodging at least three hairpins. They scattered to the floor, unnoticed.

'How did they die?' I asked. Mary looked at me, puzzled. 'The parents of the boy from the garden; how did they die?'

Her face lit up.

'I hadn't thought of that,' she said, delighted. 'It was awfully convenient that they were the most assiduous about looking for their boy, and they died. I'll check.'

Well, that was my work done. I lay back and looked across at Emma. She was asleep now, but earlier the young man in the suit had been visiting her again. He left looking very pleased with himself. Flo was out of the ward for treatment, and Emma was left alone. Mary looked over her shoulder to see who was listening and then, satisfied, leaned in close to me.

'I found something,' Mary said, pulling a newspaper out of her pocket. It was one of the gossip papers that sprang up and disappeared again all the time. This was the *Daily Crier*, and it had a rather lurid reputation.

'You read that?' I said, surprised. Mary grimaced.

'I would love to take the higher ground and say no,' she admitted. 'But it was just fascinating. To be fair to me, it was Sherlock who bought it. He thrives on gossip.'

She handed the paper to me. She had folded it over to an article all about Emma. It was mostly hints and possibilities. It managed to imply all sorts of salacious stories about her life without actually producing any facts.

'It says she's going to publish a book,' Mary said. 'There, right at the bottom.'

'This was written by Patrick West,' I said, reading the byline.

'Yes, he writes hundreds of gossip columns. He's been quiet for a while; now he's sprung up again. I could swear I heard his name somewhere else though.'

'We thought he might be the blackmailer,' I said softly. 'But Billy visited him. He's old and housebound and blind, how can he be writing?'

Mary snorted in a most unladylike way.

'Nothing stops writers. Believe me, I'm married to one. They could lose their sight, their limbs, their minds and still would find a way to write. Besides, I believe he has apprentices. Always young women, which doesn't surprise me in the least. They take all his dictation and do all his typing and run about town for him.'

'So where's he getting information from?' I countered. 'There's more to gossip columns than writing a story.'

I looked over to Emma. Now she was wide awake, and staring at us. She smiled.

'Do you want to know a secret?' she asked.

WONDERFUL
STORIES

Well, of course we did. She beckoned us over. With Mary's help, I got out of my bed and hobbled over to Emma's, collapsing gratefully onto her chair. Mary sat on her bed.

'We hear you're going to write a book,' Mary confided. I looked around. Flo was gone, Eleanor Langham was talking to Betty and her children, Miranda Logan appeared to be engrossed in her book. Still, we kept our voices low.

'Oh, I am, my dear!' Emma agreed. 'Publish and be damned, as Boney told Harriet. Now there was a man,' she sighed. 'Told me I would have made a good general. Or a policeman! I would have done, as well. But I'm a woman, and what can a woman do?'

'Live a life of quiet virtue, serving others, never complaining, always discreet and modest,' I said dryly. It was what I had been told by my mother.

Emma laughed.

'Given the choice, I would have chosen prostitution!' she whispered. 'Not that I had a choice. Sometimes, when I wake up at night, I think I'm a little girl, back in Edinburgh, picking pockets to survive. I was a useless pickpocket. Then one day I discovered I could charm the birds out of the trees and, more usefully, the money out of men's pockets, and from then on, I was set.'

'There must have been bad times, though,' Mary said. 'It can't have all been champagne and roses.' I knew she was thinking, like me, of the creatures we had seen in Whitechapel, in our last investigation, the grey, dying women selling their bodies over and over again for a few pennies.

'I know I was lucky,' Emma said softly. 'I know what happened to others. But I was clever. I didn't drink, and I kept my secrets, and I never embarrassed anyone – or married. Or fell in love. I never gave a man control over my life.'

'You don't regret anything?' Mary asked. She wasn't judging, she genuinely wanted to know.

'Not a thing!' Emma said happily. 'Oh, I know what the likes of her think,' she continued, waving towards Betty. 'She thinks I ought to repent. She thinks I'm going to Hell. She thinks I ought to beg God's forgiveness.'

'Will you?' I asked.

'Not bloody likely!' she cried, loud enough for Betty to hear, and be insulted. 'As far as I can see, all my friends are probably in Hell anyway.'

She smiled softly.

'That's why I'm writing the book,' she said. 'They're all dead now, all the men and women I knew. People are forgetting them. They forget the laughter and the music and the stories, and they just remember the stuffy old portraits. They forget how much fun it was! Soon, no one will be left alive who knew these people. I don't want those memories to die with me. Who's left who knew that Marlborough told dirty jokes to the Queen, or that Albert was the most gentlemanly man ever, even whilst throwing me out of Buckingham Palace?'

'So you'll put it in a book?' Mary asked.

'Not all of it,' Emma said, smiling mischievously. 'Listen and I'll tell you a tale.'

That afternoon she told us her life. Fighting a duel dressed as a man, escaping from France during yet another revolution, dancing through Russia, hiding politicians in her home as the mob called for their blood outside, making love on sheets of pure silk to men straight from the battlefield, charming even the most bad-tempered of politicians, secret meetings on islands with royalty, Venice in carnival.

It was glorious and wonderful, and daring. It reminded me of Irene, who wanted to sing and have adventures, and used men to give her these, but who had fallen in love and given it all up. It reminded me of Lillian Rose, the prostitute from Whitechapel who had been so badly betrayed by a man when young, and was determined to get out of that life, any way she could. I thought of the women of Whitechapel, who couldn't even dream of a life like this. And yet the glamour of her life seduced me, and I found myself envying Emma Fordyce.

As evening fell, her voice trailed off, and she became quiet. She lay back on her pillows.

'Will you remember for me?' she asked weakly. 'All of it. I'll never tell some of those stories again. Will you remember?'

'We will,' Mary promised, tucking the sheet round the frail old lady. There was only a hint left now of the sparkle in Emma's eyes.

'I could have been a general,' Emma murmured, 'or Prime Minister. I would have made a fine Prime Minister, if only I'd been a man. Still, it's all been a glorious adventure.'

She closed her eyes and went to sleep. Mary helped me back to my own bed.

'Do you believe her?' Mary asked.

'I do, every word,' I replied.

'What did she tell you?' Eleanor Langham called. 'You were talking for a very long time. It must have been a long story.'

'Only a fairy tale,' I called back.

I told Mary that Emma had known Irene, and suggested she write to her in America (Irene had given us her address there) and ask her about Emma. We planned our investigations, mine into the ward, hers into the stolen boys, right to the last minute of visiting hours. But then later, Mary left, the lights were dimmed, the ward was quiet, and I knew that soon the nightmares, as every night, would come. I had dreamed disturbing dark dreams ever since April, but now, here in this hospital, in this bed, they intensified. Instead of once a week, they came almost every night. I didn't remember the details. I didn't want to. I just knew I woke sweating and afraid, staring into the dark, frightened of the fragments of my dream.

The ward was never quite dark. Moonlight streamed through the uncurtained windows. The lamp on the Sister's desk at one end of the ward was a circle of light. The gaslight in the lavatory through the door at the right of the ward shone dimly. But all the lights did was cast shadows in the dark corners of the room. I would wake up, suddenly, and look around and swear I saw dark shapes – figures and creatures, dogs and boys. I would lie there, staring through the open door at the end, certain I saw a man watching me – only for it to turn out to be Nurse Taylor's coat hanging on the coat hook.

Night-time began with the six o'clock tea, served round to all of us. It was dark outside by this time, and the ward was brightly lit. I dreaded the lights going down. But tea time was a moment of peace in the day.

Mind you, it was a busy time, what with nurses and visitors and doctors all up and down the ward. It's hardly surprising the accident happened. The lady who served our tea collided with Flo, who was coming back from the lavatory. Flo could not stop herself falling, and as she fell, she grabbed hold of the lady's arm, spilling her full cup of tea all over Emma's bed.

Emma, luckily, was sitting up in bed, and not even splashed. Her bed, however, was soaked. In amongst Flo's apologies and Emma's amusement and the Sister's irritation, it was decided that Emma would move to the bed at the end for the night, until her own could be dried and cleaned the next morning.

The bed diagonally opposite me: the one I thought I had seen someone murdered in.

For once, by the time the lights were switched off, we were all heavily asleep. It was nearly 3 a.m. when my usual nightmare woke me. It seemed to be a struggle for me to wake up, even just to open my eyes. My limbs were leaden, so heavy I could not even lift them. I couldn't have moved for anything in the world.

I looked around. Miranda, also usually a light sleeper, was lying ungracefully, buried in her blankets. Even Eleanor, who barely slept, was snoring gently. I could just see Sister Bey sitting at the desk. There was no sign of Nurse Taylor, or the other nurse. I could hear shouting somewhere in the hospital. I guessed they had gone to help.

I stared into the shadows, waiting for them to resolve into something sensible and everyday.

'Sister, we need help,' Nurse Taylor whispered from the doorway. 'He won't quiet down.'

I felt rather than saw Sister Bey leave the ward and go to the nurses' assistance. Then I was alone, only me awake, and that shadow that refused to go away.

I cannot move. My limbs are so heavy I cannot lift them. I cannot rise, I cannot twitch, I cannot even call out. I can only watch.

It's all happening again, just like the first night. Out of the shadows comes a figure, slight and lean, all black. I can barely even see an outline, just a darkness against more darkness. It disappears by Eleanor's side, then I see it again, standing over Flo. Then the figure is gone again, and now it stands by Emma.

Why won't anyone wake up? Normally one of us wakes and calls or stirs or goes to the lavatory every half-hour. Why not tonight? Why can't I move?

But then Emma herself wakes. She turns her head and smiles, dreamily. She looks around – then sees the figure by her bed. She draws breath to scream but he – she – it – pulls out Emma's pillow and places it over her face.

But Emma isn't going to give up her life so easily. She has fought for herself all her life, and she fights now. She flails and scratches and grasps at him, weak as she is, and one hand hits his cheek, I see it distinctly. He holds her wrists down, clambering on top of her to hold the pillow down with his knee. She struggles, but she is getting weaker. He shifts his position so he can hold both her wrists in one hand as the other presses the pillow down hard on her face. She twitches, once, twice, then lies still. Her body droops and sags, her hands fall loose. He removes the pillow and her eyes open, staring silently at the ceiling.

He looks at her for a moment, then steps back.

That is when he turns and looks directly at me.

He walks towards me, his footsteps utterly silent. Quickly I close my eyes. He must believe I slept through the whole thing. He *must*. I cannot hear him, but I am aware of him standing at the foot of my bed. I couldn't fight him off if he attacked me. I'm weak as a kitten. I would be able to do nothing but lie here and die.

I ought to take my punishment. I've been thinking I deserve it. But I don't want to die. I want to live, and punish him for Emma's death.

I can hear footsteps, quick and light. Nurse Taylor has returned. I can hear her go from bed to bed, quickly checking us all, then pause by Emma's bed, and gasp, just once, a tiny sound, then a muttered low conversation.

I opened my eyes. The shadow was gone. Nurse Taylor was holding a lamp over Emma's bed.

'Poor thing,' I heard her say.

'Passed away in her sleep,' Sister Bey said, and I heard her pen scratch as she noted it in her logbook. 'Nothing we could have done even if we had been here.'

'At least it was peaceful,' Nurse Taylor said softly.

I wanted to say 'No, no, that's not right! That's not what happened! I saw it!' but my mind was fuzzy, my voice silent, my eyelids heavy. As they made arrangements to take Emma Fordyce to the mortuary, I slipped into heavy dreamless sleep again.

DEATH IN
THE NIGHT

I would have doubted the entire experience when I woke up, except that Emma's bed was empty.

I'm not sure you can understand, now, so many years later as I write this, when the streets are full of light and we can banish the darkness in the corners by the flick of a switch, just how terrifying the night was back then. It was true that gaslight had brought illumination of a kind, but it was a strange, otherworldly flickering light that made the shadows come alive. Once the sun had gone down, we lived in twilight, and it was easy to believe in creatures that lived in the dark. So you see, trapped in my hospital bed, still not able to move easily, surrounded by strangers, certain I had seen one if not two murders, it was understandable that I was terrified.

Eleanor had offered to clear Emma's locker, as she had no family, but the nurses said no, they would do it. Miranda and Flo watched as the nurses placed screens round the bed where Emma had lain. Later, when the visitors arrived, there was the same young man in a suit who had visited before. All Emma's belongings were given to him.

Flo was sad at Emma's death, but seemed to accept it.

'It is the wish of the Lord,' Flo said softly.

'As if the Lord would take such a creature to his bosom!' Betty insisted. 'She was a vile creature.'

'*De mortuis nil nisi bonum*,' Miranda murmured. She seemed angry, as far as I could tell, for someone so restrained. She seemed to vibrate, almost, with rage as she stared at Emma's bed.

'What? What heathenish thing are you saying now?' Eleanor snapped. She seemed uncomfortable, shaken even.

'Do not speak ill of the dead,' I said loudly, translating from the Latin phrase. I had heard John say it once, up in his rooms. Mr Holmes had scoffed. If no one spoke ill of the dead, he pointed out, his job would be a lot harder.

Miranda looked at me and nodded.

'Well, just say that, instead of muttering in a godless language!' Betty snapped. She appeared to be under great strain. We all were. The atmosphere in the ward was tense and angry, and we all seemed to be on the edge of a great argument.

That was when the visitors arrived.

Mary came straight to my bed.

'Typhoid,' she announced. I was puzzled. For a moment I thought she was talking about Emma. 'The boy's parents,' Mary explained, taking off her hat and throwing it on my bed, to the nurse's distress. 'The ones you told me to look into, because their death might be significant? They died in a typhoid epidemic, along with dozens of others. Nothing suspicious at all.' She looked around the room. 'Where's Emma?'

I told her the news.

'What, that wonderful woman?' Mary said, taken aback. 'It's hard to believe; she seemed so alive yesterday.'

'When she told us all those stories,' I said, in a low voice. 'Who knows what she would have told us today?'

'Yes, quite,' Mary said, sitting down on my bed. 'What did you see last night?'

I shrugged.

'I was very sleepy. We all were. I can't be sure I saw anything.'

'Oh, to hell with sure,' Mary said. 'What happened?'

'I saw it again,' I said quietly. 'The same bed. She'd had to move, and they put her in the empty bed at the end, the one with the screens around it, now. They put them there when she died. They always hide the bodies. I woke up in the middle of the night, and there *it* was.'

I looked around the room. Miranda had wandered away to the door of the ward. Eleanor and Flo were talking quietly, but fervently. Betty was surrounded, as usual, by her mass of badly dressed daughters.

'The shadow? Like the first night?' Mary asked. She never doubted me. Bless her for that.

'I can't be sure, still,' I admitted. 'I felt so sleepy, my limbs were heavy, I couldn't even move. It was like a nightmare.'

'Some drugs do that,' Mary said. 'They're just supposed to send you to sleep, but some people wake up and find themselves in a sort of paralysis.'

'We all slept heavily last night.'

'If something happened, there'll be physical evidence,' Mary said, glancing over at the screened bed.

'The sheets have been changed and the bed and floor washed.'

'Something always gets left behind,' Mary insisted, standing up. 'It's one of Sherlock's maxims.'

'But you can't investigate,' I said, hissing, trying to remain quiet. 'Everyone is watching!'

'Well, it's about the time the nurses have their mid-afternoon meeting,' Mary said blithely. 'There, you see, they're going off to the corner. They won't notice. All you have to do is distract the others.'

'How am I supposed to do that?' I snapped. She smiled mischievously.

'It's only for a moment. You'll think of something: just enough to get me in there.'

Very well, if I must. And if I really thought about it, I knew exactly what to do.

I got out of bed and stood up, still shaky, but determined to walk across the room. Betty was holding up a cardigan to her second eldest daughter, and it was awful. I walked – well, limped – over to her bed, hanging onto Miranda's bed on the way.

I stood at the foot of Betty's bed, and said loudly, 'You're not going to make the poor girl wear that, are you? It's hideous.'

I don't think anyone had ever spoken to Betty like that before, judging by the way she gaped at me. Her daughters stared at me, the youngest two angry, but the eldest two with a sort of relief. The other two just seemed very bored, and sighed heavily every few moments.

'How . . . how dare you?' Betty stammered. I was tempted to say I wasn't quite sure how I dared myself, but instead I turned to Miranda and said, 'Don't you agree, Miss Logan?'

She looked away from Emma's bed at Betty. She had never liked Betty, and she took great pleasure in drawling the word, 'Vile,' in as disgusted a tone as possible.

'My dear, ignore them, they're jealous,' Eleanor said. Flo, her eyes bright with excitement (well, she did enjoy a good scandal), came up to join us.

'Well, I know you're not jealous,' I said, to Eleanor. 'I heard you tell Mrs Bryson you thought the colour of the wool was rancid.'

This was perfectly true, and in the way of liars everywhere, Eleanor was particularly shrill in denying it – especially when Miranda agreed that rancid was a perfect description.

I didn't need to say any more. With Eleanor vociferous in Betty's defence, and Betty's hatred of Miranda and her foreign ways, and Miranda's coolly spoken insults and Flo's delighted enjoyment at it all, everyone was thoroughly distracted. The nurses were mostly still in the other room, checking stock and reading notes. I looked over my shoulder.

Mary had sneaked behind the screens that surrounded Emma's deathbed. It was perfectly obvious someone was in there, as the screen brushed against her body, but for all anyone knew, it was a nurse – unless they saw Mary's neat dove-grey kid boots.

I turned back to the argument, now in full flow. Betty's daughters looked embarrassed and fascinated. I mouthed 'sorry' at the oldest one, and she just shrugged and smiled weakly. I had the feeling Betty's temper was a common sight at home.

We were all tense and worried and wound up, and everyone took advantage of the momentary slip of good manners to release their fears. To be honest, I think we all felt a good deal better for letting go, though that hadn't been my intention.

The nurses, finally drawn by the noise, came and ushered us back into bed. Mary managed to slip back out of the screens in the general melee.

'Well?' I said, as soon as I was safely tucked up in bed and Mary was beside me.

'Blood,' she said softly, the light of triumph in her eyes. 'Just a spot smeared on the head of the bed.'

'Could be old,' I countered. She shook her head.

'It would have been cleaned off. The nurses are very efficient. It just wasn't easy to see at night. Besides, it's still bright red.'

I thought of Emma's hands flailing about, hitting his face, and then the bed behind her.

'She scratched her attacker,' I whispered.

'It's real,' Mary whispered back. 'You really did see something, Martha.'

Then I went cold, all of a sudden. I remembered. If what I had seen was real . . .

'They saw me,' I told Mary. 'They saw me watching.'

MRS HUDSON'S
FEAR

Mary had to leave eventually. Visiting hours were supposed to be very strict; the Sister was insistent, despite Mary using her husband's connection to the hospital to come and go as she pleased.

'Don't be afraid,' Mary said as she was leaving, trying to reassure me. 'I have a plan.'

I wasn't afraid. Not then. I was worn out and angry and tired. I was also desperate to go home. I wasn't in that much pain any more, though I was still weak and unable to walk far, but I was beginning to feel better. I was tired of this hospital and sick of the noise and the smells and annoyed with my fellow patients.

To be fair, they were probably sick of me too. The argument I had started had no doubt been simmering below the surface for a while now. We were all living far too close together, politely ignoring each other's snores and smells, but there is only so long a person can take the idiosyncrasies of a complete stranger that close to them before they snap – and we had all snapped spectacularly. The argument hadn't cleared the air; we all still merely sat there, brooding over our wrongs, teetering on the edge of shouting at each other again.

Miranda left around four. Her screens were closed over, and when they were opened again, she was fully dressed in a very smart brown walking suit, and was snapping closed her suitcase.

'Where do you think you're going?' Eleanor barked, as if it was any of her business.

'I am cured,' Miranda said, not turning to look at her. 'Therefore I am leaving.'

'Good riddance,' Betty said, just loud enough to be heard yet softly enough to be ignored.

'Do you like anyone?' Flo inquired of Betty, sweetly.

For a moment we all hovered on the edge of harsh words again, then the atmosphere calmed down, and everyone turned back to their reading, or knitting. Miranda came to the foot of my bed.

'I suppose there's no reason for you to stay now,' I said, glancing towards Emma's empty bed. It was enough to let Miranda know I knew she had been here for Emma. She smiled a secretive, amused smile.

'None whatsoever,' she said in a way that made it clear she was not going to tell me exactly why she was there. 'But I think we'll meet again, Mrs Hudson.'

'Will we?' I asked.

'Oh yes,' she confirmed, and left.

That left me alone with Flo, Eleanor and Betty, none of whom were companions I would have chosen. I sighed, and lay back down on my bed.

Staying here was draining me of all energy. It was all too easy to lie back and do nothing, not even read. Food was brought to me, medicine was brought to me – I didn't even have to walk to the conveniences if I didn't want to. I just had to lie here, lazily watching everyone else. It was too much effort to talk. It was even too much effort to think. All I wanted to do was to lie in this bed and do nothing and think nothing and stare into nothing.

But then I'd drift off into sleep, and in sleep the nightmares came. The ward became infected with shadows, tall thin shapes that threatened to suffocate me as the other patients watched. All I could think of was death, lingering on this ward, in this whole building.

I sat up, trying to shake off the lassitude that enveloped me. I had spent too long in hospital. I had become used to the routine and the languor of life here. Trying to force my mind to work again, I looked around me.

The screen had been removed from the bed Emma had died in, and the Sister was telling a nurse to clean the blood from the bed frame, berating her for missing it the first time. That was our one piece of evidence, but no matter. Mary had seen it, and that was enough for now. Sister Bey walked past the end of my bed, and frowned.

'What happened here?' she asked, lifting the sheets at the end of my bed.

'I don't know,' I said, puzzled.

'There's a tear in your mattress,' she said, accusing, as if

I'd done it myself. 'There's a huge rip from one end to the other. The ticking is falling out!'

'I hadn't noticed,' I said slowly, though now I thought about it, my mattress didn't feel right.

'Well, you can't sleep on this tonight,' she insisted. She looked around the ward. It was busy. A lady was being moved into the bed to my left, and the sheets were being stripped from Miranda's bed to my right. Emma's old bed was still damp: they took a long time to dry, and the nurses were taking the mattress away to air it out.

The only possible bed I could move to was the one Emma had died in.

'No,' I said softly, as Sister Bey told the nurses to move me to that bed. I was struck by a chill. 'No!' I insisted. 'I don't want to. I'm not going into that bed.'

'Of course you are,' Sister insisted firmly. 'You cannot sleep in your own.'

'People have died in that bed!' I hissed. It only seemed to make her angry.

'People have died in all these beds,' she told me harshly. 'Don't be childish. You cannot stay in your own bed, not when it's in that state.'

'Then why can't I move to Miss Logan's old bed or Miss Fordyce's?' I asked, trying to be reasonable, trying to overcome the blind panic I felt at being moved into that other bed.

'Miss Fordyce's mattress is still damp, and as for the other, the mattress needs airing,' Sister Bey said stubbornly, and I saw that I had made a mistake. She saw me as a rebellious child who needed to be put in her place, and now she had dug her heels in. Nothing would change her mind now.

'This bed is fine,' I said to her. 'I won't sleep in that bed in the corner. Emma died in it only last night; it's still warm from her body!' I heard the panic rise in my voice and felt the tears prick my eyes. I despised myself for my weakness, but I had no strength to fight them. I couldn't control my feelings. The bed in the corner had assumed monstrous proportions in my eyes. The frame was a cage, the tiny spot of blood a great smear of gore, and the sheets a shroud to choke me.

'I won't,' I insisted. 'I won't!' I said again, aware I sounded like a small child, but unable to stop myself. I was terrified.

'She's really frightened,' Flo said softly.

'Attention-seeking,' Betty commented, as she wound another stitch onto her needles.

'Some people really need to learn how to behave,' Eleanor murmured.

'Perhaps if she really is afraid . . .' Nora started to say, but Sister Bey turned on her, her pale, sharp face flushed red with anger.

'This is not a hotel,' she snapped. 'This is a hospital, and patients need to learn to do as they are told. So do nurses, do you understand?'

Nora stepped back, surprised at the Sister's anger, but I could see she was going to speak again. Sister Bey, however, just continued.

'Patients have these odd fancies,' she told Nora, as if I wasn't there. 'If you give way to one, you will have to give way to all, and then the ward would be in anarchy. I won't have that on my ward. She will be moved.'

With that she walked away to her quarters through the door at the back of the ward, leaving no doubt that her instructions were to be obeyed.

Nora sighed, and turned to me. 'I'll help you.' She took my arm to help me up. 'Don't worry, I'll keep an eye on you tonight,' she said softly.

'That didn't help Emma!' I retorted, and Nora winced as if I'd hit her. I apologized, but I was shaking as I stood up. I had to go: if I didn't, Sister Bey wasn't above getting a male orderly to physically drag me into that bed. I wouldn't sleep though. My mind was full of images of myself lying helpless in that bed, unable to move and yet awake as the shadow leaned over me and smothered the life out of me.

Yet how could I not sleep? I was already exhausted, and my medicine made me drowsy.

'Nora,' I said quietly, 'I have a friend working in the laboratories . . .' Yes, I was even desperate enough to beg for help from *him*.

'The laboratories are closed,' she told me. 'It's Sunday. Please, Martha, don't argue with the Sister. She won't accept any kind of protest. Just sleep in that bed one night, and you'll be back in your own by morning.'

Morning? I wouldn't see the morning. My last hope of rescue was gone.

'No,' I said suddenly, pulling away. 'I won't go. I'll die if I get into that bed.'

But Sister Bey was back again, her hands full of sheets for the bed.

'If you persist in fighting, we'll have to sedate you,' she said firmly, and I saw in her hand, hidden by the sheets, a silver hypodermic. 'Hold her still.' Nora held me only lightly, but the other nurse, always in awe of the Sister, grabbed my wrist painfully and held my arm out for the injection. I twisted, terrified that if she put me to sleep I'd never wake up.

'What exactly do you think you're doing?' came a cold, clear voice from the door.

Mary. Oh, thank God, Mary.

'The patient is being difficult,' Sister explained, as Mary strode in, her head high, her body stiff with anger. She looked magnificent right then.

'Difficult in what way?' Mary demanded, reaching out to support me. 'All I see is a young fit woman bullying an older, sick woman.'

'She needs to change beds,' Sister Bey insisted. She was shaken by Mary. She couldn't overpower her, not by words or deeds. 'She was refusing to move.'

'Well, she doesn't have to,' Mary said, taking my arm and leading me back to my bed. 'Here is her discharge notice from Dr Watson.'

Sister Bey read the notice, her face still and white, as

Mary pulled the screens across my bed and hurriedly pulled a dress over my nightgown.

'I'm sorry, I'm sorry,' she whispered. 'I would have come sooner. I had no idea they were going to put you in that bed. I had to make arrangements and they took longer than I thought.'

'It's all right, you're here now,' I said, as Mary knelt to help me put on my shoes. I felt so relieved she was here, and I was safe, even as I felt embarrassed at the scene I had caused.

'Can you walk?' Mary asked, standing and picking up my hastily packed bag.

'If it gets me out of here, I can dance!' I said giddily, standing up quickly. Then I had to sit down again, light-headed, as my knees buckled under me. 'I may need some help,' I conceded. Mary smiled at me, and pulling the screen back, asked Nora for help. We walked past Sister Bey, still holding the discharge notice, who just looked at me with blank, empty eyes, as if all this had meant nothing to her. At the door, I looked back at the ward. Flo smiled, and gave a little wave goodbye. Betty sniffed, and returned to her interminable knitting. Eleanor looked smug and disapproving both at once. And Sister Bey was now at her desk once more, writing in her logbook. Yet the hand that gripped the pen was white around the knuckles, and the discharge notice lay ripped into tiny pieces in front of her. She must have hated me. I had challenged her in her own personal fiefdom, and won. She must have felt humiliated. I had made an enemy.

But it didn't matter. I was leaving now and I would never come back here again.

THE ART OF
TEA-MAKING

I was alone at last. Mary and John had dropped me off at 221b and settled me in the kitchen. I had begged Mary for some time to myself. I hadn't been alone in so long, and I had missed my solitude. She agreed, saying she had a couple of things to sort out, and that she'd be back later. She kissed my cheek, and left me sitting on my comfortable chair, at my own table, finally back in my blessed kitchen, at home.

The gas was on low, so I could barely see, but I wasn't afraid of these shadows. I ran my hand over the table, knowing each cut and burn as well as I knew the scars on my own hand. I listened to the noises in the street outside, and the wonderful silence in my home, and for the first time in two weeks, I felt like I could breathe.

A figure appeared in the doorway, tall and thin, almost saturnine in the dark. In silence he moved around the kitchen, moving a cup here, a pot there, preparing his potion. He put the cup before me and I took a sip.

'Well,' I said, 'this tea is acceptable.'

Sherlock Holmes tasted his own tea and grimaced.

'I followed your steps exactly. Logically, it should taste like your tea,' he complained.

'Tea-making is an art, not a science.'

We drank in silence for a while.

'How did you know I was coming home?' I ventured.

'I heard Mrs Watson insisting that Watson sign the discharge notice,' he explained. 'I knew then you would be home immediately. She generally gets her own way with him.'

As do you, I thought.

'I hope you are quite well,' he said, after a while, as if he had just remembered he ought to say something.

'I am recovering,' I told him, equally politely. 'Mrs Watson tells me she has arranged some help for me whilst I am convalescing, so you won't be inconvenienced.'

'That wasn't—' he said quickly.

'I know,' I interrupted. 'Sorry.'

That may have been as close as we could get to an expression of concern and reassurance between us. We had both been brought up to hide our feelings and present a stoic face to the world, and we were both very good at it.

'I did not notice you were ill,' he said, after a while.

'I know,' I agreed. 'I took good care that you should not.'

'Nevertheless,' he said, getting up and pacing up and down. 'There are seventeen steps up to my room. I counted them once, and I have never needed to count them again, for they do not change. When I meet people, I meet them once, and that is enough to observe. However, I rarely have prolonged contact with them. I do not need to update my observations. Those people I see day to day have become like . . .'

'Wallpaper?' I said, quite gently.

'Quite,' he agreed ruefully. 'However, wallpaper may decay and peel away, but as the daily changes are infinitesimal, we do not notice until the wallpaper falls on our head.'

'Not in this house it won't,' I said firmly, but he ignored me.

'I must take care to notice the changes in the few people I do see day to day,' he continued, walking up and down, his hands behind his back, thinking aloud, as I had heard him do in his rooms. 'Yourself, Billy, Watson. Your illness has taught me a valuable lesson.'

'I'm so glad I could help,' I said dryly. I was feeling a little tired now.

'You were of help,' he said seriously, sitting down again. 'I must never forget there is always more to learn. I am sorry that you were the cause of that lesson, though.'

'I deliberately hid it from you,' I told him again. 'I would not have you know of my illness.'

'Why not?' he countered. 'You know of mine.'

There seemed nothing more to say to that, so we merely drank in companionable silence, each lost in our own thoughts.

'I have to know,' I said after a while, putting the cup down on the saucer. 'Did you send Billy and Wiggins to Mary about those missing boys?'

He looked up, surprised.

'Logically,' I said, 'they would have gone to you first. You're their mentor. You're the detective.'

He smiled ruefully.

'They did,' he admitted. 'But what they had was mostly rumour and conjecture. I thought perhaps it would be better dealt with by Mrs Watson and yourself. I thought it would be good training for you both, to sift fact from fairy tale, and find out what truth lies at the bottom of these stories.'

'Training?' I asked, amused.

'I admit,' he said, carefully replacing his cup on its own saucer, 'I had thought you and Mrs Watson were like the rest of your sex, incapable of logical thought or action. Although Mrs Watson had shown some genius for the work when she came to me to track down her father, I had thought marriage and a home of her own would rid her of her talent, as it does all women.'

'Did you?' I asked softly. He leaned forward and clasped his hands on the table.

'However,' he continued as if I hadn't spoken, 'certain events earlier this year led me to believe that perhaps the two of you had not entirely lost all capacity for logical thought. Or I should say, she had not lost it; I was unaware of your own talents. Perhaps you were not quite as illogical as the rest of your sex. Perhaps you could even, in time, be taught to observe and deduce and think properly. I am all in favour of as many people as possible learning to use their minds. Hence, I decided the best course of action was to give you a case of your own, and see how far you could get with it. I shall, of course, take over if you find you cannot get any further – but I shall wait until you ask me.'

'First,' I said to him, 'thank you for at least waiting until we ask. Second, what do you know about what happened earlier this year?' It was this phrase that had caused my stomach to tighten. I felt the breath catch in my throat. We had kept our secret so well, I was certain! I had not let anything slip – unless I had called out whilst under the drug-induced sleep of the operation.

He looked at me very steadily, his eyes black in the darkness of the room.

'Lestrade has a bugbear about the death in Richmond,' he said softly. 'He will not let it go.'

My hand gripped the delicate china of my cup.

'I investigated, out of mere curiosity at first,' Mr Holmes continued. 'This man had thoroughly covered his tracks. But I found scraps of papers, and several people suddenly either disappeared or came out of hiding, and names familiar to me were spoken in reference to this man. That's all I have, so far. But I have suspicions.'

I pressed my lips together. I would not talk. I would not condemn myself out of my own mouth, not to this man.

'He deserved his end,' Mr Holmes said harshly.

'Did he?' I asked, angry. 'How could you say that?'

'I have an idea of what he did.'

'You don't know how it's haunted me!' I cried out.

'Yes, I do!' he snapped back. 'Do you think I have always behaved exactly according to the law? Do you not think that I, too, might have crossed the line? Or gone further than I expected, or wanted?' He reached forward and clasped my hands, his thin fingers wrapping around mine. 'Believe me, I know.'

I sat there for a moment, in silence. I never thought of him like that. I had once or twice referred to him as an angel of vengeance, as a joke. I laughed at it. Now perhaps I saw something new in him, something John and Mary and Billy had never seen and never would.

'Inspector Lestrade . . .' I said slowly.

'Will never know,' he reassured me.

'He might. If you found out, he might.'

Mr Holmes snorted and released my hands.

'Not him,' he insisted. 'He lacks the imagination. I've already half-convinced him the whole thing was a terrible accident.'

'Why is he so tenacious about this?' I asked, not as reassured as I should be. Mr Holmes shrugged and sat back.

'Some instinct,' he speculated. 'But you will be safe, I promise you.'

I nodded. I believed him. And now, back in the kitchen of 221b, I felt safe. I sipped my tea again. It was cold, and I poured out some more from the pot for both of us.

'When you were on Dartmoor,' I asked, 'did you have nightmares?'

'Why would I have nightmares?' he said, irritated, as he added more sugar to his cup.

'It's a lonely place,' I said, sipping my tea. 'You slept in burial mounds, I understand? The moor is full of strange noises at night, Dr Watson said, and there was an escaped prisoner, too. And the Hound itself.'

'Yes, the Hound,' he said softly. He looked at me, and even there, in the half-dark of the kitchen, he could see I was not asking out of idle curiosity.

'There were dreams,' he admitted. 'It has always annoyed me that a man's mind, no matter how logical and ordered, should become prey to fantasies and fairy tales as soon as he sleeps.'

'Bad dreams?' I asked. He flared up for a moment, as if he would not answer, then nodded.

'But of course, in the daylight, there was an adequate explanation for all of them. Animals made the noises, people were responsible for the lights, the Hound, for all its horror, was not supernatural. And yet . . .'

'And yet for a moment you believed?' I whispered. 'For a moment the nightmares were real?'

'Only a brief moment,' he said to me. 'The Hound leapt at me, huge and glowing, and for a moment I believed in Hell and its devil and a great curse.' He sipped his tea. 'But I learnt the truth, the devil fell, and proved to be nothing more than a painted dog.'

'I see,' I said. 'Behind the nightmare was a kernel of truth. You had to seek out and confront that truth to stop the nightmare.'

'I suppose that was the case,' he said, almost grudging. I do not think he liked to talk to me about this. He drained his cup and put it down. 'Good night, Mrs Hudson.'

'Good night, Mr Holmes.'

He left, and went up to bed. It would always be like this in 221b Baker Street, him and me in this house. Other people would visit, and stay and sleep in here, some for years, but in the end, it was always Mrs Hudson and Sherlock Holmes in 221b Baker Street.

I sat back and tried to think about the hospital case logically, stripping away all the supernatural elements. What did I know? What was fact, and not fancy?

Emma died after she changed beds. Coincidence? Would she have died no matter what bed she was in? And how had she died? My mind had been screaming about supernatural monsters, but I knew that not to be the case. Then what? I had seen a dark shadow rise up beside her bed – and I still thought the dark shadow had killed a woman in the same bed in the same way on my first night. But I had been heavily drugged then, of course . . .

Wait a minute. I'd been a fool! That night's reaction wasn't a nightmare, it was drugs, again. And the reason no one else had woken up – not even watchful Miranda – was that we had all been drugged.

It was a moment of revelation. Drugging me might have been accidental – slightly too much of the pain medication I was still taking, or even an unexpected reaction – but drugging everyone was completely different.

For a moment I suspected the nurses. They gave us the evening medication. But of course the easiest way to drug us all would be to slip it into the evening tea. We had our own tea, but the water was boiled in the storeroom, right through the door at the end of the ward, the door we all went through on our way to the conveniences. The nurses didn't share our tea, so they would not have been affected. Any one of us could have done it – nurses, patients, a complete stranger; we didn't recognize all the doctors and cleaners and other visitors to the ward.

My mind was racing again. I remembered this feeling. This was how it felt before, when Mary and I were working on the blackmail case. This was good. This was intoxicating. This was addictive.

This was what it was to be alive.

AND SO TO WORK

Mary arrived soon after with two women, one of them drooped and depressed, in a shapeless shabby dress. She was introduced as Mrs Turner, and would do my housework whilst I was recovering. She nodded at me, not meeting my eyes, and silently went into the scullery.

The other woman was dressed as a nurse, and as she stepped forward into the light for a moment I thought she had brought me Nora.

'I've hired a nurse on your behalf to take care of you whilst you are convalescing at home. You are nowhere near strong enough to look after yourself. This is Nurse Grace Taylor,' Mary announced. 'She is Nora's sister. Now you'll be able to hear about everything that happens on your old ward. Isn't that nice?'

Clever, devious Mary.

I woke early. I had got used to that at the hospital. But thankfully I woke up in my own bed, in the small room above that of Mr Holmes. My own warm, comfortable bed, the fire still burning low in the fireplace, the door firmly shut on the rest of the house, the window showing me Baker

Street, and silence, blessed silence everywhere. With a sigh of contentment, I settled back to think.

I was interrupted by Mr Holmes, who came into the room not in his normal manner, which was to stride in as if he were the most important person there, or anywhere, which was usually justified. He held out a letter to me, the paper large and thick and lavender. The letter was opened.

'I didn't open it, or read it,' he said quickly. 'Mrs Watson did that. No doubt she knew who it was from, and knew the news was for both of you.'

I took the letter and looked at the postmark. Vienna?

'No doubt she is taking classes there,' Mr Holmes said. 'Perhaps she is contemplating a return to the stage.' He left quickly. So the letter was from Irene Adler.

My dearest Martha,

Holmes' telegram telling me of your illness was sent to New York, and sent round a few friends, and finally sent to me here in Vienna. I was preparing to come back when I received Mary's telegram, by the same route, telling me you were recovering, and asking for information about Emma Fordyce. I presume, then, you are well enough to be curious? To be investigating a little? Very well, I shall stay in Vienna for now, but here is some information for you.

I met Emma when I was a girl becoming a woman, in 1870. She was in her sixties then, but still playing the game, and still very good at it. She knew attraction was as much a matter of charm and thought and conversation as anything that happened in the bedroom, and men still loved her. As for me, I knew by then I could sing, and that was all I wanted to do in life. Well, that, and have adventures. Emma took me under her wing and guided me, kept me safe, introduced me to composers and conductors, and taught me to be clever. She also taught me about the fun to be had in the world. I would sing for her and her lovers (I was blindfolded, of course) and afterwards Emma would tell me who they were and what they had done and how they could be useful.

Emma was sweet and kind and clever, and I am persuaded many of her lovers truly loved her, and would have married her. But she would never marry. She loved her freedom, and I don't believe she ever fell in love. But this is background, and you want detail. Mary asked if there were any men who might have wanted to keep their liaison with Emma a secret. Well, there were many men, but times were different then, and most were proud of their friendship with Emma. I know of only two men who were difficult.

One was Lord Ernest Howe. He never wanted his association with Emma to be known; it was to be kept a strict secret. He had many lovers. He had three wives too (not all at the same time, they had an annoying habit of dying). He was obsessed with getting a son and heir. Both his first and second wives had died childless, and he was on his third by the time he met Emma: none of his mistresses had produced a son either, though there were a few girls.

Emma wasn't that impressed with him, I do remember that. He lacked a sense of humour, or any kindness. His third wife finally ended up in a lunatic asylum, I know. But Emma would never talk about him like she would about the other men. However, she did get letters from him, letters she would never let me read. She would lock herself away with these letters for hours on end, and when she had finished, she would burn them.

The other was Richard Pembury. Sir Richard now. Yes, that Sir Richard! The politician who speaks so beautifully in the House, and supports Reform bills and help for fallen women and so on. He and Emma had a beautiful time in Venice about thirty-five years ago. Her maid thought Emma would fall in love this time. Glowing with it, she said. But then, one day, it all just stopped. I asked her once what had happened, but she refused to tell me, saying that secrets had power. But she did warn me to stay away from him. I remember he was to be married once, but she wrote to him, and he called the wedding off. She didn't seem triumphant about it.

There, does that help your mystery? I wish I could come to help, but I am taking lessons with a great maestro. I think I shall sing again – through choice, not necessity. My husband is kind, and understands the lure of the stage, though I'm not sure he knows how great the lure is. Then I shall come to London, and send you tickets

*– but I won't send one to Mr Holmes. If he wants to
hear me sing, he can pay for it.*
  Love to Mary, and of course to you.
  Yours, Irene.

Like Irene herself, the letter left me excited, but exhausted.
I put it to one side.

At first I thought about the incidents at the hospital, but
my mind just kept going round and round in circles, and
nothing new sprang out at me. I decided to put that case
on the back burner and think about Mary's case. Therefore,
a couple of hours later, when she came in, before she spoke,
I said to her:

'Boys may get lost, but they don't just disappear.'

'Well, good morning to you too,' she replied, taking off
her coat. 'Did you sleep well?'

'Moderately well,' I replied. 'I've been watching Baker
Street.'

She moved over to the window and peered out.

'It's very busy this morning,' she said. The street was full
of street sellers, important men in suits, less important men
lounging about, hansom cabs, carriages, horses, carts, boys
running messages, boys delivering goods, boys just running
about and getting in everyone's way.'

'Boys, street boys, just move on,' I said to her. 'I've been
thinking about it since I woke up.'

'Aren't you supposed to be relaxing and recovering?'

'I am relaxing. They change streets, change towns

sometimes. Or they get taken up by the beadle, or the police. Or they end up in the workhouse, or the infirmary.'

'I do have something to tell you, you know,' Mary continued, perched on the windowsill.

'Those boys, however, just disappeared, didn't they?' I went on, eager to get my thoughts out. 'They didn't leave any clue as to where they had gone, did they?'

'You're just like Sherlock,' Mary said, amused.

'What's that supposed to mean?' I asked, affronted. Mr Holmes was the rudest man I knew!

'Once you have a thought in your head, you must follow it through to the logical conclusion, no matter what is in your way,' Mary told me. 'In his case that's usually villains, but in your case it seems to be ordinary conversation.'

'Sorry,' I said, lying back in bed. Well, perhaps I had been a little rude. Perhaps a mite over-excited. 'Good morning, Mary, how are you?'

'That's better,' she said. 'Good morning, Martha, I see you had a letter from Irene. It arrived whilst you were ill, I hope you don't mind I opened it.'

'No, not at all, the information was for both of us. We can talk about it now.'

'Yes, and I have an idea about that,' Mary said, smiling to herself.

'What?' I asked. 'What are you planning? Tell me, Mary.'

'In a minute,' she said, getting off the windowsill and walking up and down, across the foot of my bed. 'Go on with what you were saying. About the boys, not Irene's letter.'

'Intrigued now, are you?' I asked.

'I went to the docks last week,' she told me, serious now.

'The docks? Alone? Are you insane?' I exclaimed. The docks were dangerous, especially for a young woman alone. She shrugged.

'I took John's gun,' she reassured me, although I wasn't reassured. 'I disguised myself as a Swedish woman looking for her brother.'

'Why Swedish?'

'In case I got something wrong. I could blame it on being Swedish,' she said eagerly.

'And the accent?'

'Who knows what the Swedish sound like?' she told me. She continued to walk. 'It is glorious down there, Martha. The smell, for a start! All these spices in the air, so heavy it almost chokes you. Spices and tobacco and tea from all over the world, just sitting there on a London dock. And the mast and the ships rising up above you. They're huge, they make you dizzy just to look at them. It's like a forest on the water. And the people. All kinds of people from all over the world. You can hear ten different languages in ten minutes. Russian, French, Portuguese—'

'Swedish,' I interrupted.

She smiled at me.

'I wasn't caught,' she said.

'I'd doubt you'd be standing here if you had been,' I pointed out. 'All right, go on. You told people you were looking for your younger brother?'

'Yes,' she said, leaning on the rail at the end of my bed. 'So of course, people told me about other boys that had gone missing.'

'Misery loves company,' I said.

'And they had. Three boys in the past two years. Just vanished, poof, like that,' she said, snapping her fingers. 'And not left on a ship or fallen in the river because they would have heard something after so long. Bodies come to the surface eventually, sailors return home. No, just gone.'

'Very mysterious,' I said, sitting back in bed and wrapping my shawl round me. 'Just like the Pale Boys.'

'The Pale Boys?' Mary said, puzzled. 'Aren't they just a legend? A sort of fairy tale for street children? I know I talked about them, but I don't actually believe they exist.'

'There is a hound from Hell, and there are painted dogs,' I said softly. 'Every legend has a grain of truth.'

'I see,' Mary said gently. She didn't have to say she knew I'd been talking to Mr Holmes. It was blatantly obvious.

'So what next?' she asked.

'Well, I'm going to get dressed,' I said, flinging back the covers and standing up – then I stopped, and sat back down again heavily. I had felt fine in bed, but now my head spun, my stomach ached and my knees felt they would give away underneath me. 'Maybe not . . .' I gasped. Mary was by my side in a second, forcing me back into bed.

'Don't you dare get up!' she snapped. 'You came out of hospital much too early. You need at least two more days' bed rest before you can get up.'

'I can't, I have things to do,' I argued, but wearily.

'Mrs Turner can do your work,' Mary told me, plumping my pillows. 'She's trustworthy, and competent.'

'But Mary . . .'

'You can come down to the kitchen in a few days, if Nurse Taylor says so.'

I didn't want anyone else interfering, telling me it wasn't suitable for a lady like me; that I should take up knitting instead.

'Very well, I'll rest,' I said, rather bad-temperedly. 'What are you going to do?'

Mary leaned over me, tucking in my disarranged sheets.

'As a doctor's wife, and as an author's wife,' she said lightly, 'I get invited to join an awful lot of committees. Ladies doing worthy work, that sort of thing.'

'It sounds like it would bore you to tears,' I said suspiciously.

'Oh, it does,' she admitted, standing up to admire her handiwork, and not meeting my eyes. 'But they do get a chance to visit an awful lot of influential men. Business leaders, Lords, Members of Parliament . . .'

Her voice trailed off as I realized what she was saying. She looked at me, and sort of smiled, in her special 'please forgive me' way.

'Mary?' I questioned.

'Well, it turns out,' Mary said, quickly buttoning her coat, 'that one of the many committees I am on has arranged a meeting with Sir Richard Pembury. This afternoon, in fact.

And I've got myself invited along,' she went on, not letting me interrupt, as she fastened her hat. 'I think I can contrive to get myself alone with him, and then who knows what I'll winkle out of him. Ta-ta!' she said cheerily, sweeping out in the full knowledge that there was absolutely no way I could stop her.

THE HONOURABLE
MEMBER OF PARLIAMENT

Grace Taylor visited my room soon after Mary left. She looked around, hands clasped in front of her.

Now I could see her properly, I could notice the differences between her and Nora. Grace's hair was lighter, and she was slightly shorter. She didn't carry herself with the same authority as Nora, and she seemed quieter, to have less of a presence.

'Mrs Watson has hired me to live here, and look after you for a while, as you recover,' she told me. 'She tells me you are likely to try to do too much too soon, and you don't like to be dependent on anyone.'

'That is true,' I admitted.

'Well, you've been ill, very ill, and you'll be ill again if you don't allow me to care for you, do you understand?' she said firmly, but kindly. I nodded meekly.

'How do you feel?' she asked me, coming over to the bed.

'Well,' I said. She looked at me dubiously. 'Weaker than I expected,' I admitted.

She gently lifted up my nightgown to look at my wound, unwrapping the dressing with her cool hands. She seemed pleased with what she saw, and gently washed the site.

'It's quite a coincidence, your sister nursing me in hospital and you nursing me at home,' I said.

'Not really,' Grace said softly. She patted my wound dry and reached into her Gladstone bag for a clean dressing. 'Nora is acquainted with Dr Watson, and when he said you would need a nurse, she mentioned me. Hold still, please.'

She wrapped a new dressing round my stomach as I sat as still as I could.

'I didn't realize they knew each other so well,' I said, as she pulled the nightdress down. 'I knew they worked together in the hospital but . . .'

'Dr Watson is helping Nora to train as a doctor,' Grace said, as she pulled various bottles out of her bag. 'He's lending her books.'

'That's kind of him. And brave of Nora.'

'She's very determined,' Grace said, with a sigh, as if Nora's stubbornness got on her nerves. 'That's why she prefers the night shift: she has time to study. Are you in any pain?'

'A little,' I told her. 'That explains why Nora was working there. I had the impression she didn't like it much.'

'Drink this,' Grace said, handing me a glass of water. She had poured two drops into it from a small green bottle. I obeyed, watching her.

'I shouldn't tell you this, but Nora liked you,' Grace said. 'The other patients could be difficult though. They were all there because their families had made large donations to the hospital, or were friends of the directors. They think of the nurses as their servants.'

'That must be awkward,' I said, as Grace opened my wardrobe door and started to inspect my dresses.

'It is,' she admitted. 'You won't be able to wear corsets or a bustle for a while, I'm afraid.'

'I'll feel undressed without a corset!'

'At first, but you'll get used to it,' she said, taking down an old dress – black, of course. 'You'll heal faster without a corset.'

She turned to face me.

'I'll stay overnight for the first week, in the room next to yours. For the second week, I'll be here from when you wake until you go to bed. After that, all being well, I shall be here three times a day to administer your medication and change your dressing. Is that acceptable?'

'Perfectly,' I told her. 'I'm not sure what you'll find to do all day anyway.'

'There's plenty for a good nurse to do,' she said calmly. She hesitated for a moment, then added, 'Nora said I was to tell you anything about the ward you wanted to know, if you asked.'

'Well, I miss it,' I lied, convincingly.

'Patients often do,' she agreed. 'It becomes a home from home, and the other patients become like family.'

The kind of family that dislikes, distrusts, hates and possibly murders each other, I nearly pointed out. Instead I asked about Betty, Flo and Eleanor. Were they still there?

'Eleanor Langham has gone home,' Grace said. 'She has a recurring chest infection which affects her heart. She comes in to recover, then goes home as soon as possible. She doesn't like to be away from home too long. She'll be back soon, though.'

'She's that ill?'

'She never seems to recover. Betty Soland has gone home too, since you left. Flo Bryson is still there, though.'

'I never understood what was wrong with Mrs Bryson,' I admitted. 'She was supposed to have a lung infection, but to be honest, she showed no symptoms. Not even a cough.'

'No, Nora never understood her presence there either,' Grace said darkly. 'Maybe Flo just liked the company. Now, you must stay in bed, but if you rest and eat, I think you'll be well enough to come downstairs in a few days.'

I slept and thought and slept some more, until the next morning, when Mary swept in, looking exquisite in blue.

'Good morning,' she said, standing at the foot of my bed.

'You met Sir Richard Pembury?' I asked eagerly. She nodded, and moved over to the window, perching on the sill.

'It's a long story, so listen, and don't interrupt,' she told me. 'The committee I chose was one to rescue fallen women. There seem to be a lot of them. Sir Richard interests himself in social issues, so he was an obvious person to meet. The title is earned, not inherited, by the way. He rose from being the youngest son of a clergyman. That shows his determination. He has a certain strength of character.'

'This isn't the story,' I said, impatient. She nodded, and

looked out of the window at the blank grey sky, already smudged with smoke.

'There were four of us who saw him, all painstakingly respectable. We visited his home, in Mayfair. It is exactly the kind of home you'd expect a man like him to have, right down to his terribly stiff butler. It felt like an ancestral town house that had been in his family for years, but that's not right, is it?'

'No, it isn't,' I confirmed. 'I read a profile on him in *The Times* when he took on his present position in the government. His family were never rich; he himself started as a clerk in a shipping office.'

'Well, he hides it well. He has big old furniture, soft, well-worn carpets, servants that act like they've served him for generations. We were shown into his study which, again, was exactly how you'd imagine it to be, with a huge mahogany desk, a Turkey carpet, books lining the walls floor to ceiling, and Sir Richard himself, holding out a hand to us. He seemed pleasant, old, of course, easily in his seventies, but upright. His hair has gone white, and is just a shade too long, he has pleasant brown eyes, and is neither slim nor fat.'

'Just what an MP ought to be,' I commented. Mary nodded.

'We sat down and drank tea and ate tiny sandwiches and talked and he agreed with everything we said, and he pointed out the difficulties, and how we could get over them, and promised he would help, and everyone went away satisfied and utterly charmed,' Mary said, shifting her position so she could look right at me. 'Everyone felt like they'd achieved something good that day, and he made us feel like that.'

'I see. He's a good man then,' I said, disappointed.

'I haven't finished,' Mary said, smiling slightly. 'Somehow, as the others left, I got myself behind the door, and when they had all gone and he had sat down, I stepped out and said to him, "Emma Fordyce".'

I really should have told Mary she was reckless. I should have told her she shouldn't be doing that sort of thing. Mary even paused for me to say that. But I had learnt that Mary was the sort of person who happily walked into dangerous situations, not out of bravado, but simply to see what would happen next. I merely nodded at her to continue.

'"Who?" he said. "Have you forgotten something?" I stepped forward, trying to look a bit menacing.

'"Emma Fordyce is dead," I said.

'"I'm afraid I don't know that name," he said, and he took up a piece of paper, but he was lying, I knew it. Do you know what Sherlock says – if you pretend you know everything already, nine times out of ten they'll end up confessing.

'"You do," I insisted. "And now she's dead."

'"I'm sorry about your friend, but I cannot help," he said to me. "Now let me show you out."

'He moved towards me, but I stepped aside, and said, "But she left behind a manuscript."

'He froze. I continued.

'"I've read it," I said. "It's very interesting. And I should imagine very expensive."

'"I don't know . . ." he started to say, but he faltered, and I knew I had him, Martha. I had him!

'"But maybe Patrick West will pay more," I said, and then he snapped. He darted towards me, fast as a snake, and grabbed my wrist and twisted it up behind me, and pushed me against the bookcase. It hurt, and I was terrified, but I had scored a blow, Martha.

'"You tell no one," he hissed, and I twisted so I could see his face. He wasn't the polite old man any more. He was vicious and cruel. I could see it in his eyes, and the spittle at the corner of his mouth and the way he ground his teeth as he snarled at me and that trace of pleasure in my pain.

'"People know I'm here."

'"Who, a blind old gossip writer no one listens to any more?" he mocked, and twisted my wrist a little higher.

'"Sherlock Holmes!" I gasped out. I hate to use his name, Martha, but it was useful then. He let go and stepped back, and pulled his coat straight.

'"She's dead," he said, panting as he regained his control. "It's just the rambling of an old woman. Whatever that bitch wrote was a lie, do you understand?"

'"I understand," I said. I wasn't in any state to argue.

'"You publish, and I'll find you," he said to me, his eyes still evil.

"'Will you?" I asked, trying to be insouciant, as I'm sure blackmailers are in these circumstances.

"'I found Emma," he said, and he smiled, and it was horrific, the smile of a shark before it eats its prey. And yes, I know sharks don't smile, but if a shark could smile, that's exactly what I would imagine it to look like. I left, quickly. And that was that.'

'And that's his secret,' I said softly. 'His temper.'

'More than a temper,' Mary said ruefully, rubbing her wrist. 'His Mr Hyde. But many men, and women, are like that. It's not enough to kill for.'

'It could be, if he did something in that temper,' I said. 'It could certainly be enough to hold back his career if it was known he was prone to that kind of violence.'

I lay back on my pillows. It could be enough. For it to be known you could get so angry you could hurt, maybe even kill. Cabinet ministers were supposed to be calm, fatherly examples to us all. I closed my eyes.

'You're exhausted,' I heard Mary say. 'I'll leave you alone.' Her voice drifted as I slipped back into sleep.

I woke later on that same day to find John leaning over my bed, checking my pulse. I think he had been talking to me some time, but I had not been aware of it.

'Mary's getting rather caught up in this "missing boys" story,' John said to me, in a low voice.

'What?' I said sluggishly. I must have been awake for a few moments: I had been vaguely aware of John checking

me over and talking to me, but I was still feeling rather
drained. I had slept badly, my dreams full of hospital wards
and angry men.

'You think it's just a story?' I asked, when John repeated
himself.

'I've no idea,' he admitted. 'It's just – she's becoming
obsessed by it. She talks about it all the time, and when
she's not talking, she's thinking. I'm worried it may be too
much for her.'

'Mary's stronger than you think,' I told him.

He shook his head. 'Mary's more fragile than you think,'
he told me. 'You're the strong one.'

READING BETWEEN
THE LINES

Three days. Three days I lay in bed! I am ashamed to think of it now, but John insisted, and his agreement that I be released from hospital early had come with certain conditions, including that I couldn't get up until he told me so.

Besides, he wasn't going to let me go anywhere until I told him what I had observed at the hospital.

'I didn't actually see much,' I had to admit. 'There were arguments and tension, and people enjoying and misusing whatever little power they had. I also saw kindness and gentleness, and some truly awful clothes.'

'Do you think something is going wrong there?' John asked, standing by the window, fiddling with his watch-chain.

'I think Emma's death wasn't natural,' I insisted.

'The post-mortem showed nothing,' he said unhappily.

'Mary says suffocation doesn't always present evidence.'

John smiled, and nodded, his pride in his clever wife overcoming his worry.

'Can I get up now?'

He agreed, partly because I was so insistent, and partly to keep an eye on Mary. Restless Mary could become reckless

Mary. I told him I felt much better than I did. I couldn't bear to be up here any more. The solitude was acceptable, but there was someone in my kitchen, doing my job, looking after Mr Holmes, and I had to keep an eye on her.

Halfway down the stairs I regretted my decision. I was supported by Grace, but still felt very weak and shaky. I could hear Mr Holmes playing his violin as I descended, but when I stopped, he stopped. I reached out for support, and became aware I was leaning against his door. I stood there for a moment, listening to the silence within. He was waiting for me to go on or give up. I could never give up in front of him. I took a breath, drew upon my strength and carried on down the stairs, hearing the music start again behind me.

I went down to the kitchen, my kitchen, at last. I couldn't quite believe it was all still there, the brand-new gas range, the windows out to the street and the back yard, the porcelain pastry board below the air vent, and that scarred and burnt kitchen table. It all felt oddly like something that I dreamed, but when I stepped through the door, there it all was. First I saw Mary, standing by the range. She looked so young and so strong. She didn't even look tired any more. I decided John must be worrying unnecessarily, because he loved her and wanted to protect her.

Grace handed me over to Mary, who hugged me close, and sat me down in the armchair by the range very carefully, as if I was made of porcelain. Grace went to look in the pantry, I presume to check what I could eat. I looked around my kitchen, which seemed so familiar and yet so strange. I had been gone too long. I would need time to fit in again.

In the centre of the room stood another woman, the woman I'd been introduced to before as Mrs Turner, although I had been only vaguely aware of it then. She was of middling height, but very thin. Her face was drawn and grey, and her hair was mostly grey too, though you could see it had once been brown. Even her clothes were grey and brown, patched, and of cheap material, but carefully sewn. Either she or someone she knew was an expert seamstress. I nodded to her, but though she nodded back, she looked away again nervously.

'Martha, this is Mrs Turner,' Mary said, as she adjusted my cushion for me. I shifted uncomfortably – I was quite capable of adjusting my own cushion – and, getting the message, Mary went to stand by Mrs Turner. 'I've brought her in to help you whilst you recover.'

'How kind of you,' I said, wondering if Mrs Turner was a blessing or curse. She was obviously one of Mary's waifs and strays. Mary could never resist helping anyone in trouble, no matter what the cost, or the outcome.

'She can clean and dust and do laundry,' Mary continued, her eyes pleading with me to be kind to Mrs Turner.

'There's no need to do laundry here, it's sent out,' I said. I had always hated laundry day – the damp, the heat, the clothes drying for days, the repeated washing. 'Can you cook?'

She cast one scared look up at Mary, and said to me, 'Only basic things, ma'am.'

'You don't need to call me ma'am, Mrs Hudson will do,' I told her. 'That's all right, I can cook.'

Grace turned round to argue, and I said quickly, 'I'll instruct you what to do. What other skills have you?'

'I'm a good seamstress,' she said softly. 'I can take your dress in for you.'

My dress was hanging loose. I must have lost a considerable amount of weight whilst I was ill. It was not the reducing diet I would have chosen.

'Thank you,' I told her. 'Well, cleaning, lighting the fires and so on will be your main duties. You'll need to take food up to Mr Holmes, too, though you'll only clean his rooms if he's out. He hates having people fussing around him.'

'Mr Holmes?' she said, her voice low and scared. I'd never seen anyone quite so shy and nervous.

'He'll be nice to you,' I reassured her. 'He's only rude to people he's close to.'

'He called me a damned interfering woman yesterday,' Mary said happily. 'We're good friends.'

And that was that, Mrs Turner was hired. Grace took her out shopping as I would need special food for the next few days, and Mary and I sat down round the kitchen table.

It wasn't silent in there. The noise of Baker Street filtered through the area door, all the cabs and carriages and calling. The air vent that led up to Mr Holmes' room was half open, and we could hear the Chopin pieces he was playing. But in the kitchen, we didn't speak. Mary smiled at me, and I smiled softly back. It was our way of saying we were glad I was back.

'I've been doing some research,' I told her. I had Billy and Mercer, the man who dug up the tedious background details for Mr Holmes, find all the mentions about Lord Howe in past newspapers they could manage. 'It didn't escape my notice that most of the gossip items came from Patrick West's columns.'

'He doesn't like him,' I told Mary. 'Mr West is very scathing about Lord Howe.'

'I'm surprised he dare,' Mary said.

'Oh, he never says anything definite,' I told her. 'You have to read between the lines. A certain Lord H goes to Spa, and then two columns later Emma is mentioned going to Spa to meet a lord. Separately it means nothing but together . . .'

'All the secrets are told,' Mary said, almost under her breath, as if we were being eavesdropped on. 'And, well, what did you find out?'

'Not much,' I admitted. 'It feels like there's a story there, but no one's ever quite grasped it. He comes across as a humourless man, very proud of his heritage, the sort of man who never believes anything he does is wrong because someone as important as him could never be wrong.'

'Doesn't sound like Emma's type,' Mary said dubiously.

'Perhaps he had hidden depths,' I said, though I doubted it. 'Perhaps he paid well. But she was only one of many mistresses.'

'I read Irene's letter. Married three times and no son! Finally got his Jane Seymour in his last wife. What these men will do for a boy.'

I shook my head. Something felt wrong, but neither Patrick West nor I had managed to put a name to it.

'Oh, she gave him the son all right,' I said. 'He even took her abroad to a special doctor to make sure she got the best treatment. She suffered a great deal, but a son was born, and survived. He'd be about forty now.'

'And the mother?' Mary asked.

'Oh, she survived, too. But she never got over the trauma of the birth. She'd never look at her son, or touch him. She started to say he was evil. She went mad. She ended up locked in an asylum.'

Mary shuddered.

'Was this when Emma was his mistress?' she asked. I nodded. So there it was. Another story from Emma's past, another tale she wouldn't tell, another man with a secret.

'He's very powerful,' I murmured. 'He could arrange a death.'

'In a hospital? With everyone watching?'

'Where else would be so perfect?' I pointed out. 'People die in hospital all the time. It's expected.'

'But there's no proof,' Mary said quickly. 'Just speculation and maybes and perhapses, but nothing concrete. We need some evidence. We need some data! What about the first woman who died? That first night you were there?'

'I'm not absolutely sure that happened,' I told her, biting

my lip. I had been in so much pain, and groggy from the drugs they'd given me, and scared and alone. 'It could have been just a nightmare.'

'Nothing that can be proved, then,' Mary said. 'We'll leave that to one side, and concentrate on what we know actually occurred.'

I smiled. So like Mr Holmes! But both our cases were just as nebulous as each other. Just ideas and feelings and fancies from a sick woman, and an over-eager woman.

'Mary,' I asked, 'who is Mrs Turner?'

'Oh, one of John's charity cases,' she said, looking down.

'You're no better at lying then,' I told her. She looked up.

'All right,' she admitted, 'Mrs Turner is a woman I found whilst looking for the boys.'

'A witness?' I asked.

'Sort of,' Mary said slowly. 'Ten years ago she was admitted to a workhouse with her five-year-old son. She was very ill. She recovered, and got the chance of a place in a country house, but she couldn't take her boy. She decided to go, and save up and come back for him. She was there for five years, then came back to claim her son – only to find someone else had taken him.'

'How awful,' I said. To work and work for your boy, all that time, just waiting and hoping, then find him snatched away.

'As far as the workhouse was concerned, he was claimed by his mother and that was that. Mrs Turner had a bit of a breakdown, but when she recovered, she started to look for him. That's when I found her, hanging around the work-house, watching every woman that came in and out of there.'

'So is it a woman taking these boys?'

'A woman could be the ringleader,' she said. 'Or maybe she's just a dupe, or . . . Martha, I don't know what to do next.'

'Wiggins and the others are coming Tuesday,' I said gently. She was getting quite distressed, and it tugged at me to see her like that. 'I'm going to ask them about the Pale Boys.'

'You think they're the missing boys?' Mary questioned. 'But some of those boys went missing years ago. If they were alive they'd be grown men now.'

If they were alive. What a thing to say. It was obviously something Mary had thought, but I don't think she had said it until then.

'Mary,' I said slowly. 'You didn't tell Mrs Turner we'd find her boy, did you?'

'What else could I say?' Mary said quickly, getting up and pacing round the kitchen. 'You didn't see her, Martha, standing outside that workhouse day after day, begging people to tell her where her boy was.'

'But Mary . . .'

'I know!' she cried out. 'We may not find him. He may not be alive! But someone has to look. No one else would. Everyone else just said good riddance, street boys, who cares, let them rot! No one else would do anything! I have to help, Martha, I have to!'

'We will help,' I said quietly, and she nodded in agreement.

I watched her, clasping her hands, her cheeks red with passion, pacing round the kitchen, and I wondered if Mr Holmes had done the right thing giving this case to Mary Watson.

THE TALES OF
THE IRREGULARS

Tuesday afternoon came, and with it, the Irregulars.

Wiggins arrived first, slipping through the area door. He didn't hug me. He just stood and looked at me for a long while.

'You all right?' he asked eventually.

'I will be,' I replied. He nodded, just as Mrs Turner came in. She saw him and looked stricken.

I remembered what it was like after my boy died. For a while, I dared not go to the village near my home: every boy looked like my boy. I found myself following strange children down the street, half convinced they were my dead son. But at the same time I couldn't bear to see children happy and alive and well, and with their parents. To spare her, I sent Mrs Turner upstairs to clean my room.

I had, with the help of Mrs Turner, Mary and even Grace (though it wasn't part of her duties), made a batch of cakes for the boys, and they came tumbling in, eager to eat and talk, and reassure themselves I was well. I was touched by their concern for me, and found myself unexpectedly tearful once or twice.

'It's because you're still weak,' Grace told me, as I wiped

my eyes in the scullery. Weak: how I despised that word. Weakness was for others, people I took care of. I wasn't supposed to be weak.

I had thought I would have to introduce the subject myself, but when I walked back into the kitchen, the boys were crowded around Mary, telling her tales of the Pale Boys.

'You only ever see them at night,' Micky, the youngest, told her.

'Pale face, just floating in mid-air, like a ghost!' another boy, Mike, thin, with sandy hair, told her.

'Just like 'eadless ghosts!' Jim, who only had one eye, insisted.

'Don't be an idiot,' one of the older boys, Frank, said. 'They only look like that 'cos they wear all black, innit?'

'I saw them,' Jim told him. 'Just before dawn, it was, just floating down the street. They weren't real, I tell you.'

'They're not a fairy tale,' one of the other boys insisted. He was new, and I couldn't remember his name. The number and members of Wiggins' Irregulars changed all the time. This boy was very quiet, and still. 'We've all seen them,'aven't we?'

There was a chorus of agreement, with only Wiggins remaining silent. The boys shouted out over each other, eager to tell their tales.

'All in black.'

'White face and black eyes!'

'Just walking around, like they don't care.'

'Middle of the night, it were.'

'Never seen them in daylight.'

'Bet they can't come out in daylight!'

'They don't eat, or drink neither.'

'They don't even breathe. I seen 'em! They've got no breath when it's cold.'

'They can get through locked doors. Nowhere's safe from them.'

'They leave corpses wherever they go. They just walk past you and you die. Don't even have to touch you.'

'Enough!' Wiggins snapped. The boys immediately fell silent. 'Look,' he said, quieter. 'Maybe there are boys in black. I ain't never seen them.'

'P'raps they're scared of you, Wiggins,' Micky said softly.

'Lots of people are,' the quiet boy said, staring up at his leader in awe, like knights would have looked at kings, once. Wiggins smiled, a dry smile with no humour in it.

'Maybe,' he admitted. 'Maybe they just avoid me 'cos I'll see right through all this ghost crap they've got you believing. Right, Jake, you said you saw them, tell Mrs 'Udson. Everyone else keep quiet.'

He sat down and Jake, who turned out to be the new, quiet boy, started to talk.

'It was before I knew you,' he said. 'I was trying to find a place to sleep in the park.'

'Park's no good,' Micky said authoritatively. 'Colder than the streets and full of perverts.'

'Well, I didn't know that then, did I?' Jake said, as

138

Wiggins silenced Micky with a look. 'I found a place in those bushes past the boating lake, just at twilight. That's when I saw them. Just faces at first, coming towards me. Floating in mid-air, like. I nearly ... well, I nearly peed my trousers, if you know what I mean. Anyway, then I saw they were just boys but in black, so I could only see their faces in the dark. But they were silent, you know? Not just walking silent, but not talking or laughing or coughing either.'

'How old were they?' Wiggins asked.

'Like us,' Jake told him. His accent was northern, and I wondered how he had ended up in London. 'Some young, some about fifteen or so. They didn't see me. You know me, I know how to hide. Went into the bushes, didn't dare breathe, case they heard me. They walked straight past me, down the path, and I thought they'd gone, but then I heard a scuffle, and a gasp, and I waited a while and went and looked. Couldn't sleep 'less I knew. There was a woman down there, just an old woman, she was all hunched over, and when I touched her, well, she was dead.'

'She could have died of cold,' Wiggins objected. Jake shook his head.

'She were still warm. Life had just gone out of her.'

Wiggins sighed, his shoulders stooped for a moment. I thought he would look at me, just a second's support, but he didn't. He did this alone.

'No one goes near the park alone after dark,' he said eventually.

'Never do,' Micky said. 'Those trees are strange.'

'They're not ghosts,' Mary said suddenly. 'They can't walk through locked doors and they can't steal your breath and they have to eat.'

'You can prove that, can you?' Wiggins asked. She looked at him, and nodded.

'Where have you all seen them?' I asked. 'If I got a map, could you show me?'

'Course we could,' Wiggins said. 'Least we could do.'

Billy went to get the map.

'What are you doing?' Mary whispered.

'Every dog has a kennel,' I said softly. 'Even painted ones.'

'What?' she asked, then got my point. 'You know, you can carry a metaphor too far,' she told me with a smile.

When Billy unrolled the map, I had a shock. It was covered in red crosses. It was the map I had used to track down the blackmailer, back in April. I must have gone white, because Grace quickly poured me a glass of water.

'I thought you threw this away,' Mary said to Billy, under her breath. The boys had crowded round her and didn't hear him.

'I meant to!' he insisted. 'I put it under my bed, I must have forgotten.'

'What's all the red marks?' Wiggins asked.

'Something Mr Holmes was doing,' I lied easily, then felt guilty as I met Wiggins' eyes. He knew I had lied. He turned back to the map, his face full of suspicion. He hadn't been there when I had used this map before.

'So,' Mary said, 'everyone show me on the map where you saw the Pale Boys.'

They gathered round, trying to match the carefully drawn lines to the crowded, filthy, battered streets they knew. More than a few arguments broke out as they matched road for road, or tried to find an alleyway that didn't exist on any map.

Eventually, we had a pattern. The sightings all seemed to be concentrated in the streets at the north end of Regent's Park, near Albert Road.

'That'll do,' Grace said firmly. She had seemed to take the invasion of the kitchen by an army of filthy street boys with equanimity, and they had taken to her, once they realized she was here for me, and not to clean or dose them. But now I was exhausted, and she and Mary guided them out. Wiggins lingered.

'You lied to me,' he said, his brown eyes full of repressed anger.

'Yes,' I admitted. 'It was something that it was better for you not to know.'

'I decide what's good for me to know,' he snapped.

'Not this time,' I insisted, leaning back in my chair.

He thought about it, then said, 'Don't lie to me again.'

'I can't promise that,' I told him, truthfully. He grunted.

'I deserve better,' he told me.

'You do,' I agreed. And with that he had to be satisfied. He left then.

Grace and Mary came back into the kitchen.

'What was all that about?' Grace asked.

'Just a game,' I replied. I had no compunction about lying to Grace.

It became dark very early, and the lamps were lit at three. Mrs Turner and Mary went home, Billy went to bed early, and by seven I was ready for my bed too. Grace guided me up the first set of stairs, where I paused by Mr Holmes' door.

It was slightly open, and swung wide at my touch. The room was a mess, covered in cut-up newspapers and glue pots and big paper books. He and Dr Watson had obviously tried to have a clear-out of his old newspapers and paste them into his reference books, and, like all clear-outs, it had created a huge mess.

He sat in the centre of the floor, and on his lap, unfolded, was the map of London Billy had brought down earlier. I could see the red crosses and lines on the map clearly. I had used those marks, extrapolated from old papers, to track down the blackmailer. Obviously Mr Holmes had known I had used this, but did he know how or why?

He looked at me, with an expression of surprise – not that I was there, but that I had puzzled him. If we had been two normal people, that would have been the time we would have spoken. I would have said it was a trap, and he would have said it was a trap set for him, and how had I worked it out?

But we were not two normal people. We were Sherlock

Holmes and Mrs Hudson. He was too proud and I was too reserved. So I merely said:

'Is there anything else you require this evening, Mr Holmes?'

'If there is, I'll get it myself. Go to bed,' he said, not harshly, but not kindly either. I nodded in compliance, and allowed Grace to take me upstairs.

THE WOMAN
WHO WATCHES

Still, Mary and I had two cases to solve. By Friday, only a few days later, I felt better, and was also sick of the house and bored to tears. (Mr Holmes was in Paris, investigating the case of Madame Montpensier's missing stepdaughter.) I was desperate to get out for a walk, and to have something to do.

I had asked Grace for Eleanor Langham's address, saying I wanted to visit her now we were both home. I felt the only way to continue my investigation, and also to shake away the dread of the hospital ward, was to visit these women. I wanted to see them not as fellow patients, but as people in their own homes, surrounded by their own things, with their own family. I knew how different people could be in those circumstances. I certainly was. Outside of that ward, I was stronger, no longer the weak, trembling creature afraid of a hospital bed. To my relief, Eleanor handily lived just round the corner, on Park Road.

Grace wanted to accompany me, but I insisted I wanted only Mary.

'I don't mean any offence, Grace,' I told her, 'but I'm sick of the sight of your face.'

She only laughed, and said patients often felt that way as they recovered. Since Mary, as a doctor's wife, was perfectly capable of looking after me, we were left to ourselves.

Eleanor Langham lived in a huge white house on the western edge of Regent's Park. It was ornamented and curlicued and obviously very expensive. It made me pause for a moment – but only a moment.

I presented my card to the very tall, very upright butler. I wasn't sure if I would be welcomed in, as it was not the conventional time for visiting. Eleanor and I had not got on very well in hospital, but I was relying on her overweening curiosity to see what I wanted. I couldn't blame her for that: I was just the same.

As the butler went to check whether our presence was acceptable, Mary looked through the cards left on the side table. Silently she held one up for me. Sir Richard Pembury had called – but not been seen, as the folded corner of his card showed.

I was right about Eleanor's curiosity. The butler showed us up to the first floor, explaining that Mrs Langham was, by reason of her health, confined to a suite of rooms. As we climbed the stairs I heard the laughter of children somewhere in the house, hastily shushed.

Eleanor welcomed us into her drawing room. It was very correctly decorated, everything in its place, everything as all the good guides suggested it should be. It felt like a showplace, but not like a home. It was discomfiting. My own home was neat and tidy (outside of Mr Holmes' rooms), but had idiosyncrasies that reflected my own taste, such as a lack of little china ornaments, which I despised. You would too if you ever had to dust them. Mary and John's house was a muddle of papers and books and medical instruments and all kinds of things, but was utterly charming. This room – in fact, all the house I had seen – felt like the contents had been ordered en masse from a pattern book, and never altered.

The wallpaper was a fashionable green, as were the thick velvet curtains. A piano stood in one corner, with an Indian shawl thrown over it. Horsehair chairs were scattered about the room, in between various spindly tables. The only touch of individuality was a mass of photographs placed on the piano, and most of those were of royalty and public figures, rather than family. And in the centre of it all sat Eleanor Langham.

I had never seen her clearly in the hospital. She had sat far away from me, and I had been dazed with pain and fear. Now I could see her, I could tell her body was pulled tight with tension. Her fingers grasped each other so tightly the skin was white. The muscles and tendons beneath her skin were as tense as violin strings. For a moment I thought it was us that had made her like this, but I could see the nap of the velvet-covered arm of her chair was worn where she had pulled at it, and I realized she was like this all the time.

'How do you do, Mrs Langham,' I said softly. 'Do you remember me?'

'Of course,' she said, her voice cold and polite. 'The Mrs Hudson who is not Mr Holmes' housekeeper.'

'How kind of you to recall,' I said sweetly. 'I heard you were at home, and I realized I lived nearby, and I was eager to see you recovered. And I wished to introduce you to my friend, Mrs Watson.' I nodded at Mary, who held a hand out to Mrs Langham. She did not shake it. I don't think she approved of these modern manners of women.

'Watson?' Eleanor said.

'Dr Watson's wife,' Mary added, cheerfully. 'Martha – Mrs Hudson – spoke so often of you, I just felt I had to come and meet you myself.' Eleanor's face remained stony in the face of Mary's effort to charm her. 'I can see why you made such an impression,' Mary added.

I sat down in a chair opposite Eleanor. The chair was, as I suspected, stiff and uncomfortable. Mary roamed the room, looking at the pictures. She would occasionally pick one up and then put it down, not quite in the same place. She seemed to be doing this accidentally, but I knew it was deliberate.

'Good morning, Mrs Hudson,' Eleanor said, her voice cold. 'What a pleasure to see you looking so well.'

'And you also,' I lied. 'I do feel that those of us in that ward formed a bond, a companionship of sorts, don't you?'

'Of sorts,' Eleanor said, not really paying attention. She was trying to see what Mary was doing. Mary had wandered behind her to the window. She pulled back the curtain to show me a telescope on the windowsill, on a stand, trained on the park. Eleanor must be able to see a great deal from up here.

'I hear only Florence Bryson is left now,' I said, trying to keep the conversation going.

Eleanor snorted. 'That woman treated the place more like an hotel than a hospital. I do not believe she was really ill at all.'

'Well, perhaps,' I said gently. 'She was very close to Emma, though. It was such a shock when she died.'

'I'm only surprised she lasted that long. She had a very wicked life,' Eleanor said. I was beginning to remember why I disliked her so much.

'She did die very suddenly,' I insisted. 'One minute she was well, the next dead in the middle of the night, when everyone was asleep.'

'You weren't asleep,' Eleanor said, and her voice grated on me, catching, like a thread on a broken nail. 'You had nightmares. You had nightmares every night. You would scream. Tell me, what was that about?'

I swallowed, though my throat was dry. I knew I had dreamed, but I had no idea I had called out loud. What else had I said?

'It was a story my nurse told me when I was little,' I said to her. 'It has given me nightmares ever since. Ridiculous, for a grown woman.'

'Ridiculous,' Eleanor agreed. Mary returned to the photos.

'So if you were awake to hear me call, you must have been awake when Emma died,' I suggested, determined to get my answer and get out of that room. It was stifling me.

'No, that night I slept,' she said, frowning. She was annoyed! She was annoyed she had missed Emma's death.

'So you saw nothing?'

'What did you expect me to see, the Angel of Death?' she said, smirking. 'What did you see?'

What did I see? Well, I saw a ward full of sleeping women, including her. I remembered clearly seeing her shape under her bedclothes.

'Nothing,' I said firmly. 'The ward was so dark, and the lamps threw such shadows.'

'Shadows,' Eleanor repeated. 'I didn't . . . Put that down!'

The last was directed at Mary, who had picked up a picture of a boy. The picture was old, and I could barely see it, but it did have a black ribbon wound through its ornate silver frame.

'I'm sorry,' Mary said, putting the picture back down carefully. Eleanor reached for it, though, and Mary handed it to her. Eleanor snatched it, and wiped the picture with her sleeve, as if Mary had made it filthy by touching it.

'Your son?' I asked. 'I think I heard him downstairs.'

'That was my other sons,' she said dismissively. She smiled at the picture. 'This was my eldest son, James. He died, eleven years ago.'

Oh, now I understood. I knew that pain, the loss, the

aching emptiness of losing a child. I knew how the agony could twist and bind you, until just breathing hurt, and you hated the entire world for being alive. I had my work to sink into, but what had she had? Just an endless round of courtesy and tea and long days of nothing, allowing her grief to dominate her.

'I'm so sorry,' I said softly. 'I too have lost a son.'

'Yes, I remember you and Florence made good friends over your dead boys,' Eleanor sneered at me viciously, and I drew back, shocked by the venom in her voice.

'How do you know Sir Richard Pembury?' Mary said quickly. She still stood behind Eleanor, who had to twist to face Mary. 'I noticed his card downstairs.'

'He is an old family friend,' Eleanor said, proudly. 'I have known him since I was a child.'

'He's an impressive man,' Mary said, leaning in a most unladylike way against the windowsill. 'I met him myself a few days ago.'

'Most impressive,' Eleanor murmured, smoothing the worn nap on her chair.

'And do you know Lord Howe?' Mary asked, pushing the point.

'No more than anyone else in my social circle,' Eleanor snapped. 'Why are you asking these questions?'

'I'm being nosy,' Mary told her.

'But why those men?' Eleanor snapped. 'Why do you want to know about them? Why are you hiding behind my chair?

Come out into the room where I can see you! Get out of the light!' she screeched.

It was at that moment that the door opened, and the tall, older man with the military air that I had seen visit Eleanor in hospital came in. He went straight to her and kissed her on the cheek, stroking the back of her hand where it grasped the picture. She did not respond, not to the kiss, the love in his eyes, nor when he took the picture from her, and replaced it on the piano.

'This is Mrs Hudson,' Eleanor introduced me. 'She was in the hospital with me. And her friend, Mrs . . .'

'Watson,' Mary said, holding out her hand to Mr Langham. He shook it, slightly surprised. At the repeated name 'Watson' Eleanor's eyes had widened and now she stared at me suspiciously.

'It's a pleasure to meet you,' Mr Langham said. 'It's kind of you to visit. Eleanor doesn't get many visitors.'

'Can't think why,' Mary murmured.

'We were just leaving, actually,' I said, standing. I felt quite shaken. 'Such a pleasure to see you again.'

'I think we'll take a walk in the park,' Mary said lightly. 'You might see us.'

'The park looks lovely today,' Mr Langham said. 'The nurse has just taken the boys over there. I thought I might join them.'

'No!' Eleanor cried, and her hands pinched each other so tightly one of her nails drew blood. 'I need you here,' she said in a softer voice. Mr Langham shrugged, and agreed, and showed us to the door.

I looked back as we left. Eleanor didn't see me. She was staring at her husband. Whilst he had looked at her with love, she stared at him with absolute hate.

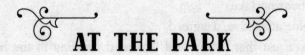

AT THE PARK

We really did go over to the park. Regent's Park was large and sprawling, but we stuck close to the paths beside the boating lake. In summer these would be flower-lined, but now it was all just mud and damp grass and bare trees, and mist hung in the distance, obscuring the bandstand and the cafe. I was tired and wanted to sit down, and Mary wanted to see if she could find Eleanor Langham's children. Or so she said – we followed the same path the boys had seen the Pale Boys on.

'She knows them both,' Mary said, diving straight in. 'Lord Howe and Sir Richard.'

'That doesn't really prove anything,' I said, glancing back at the house. 'She's rich, very rich, judging by that house, and everyone at that level of society knows each other.'

'Sir Richard didn't start off rich. Not when she was a girl, anyway. His political career didn't even start until his mid-thirties, after he'd made his fortune in business, and trade and high society don't mix. They couldn't have known each other then.'

'No,' I said. No doubt there was an explanation for that too. I was very tired, and not really thinking.

'I hated that home,' Mary said to me, as we walked towards the boating lake.

'Not attractive,' I agreed.

'Not just that,' Mary said. 'It was the feeling in the house – not even really a home. As if everyone was hiding something, or not telling something – I can't quite say what it was.'

'Hiding something, I think,' I said, as we walked along the lake. 'She was like that in hospital, always watching.'

'You watch,' Mary pointed out.

'She was always judging, then, and finding the worst of everyone. You can't accuse me of that.'

'No, no one could accuse you of that,' Mary said, squeezing my arm affectionately. 'Look, I think that's them.'

Ahead of us were two boys, around ten and seven, playing with an excitable spaniel. They looked ordinary in their dark suits, light brown hair flopping over their eyes. They were being followed by a young plump girl with rosy cheeks – obviously their nurse. She called after them, in a voice with a thick Irish accent, trying to get them to behave, but both she and the boys were laughing. They looked happy, but with an air of nervousness, as if they had escaped and were waiting to be caught.

The spaniel, recognizing someone who would love him, ran straight up to Mary. She bent down and ruffled his fur, calling him gorgeous, and immediately endearing herself to the boys.

'I'm going to sit down. You charm the boys,' I said, heading for a bench. Mary was better with strange children than I was. I never knew what to say to them. Except the Irregulars, of course, but then Wiggins took care of them, and I never really considered him a child.

It was a cold day, but sunny. It had been damp lately, but not today. The air was sharp and bright, and felt good to breathe. I could hear children laughing, and ducks quacking over at the boating lake. I could see soldiers in their bright red uniforms strolling with pretty girls, well bundled up, and a caretaker painting a bench with as much care and pride as a Royal Academician painting a masterpiece. I sat in the sunshine and smiled and watched.

I had so nearly lost all this. I had so easily closed my eyes and drifted away.

The sense of sorrow at the thought that I might have left all this made me gasp, and I leaned back on the bench. I closed my eyes, feeling the sunshine on my face, trying to calm myself down. My thoughts wandered away from the park, away from the day to that night in the ward, the shadow by the bed, the women asleep in their beds.

'No!'

To my surprise, I had said it out loud. I looked around. No one had noticed. I wasn't crying in fear, but in anger, at myself. I had forgotten Mr Holmes' precept – do not see: observe.

The atmosphere in the ward, the night, my own pain, the drugs – they had all combined together to create a moment of terror. But what had I actually seen? What was the dog beneath the Hound?

I had seen something stand beside Emma's bed. Not a

shadow, a shape, a human shape. Slim and short – so a woman, or a child or even a short man. But something real, nonetheless. Emma had scratched them!

The women in the beds – but had I seen them? I had merely seen shapes under covers, just white lumps in the dark. I had no way of knowing if what was under the sheets was a woman or a mound of pillows. Someone could have crept out of her bed as we slept.

Let me see now – no, none of the women had a scratch on them next morning. But that only meant the creature by the bed was not one of the women. It didn't mean he didn't have help from one of them. One of those women could have got out of bed, let him in. Perhaps he had been hiding in the stock cupboard, or the bathrooms, having climbed in through a window. Perhaps she had let him in from the corridor to the rest of the hospital. One of those women could have caused the disturbance in the other wards that had distracted the night nurses and Sister. By all accounts the patient that had the violent fits was prone to them if he was scared. And who exactly had called for help from our ward anyway?

I opened my eyes. Well, I thought, I could be proud of myself. I had shaken off the wild imaginings of that night and actually deduced some possible facts. I didn't know names, or how, but I knew it was possible for someone to have killed Emma, and perhaps even the woman who died the first night I was there, without any supernatural intervention.

I was smiling widely when Mary, exhausted and mussed from playing with the boys, came to join me.

'What are you grinning at?' she asked. 'No, tell me later
– me first.'

'You talked to the boys?' I asked.

'And the nurse, too,' she agreed, panting a little.

'I hope she didn't see you,' I said, gesturing towards
Eleanor's house, where she sat with her telescope trained on
the park.

'We stayed in the trees,' Mary said. 'They hide from her,
too. That nurse is very talkative! I get the feeling she's not
allowed to talk at home.'

'Or laugh,' I said, remembering the hastily hushed laughter
as we entered the home.

'No, the Langhams don't keep staff long,' Mary said. She
was building up to something, I could tell. 'Eleanor watches
everything they do, and finds fault with it all. Luckily Mr
Langham is very understanding, and always gives them a
good reference, but barely a month passes without someone
leaving and someone new coming in.'

'So what you're saying is it would be easy to slip someone
into that household?' I asked, amused.

'I swear there are secrets in that house. I'm not sure how
it can tie into Emma's death, but we have to start somewhere.'

'I agree,' I said to her. 'So, has their governess just left?
Are you planning to replace her?'

She turned to look at me, her face very serious.

'No, not the governess. The boot boy,' she said to me. 'I
said I had a replacement. I suggested Billy.'

NOT A BOY
ANY MORE

'No!' I said again, as I marched into the kitchen. Mrs Turner stood up hurriedly to take my coat, and Grace frowned at me.

I hadn't spoken to Mary all the way back from the park, although she had begged me to discuss her idea. She had tried to persuade me that Billy would be safe, Billy knew what he was doing; he had probably done more dangerous things than this when he was with Wiggins. Finally she started apologizing to me and begging me to speak to her. I hadn't dared until I was safely in 221b. I was too angry. Didn't she understand how much this boy meant to me? Ever since we had taken him in when Wiggins brought him to me, ever since I had agreed to make him Sherlock's apprentice, he had been like a son to me. His parents had died, my son had died, but we had found consolation in each other. How important it was to keep him safe. I couldn't shove him into a stranger's house, a possibly murderous stranger, and leave him alone there!

Grace and Mrs Turner had tactfully withdrawn. I paced around the kitchen, as Mary stood by the table, trying to calm me down.

'I didn't mean he should go in there alone,' she said to me. 'I was going to suggest that Wiggins station a couple of his boys outside the house, day and night, to keep an eye on things. He can run to them for help, or they can get help if he calls out.'

'It's not enough,' I insisted.

'It's not as if we even know anything or anyone in that house is dangerous,' Mary pleaded. 'It's just an atmosphere, a few secrets.'

'It's still dangerous!'

'He'll only be a boot boy! No one pays attention to the boot boy.'

'No, Mary!' I shouted. She looked at my face, and perhaps finally saw clearly the fear I had in the bottom of my heart of losing this boy. She sighed, and sat down on the chair.

'You're right, it's too dangerous,' she said softly. 'I'm sorry I suggested it.'

'I'm not.'

That was Billy, standing at the top of the stair to the kitchen. I hadn't seen him. He must have heard the whole thing.

'You don't know what she's asking,' I said wearily.

'She wants me to go into a house in disguise as a boot boy,' he said. 'Like the sort of thing Mr Holmes does.'

'It's not the same,' I snapped.

'Why? Because he's a man and I'm a boy?' Billy asked, coming into the kitchen and standing next to me. How he had grown! He was as tall as me now, his face losing the last of his childish softness. I wanted to take him in my arms and hold him, and knew he would submit gracefully, but hate doing it.

'Yes, I suppose,' I said softly.

'That's not fair,' he told me, not whining, but making a statement. 'Boys younger than me work all the time, doing far worse jobs. Dangerous jobs, too, down the mines and up chimneys.'

'You're going to talk me into it, aren't you?' I said to him. He was determined, his jaw set, his gaze strong.

'Mr Holmes has taught me lots,' he continued, 'and so has Wiggins. And Mrs Watson is right: no one notices the boot boy. And we can rely on Wiggins to have someone watching all the time.'

'It's not safe,' I said in a last-ditch attempt.

'If you don't think that's safe, you should know what I do when I'm out with Wiggins,' he said darkly.

'I don't want to,' I said. I preferred to think of them as two boys running round town having fun. I didn't want to know of the battles they fought, the dangers they faced.

'I live in this house,' Billy said gently. 'I see Mr Holmes and Dr Watson risking their lives all the time. And I see you and Mrs Watson doing it too now and I know why you do. I know you want to help people. I want to help them too. I want to be part of this too. I don't want to be sat in the corner, waiting for you all to come home, maybe hurt, and not be able to do anything.'

'Billy,' Mary said softly. 'Martha said no . . .'

'I've changed my mind,' I said quickly, before I could change it back again. 'You're right, God help you, you're right.'

He sighed happily, as if he weren't expecting this outcome.

'Right,' he said, squaring his shoulders. 'Where am I going?'

Wiggins was found quickly, and agreed to have two boys waiting outside the Langham home day and night. They'd hang around, like ordinary street boys, and could hide in the park if necessary. If there was any sign of trouble, they'd get help, quickly. Wiggins would join them every day to personally get a report from Billy.

'One of my boys could do this,' Wiggins objected.

'No, they couldn't,' Billy told him. 'For a start, they don't know the duties. And besides, they look like street boys. Two days there and someone would be stealing the silver and blaming it on them. Whereas me,' he grinned then, 'I look innocent as the day is long.'

He did. In some clean but shabby old clothes he looked like a good honest boy down on his luck seeking a good household. Wiggins gave him advice all the way there.

'Knock the edge off your accent,' he told him. 'You sound too posh. Once you're in, don't ask questions, it makes people suspicious. Just listen. Stay quiet, keep your head down, and listen. People think servants and children are just part of the furniture, they say anything in front of them, but the minute you speak, they shut up. You ready? See you tomorrow, if you get in, or in ten minutes if you don't.'

We left Billy at the kitchen door, clutching a reference from Mary, and a letter saying she'd heard from the nurse a boot boy was wanted. Wiggins and I sat in the park. I could smell something burning. Something is always burning somewhere in a park in autumn.

'Why don't you believe in the Pale Boys?' I asked Wiggins.

'Ain't got no time for ghost stories,' he said. 'My boys have got enough to be frightened of without being scared of made-up stuff, too. They gotta learn to like the dark. I ain't going to have them be scared of it, 'cos they gotta live in it.'

'Oh,' I said softly. Wiggins painted a grim picture. I had always rather liked scary stories, but I had nothing in my childhood to frighten me.

''Ow long's it been?' he asked. His feet banged back and forth on the ground beneath the bench. I pulled out my tiny gold pocket watch.

'Half an hour,' I said. Wiggins stood up.

'That's it then, he's done it,' he said, staring away over the park. He sniffed once. 'Fair play to him.'

'Yes, he's done it,' I replied. 'He's a brave boy.'

'Nah, he's just a boy,' Wiggins replied. 'Looking for a bit of adventure.' Wiggins gingerly placed his hand on my shoulder. He rarely touched me, rarely showed affection to anyone outside his gang, but he was trying now. 'Don't worry.'

'I won't.'

Wiggins offered to see me home, but I pointed out acerbically that not only was I the grown-up, I also only lived around the corner. He left me, and I sat alone, thinking, allowing the stillness of solitude to melt into me. By the time it was dark, I was at peace again.

I did feel a little nervous as I went home, thinking about the Pale Boys, but they didn't come.

Not that night, anyway.

HALF-SICK
OF SHADOWS

Mary was still in the kitchen, reading a book by candlelight, when I got home. She looked up eagerly as I entered and took off my coat, putting the kettle on to boil.

'Where's Mrs Turner?' I asked.

'I let her go home for the evening. Grace is upstairs waiting for you.'

I nodded.

'It went well,' I told her. 'He's in the house now.'

She nodded, then burst out with, 'Are you still angry with me? Please don't be, I can't bear it.'

Was I angry? No, not any more. It had been a good idea, and it had worked, and Billy had wanted to do it. It was only my own fear that had driven me beyond logic into anger.

'No, of course not,' I told her. 'Not now, anyway.'

She sat down, appeased, but there was still a tension between us. I reached out for the book she was reading.

'Improving your French grammar?' I teased, as I read the title: '*Étude médico-légale et clinique sur l'empoisonnement.*'

'That book is a bit of a struggle,' she admitted. 'But John says it's the best, and if I want to learn, I should read it.'

'Learn what?'

'Do you remember before, when I looked at that man and knew he'd been murdered, and hadn't committed suicide?' I nodded. He had been one of the suspects in the blackmail case, until he had died himself. 'Well, I wanted to learn more about what you can tell from bodies after they're dead, how they died and so on. Not as an expert, just an intelligent layman. John's teaching me.'

'That sounds . . .'

'Morbid?' she said, laughing.

'Fascinating,' I corrected her, 'but yes, also morbid.'

I looked through the book. It was certainly gruesome.

'John thinks you're fragile,' I said suddenly. She looked puzzled.

'Well, I'm not,' she said, turning back to the book. 'It is fascinating,' she said, leafing through the pages. 'How can anyone be bored when there is so much to learn in the world?'

Lucky Mary. Blessed with a good education, then an employer who allowed her to use her imagination and creativity, and now a husband who firmly encouraged her to use her mind, how could she know what it was like for the rest of us? Stuck in the same cycle of work, or home life, day after day, always doing the same jobs, that whether hard or easy rarely taxed our intellect, reading the same books, seeing the same people, having the same conversations over and over again, year after year after stultifying year. Never allowed to break out of the cycle, because that would be unladylike, not a woman's place, not the correct or modest thing to do. Always living in the shadow of men.

'"I am half-sick of shadows",' I murmured.

Mary, reading her book and not recognizing the quote, replied, 'Turn the light up, then.'

Well, she was right.

'Be here tomorrow,' I said briskly. 'First we're going to pay a visit, then we're going to Sarah Malone's house. I want to find out what she was confessing to Miranda Logan when she died screaming.'

Grace was waiting for me up in my room. She undressed me and took off the bandage, not speaking a word. At first I thought she was angry with me for staying out late, but in the light of the gas lamp I could see she was distracted.

'You're healing well,' she told me, as she smoothed cream over my scar. 'You don't need me here at night any more; I'll just be here in the morning and evening, and at lunchtime, if that's acceptable?'

'Perfectly,' I said to her, as she measured out my nighttime dose of medicine. 'Grace, is everything all right?'

'Of course,' she said, standing up straight, and bridling a little. 'Why wouldn't it be?'

'Nothing, it's just you seem a little distracted.'

She stared out of the window a moment, as if making up her mind.

'Nora said to tell you,' she said, half to herself. 'But what kind of nurse would I be if I burdened my patient?'

'If Nora said to tell me, you'd better tell me.'

So she did. Nora had been worried about the deaths on the ward, as she had revealed to me before. She had checked the official logbooks – no one could get hold of Sister Bey's personal one – and found that the deaths, at least five of them, often happened when the staff were called out of the room to help with a particular patient.

'A man in one of the main wards,' Grace said, as she helped me on with my nightdress. 'He ought to be in an asylum really. Most of the time he is perfectly quiet, but two or three times a month, he suddenly gets a fit on him, and starts screaming and shouting and smashing up the ward.'

'The nurses on his own ward can't deal with him?'

'He's very strong. And besides, he upsets the other patients, and they need soothing too. Here, drink this.' She handed me my medication.

'So everyone in earshot runs to help,' I said. She nodded.

'It's understood that they all help each other, especially at night, when there's so few of them. And, as it turns out, Sister Bey is the only one who can calm him. She just whispers in his ear and he quietens, eventually. They have to beg her to come though. She never comes running like the others.'

I got into bed. Sister Bey, with her two logbooks, never going near a patient, always sitting and writing. Now here she was, at the centre of the distraction.

'What causes this man's fits?'

'No one knows,' she said, as she tucked me in. 'He claims to hear a woman's voice whispering in his ear telling him he's going to die, but no one ever sees anything. Mind you, it's easy to hide on those pavilion wards. There are so many people around, and it's so dark.'

Nora too had had her suspicions, and vowed next time the man started to scream, and Sister Bey came to help, she would quietly go back to the private ward before Sister Bey returned. Last night, that was what had happened.

'The ward was full,' Grace said, sitting on my bed. 'Flo Bryson is still there, from your time, Betty Soland had gone, but is back after a relapse, oh, and Eleanor Langham is back.'

'Really? Already?'

'Just for a day or two, for tests. She'll be home again tomorrow. And Miranda Logan came to visit Flo, but of course Miss Logan would've been long gone by then. Are you warm enough?'

'Yes, yes, go on,' I said impatiently. 'All the beds were full? Including the one opposite the one nearest the door?' The Death Bed, I called it, but I couldn't say that to Grace.

'Yes, all of them,' Grace repeated. 'Well, the man started to scream, and a woman screamed too, because he'd become violent and was hitting the other patients. It was Bedlam, quite literally. Well, Nora ran to help, and then ran back to get Sister Bey, who came after a few moments.'

'Then Nora came back to the ward?'

'She waited to make sure Sister Bey was fully occupied

before she left. She slipped away as the Sister was bent over the patient's bed. She is certain that Sister didn't follow her.'

'What happened when she got to the ward?'

'Well, that's the awful thing,' Grace said. 'She'd barely got in when someone smashed that lamp on the desk over her head. She was knocked unconscious. She's lucky she isn't dead.'

IN THE GRAVEYARD

Early the next morning, very early, so early the gas lamps still flared in the cavernous station, Mary and I caught the train to Teddington. There, as a pale and sickly sun struggled up, we walked for twenty minutes, with a rest every so often so I could catch my breath, until we found a low stone church. It had a graveyard surrounding it, the heavy mist swirling around the crooked ancient gravestones. Only one stone was new. This was Emma's.

She had told me about this place. In spring the church-yard was full of flowers. 'I want to be buried amongst flowers,' she had told me. But as it was still winter, I carried a bouquet of flamboyant hothouse roses. I believe she would have loved them.

But we were not the first. Though it was early, and damp and cold, the kind of cold that seeps into your bones and freezes your heart, others had got there before us – two men.

One was in his forties, fair, thinning brown hair blowing in the breeze, thin shoulders huddled into his black coat. The man beside him was older and taller. His hair was white, uncovered, his hat in his hand. His face was deeply lined, his hook nose prominent, and he looked as massive and ancient as the tombstones around him. He stood there, gazing at Emma's grave. Judging by the younger man's impatience, they had been there a while. I recognized the older man. I had seen pictures in the papers.

Lord Ernest Howe.

'Wait,' I whispered to Mary. Lord Howe did not move, nor speak. He had brought no flowers to lie on the grave. There was no expression on his face. He merely looked at Emma's tombstone, but I could not tell what he was feeling.

The younger man looked up and whispered to Lord Howe. He looked up sharply and saw us.

'Who are you?' he commanded. This was not a man used to disobedience.

'Mrs Hudson,' I said, coming forward. 'I was in hospital with Miss Fordyce. I wanted to pay my respects,' I said, holding out my flowers.

He nodded.

'I expect you're wondering why we're here,' the younger man – obviously Lord Howe's son – said, but Lord Howe interrupted him.

'It's none of their business why we're here,' he snapped.

'We know she was your mistress,' Mary said, coming forward. He demanded how, and she told him she had read it in a newspaper. He nodded.

'Newspapers,' he said sharply. 'Bane of my life. I'm not ashamed. She was a fine woman. Everyone did it in my day.'

'She told us stories,' Mary said, trying to probe.

'Not about me, I guarantee it,' he said. Mary shook her head in agreement.

The younger man shifted nervously, but Lord Howe remained stock still. He glared at me. The man had power. I could feel it ripping across the graveyard. This was a man who not only got exactly what he wanted, but saw no reason why he should not.

'So she told you things, did she?' he said to me.

'Not about you,' I told him. He grunted, satisfied.

'Very sensible of her,' he said, looking down at the grave. 'She was always sensible. Strong and clever too. Not like the milksops I married.'

'One of those milksops was my mother,' the boy snapped.

'And look at her!' Lord Howe snapped back. 'Mad then dead. What was the point of her? I should have married Emma Fordyce.'

'She'd never have had you,' Mary said. 'Nor any man.'

He laughed, once.

'Well, can't say I loved her. Never loved any woman,' he said, but a quick glance at his son showed where the love had gone, obsessive and strong, invested in his heir. He glanced back at the gravestone. 'But she is the only woman to give me a great gift.'

He nodded sharply, and the two men walked away into the fast-thinning mist, towards the river. I watched them go.

'So that's the son that cost so much,' I said softly.

'Dead wives and mad wives,' Mary said. 'No price too high for Lord Howe's heir.'

'No, no price . . .' I murmured. 'Unless it came as a gift.'

I laid the roses on Emma's grave, and we walked back to the station.

'Imagine you wanted a son,' I said to Mary. 'Not you as you are now, I mean you as a grand lord with a long line of ancestors.'

'All right,' Mary said.

'You've married twice, and nothing has happened. Then you marry a third time, and this one is young and physically strong and likely to last a while and yet still no son.'

'How long were Lord Howe and his third wife married?'

'Ten years before the boy appeared. Listen. Suppose your mistress fell pregnant?'

'Emma never said she had children.'

'And then, let's suppose,' I continued, 'that all three of you go away to the Continent at the same time – Italy, they were all in Italy.'

'Everyone goes to Italy at some point,' Mary objected, but I continued.

'The mistress has the child, and hands him over to the lord and his wife, to raise as his own, as his heir.'

'That's . . . that's . . . why would Lady Howe agree?' Mary asked, stopping in the middle of the street. 'Come to that, why would Emma agree?'

'Emma never wanted children, and besides, the baby would have had a much better life with his father than his mother,' I said quickly. 'As for Lady Howe – she would have been too scared of Lord Howe to disagree. She had failed in her wifely duty.'

'And the guilt of raising a child drove her mad?' Mary asked. 'She was supposed to have said the child was not hers . . .'

'Maybe now, on her deathbed, Emma wanted to see her son,' I speculated. 'But that could destroy it all, and hence . . .'

'Lord Howe had her killed,' Mary said softly, then shook her head as if waking herself up. 'No, this is ridiculous!' she pronounced, walking on. 'It sounds like a bad play.'

'Years of living with Mr Holmes has taught me even the worst melodrama isn't as ridiculous as real life can be,' I replied.

We went back to 221b, Mary to the kitchen and me upstairs to have a doze before our second task.

I awakened when the door opened and Mrs Turner came in, carrying a tray, and with a black dress draped over her arm. She wished me good morning in her quiet voice, and laid the tray on the bed. (Scrambled egg – soft food for the invalid!)

'Can I please try this dress on you, to make sure it fits?' she asked.

'Is that one of mine?' I asked, surprised. It looked quite different – not in colour, but in style.

'You lost some weight whilst you were ill, and I noticed your dresses were a little loose,' she said, blushing fiercely.

'I took the liberty of altering one to fit, if that's all right. I can put it back . . .'

'It's perfect,' I said quickly, getting out of bed and allowing her to slip it over my head. She had made the dress neat and smart, and updated it subtly, altering the cut to make me appear slimmer and a mite taller.

'The bustle's gone,' I said.

'No one will be wearing bustles by next year,' she promised, as she hovered around the dress, pulling a thread here and seam there. She seemed more confident now she was focusing on the dress, and not me.

'I'll be ahead of fashion for once,' I said, amused, as she pulled it off. 'It fits perfectly, thank you.'

'Not quite perfect,' she said. 'I'll make a few alterations and get it back to you. I might fasten some lace to the neckline, if you have some?'

I nodded, and pointed to a drawer. As she drew the fine lace (given as a present and never worn) through her hands, I decided to take advantage of this more relaxed mood of hers. Obviously clothes were to her what was cooking was to me, and I was always at my best when cooking.

'You were a lady's maid, then,' I said. Only lady's maids and dressmakers could judge how a dress would fit by eye alone.

She nodded, holding a piece of lace up to the light.

'I loved that work,' she said softly. 'If I could have had my son with me it would have been heaven.'

'You came back for him though?' I probed gently. She put the lace back and chose another piece.

'The woman I'd been maid to died and left me enough money to open a little shop. I came back – and he was gone.'

She froze for a moment, staring into mid-air. I looked at her face, expecting to see tears, or a trembling lip, but she was as stone, every muscle in her straining, her expression utterly blank. Only her eyes were alive, staring into space, seeing something utterly beyond these four walls, something that tore at her inside, something she was struggling to control. Wherever she was, she was not here, and she suffered in utter silence. I thought I'd lost her, but after a moment she shook her head, as if shaking off the pain, and turned back to the lace. She'd had a breakdown, Mary said. Perhaps she was afraid if she expressed her pain, if only for a second, she'd break down again. She had to be strong for her boy. She had to control her feelings utterly.

'The workhouse said you'd already taken him?' I queried gently.

'They did. Some woman turned up and claimed to be his mother, and she was allowed to take him. No questions asked. They were just glad to be rid of him. They'd have asked more questions if it'd been a man.'

'Why?'

'Because a man might claim a child to be his apprentice, or his servant. If that's so, they want money. But what woman would take a child but his mother?'

So, a woman. A woman had taken him.

'It had happened before,' she said, laying the lace she had chosen against the dress. 'I asked. I spent all my money asking people and paying them to tell me. I never got the shop. I just stood outside the workhouse all day, waiting for him to come back. May I use this?' she said, holding up a small piece of very white lace.

'Please do,' I said. 'You said she'd done it before?'

'I found people: other mothers like me. They'd lost their sons, too. This woman just walked up and took them,' she said, not looking away from the dress, as if the material in her arms was the only real thing in the entire world and all she had left to hold on to.

'Did anyone see her? What did she look like?' I asked, perhaps a little too eagerly.

She looked up slowly. 'A woman. Just a grey-haired, nice old woman,' she told me. 'She looked like a mother.'

That was all I dare ask her. I didn't want to upset her any more. She never said a word about it when she gave me the finished dress later. The lace collar was a perfect touch. I looked five years younger. She would have made a fortune in her shop.

Despite Grace's disapproval, Mary and I left again, though this time I insisted we catch a cab for our second task of the day. Sarah Malone's home was just at the other end of Regent's Park, a brisk thirty-minute walk, but I was still tired from the day before. As Mary held out her hand for a cab, I pulled back.

'Not the first one,' I told her. 'Nor the second one.'

'That's Sherlock's rule for when he thinks he's being followed,' Mary commented. 'What's wrong?'

'I have no idea,' I told her. I had felt a tingle on the back of my neck, just a slight one, as if someone was watching me steadily. But, when I turned to look, no one was there.

Well, I say no one. Baker Street was never entirely empty. A grocery boy was arguing with the telegraph boy. Several businessmen marched up and down, not as important as they thought they were. A one-legged veteran sold matches. A woman huddled up in a plaid shawl hurried along the street. Two of Wiggins' boys were following a corpulent man with a gold watch-chain. A dainty woman in purple stepped around the horse manure as she crossed the street. A young woman swaddled in three shawls walked up and down selling ham sandwiches. 'I thought someone was watching me.'

'They're more likely to be watching for Sherlock than us,' Mary said reasonably. 'Come on, here's the third cab.'

I couldn't shake the feeling though. As the cab turned out of Baker Street and into Park Road, I thought I saw a familiar face. I peered out of the window, but she had gone in a flash.

'What?' Mary asked. 'Who did you see?'

'Lillian Rose,' I told her. The clever, wily prostitute I'd met when tracking down the blackmailer, half his victim, half his cohort. We'd sent her to Scotland. What was she doing back here, in London?

THE HOME OF
SARAH MALONE

Again following Sherlock's rules, we got off a few streets away from our final destination. As we strolled to Sarah's house, taking the opportunity to see if we were being followed, or if anyone else had got there first, I looked around. We were on Henry Street, near the north end of the park.

'I thought I knew this area,' I said to Mary. 'I used to own several houses here.'

'Boarding houses?'

'No, these were mostly homes I rented out. That was one of mine. And that one.' I gestured to a three-storey dove-grey house, set back from the road, surrounded by a garden. It was one of the stylish, huge houses built during the Regency for newly rich families to entertain, but the family that had owned it had long ago lost their money, and the house. I had bought it very cheaply, though I had never really been able to find tenants for such a place. It had been a neat, clean house when I owned it. Now the 'To Let' board was lying in the ragged garden, covered by brown decaying leaves, and the house was dishearteningly silent.

'Martha,' Mary said, pulling my arm. I walked on, but something was niggling me about the house.

Sarah Malone, the woman who had died so agonizingly in the bed next to me, had never left my mind. Her suffering had been as much mental as physical, and her confession had lifted a great weight. I had to know what her secret was.

Mary had gone into the hospital records – with no trouble: apparently the clerks were quite ready to do anything for her – and found Sarah Malone's address, as well as the fact that there appeared to be no next-of-kin. Whilst solicitors for the Crown searched for one, her home was left undisturbed.

As for how we'd get in, Mary had been taking lessons from a friend of Wiggins, and now had her own slim wallet of lock picks.

Sarah Malone's home was in a tall, narrow building of red brick and white stone. It was pleasant, and quiet, and felt like the kind of place where people kept to themselves.

The front door opened quite easily, it had been left on the latch by a careless resident, and we walked up to the second floor to Sarah's apartment. A young man passed us on the stair, but we simply carried on as if we had every right to be there, and nodded to him. He nodded back. Irene Adler had taught us that trick well.

Mary had been a good pupil, and we were through the door of the apartment in moments. It was a nice set of rooms, even now, when it was dusty and cold. The rooms were airy and light, and very neat. The front room was well-furnished, with a pretty green wallpaper and velvet curtains to match the seats, but looked unused. There were no books lying around, no sign of any meals, not even impressions on the cushions. It all looked as if it had been bought yesterday. We walked through to the bedroom.

This room was painted in plain white, the only decoration a crucifix hung above the bed. The bed itself was a narrow wooden one, and it creaked when I sat on it. Beside the bed on a cane chair lay a Bible and a prayer book.

'It's very simple,' Mary said. 'Like a maid's room.'

'Perhaps she was a maid at one time,' I said, picking up the Bible and leafing through it. Nothing fell out. The pages seemed stiff, though they were cut. 'Sometimes people from poor backgrounds who make good cannot sleep amongst luxury. They've grown too used to the servants' room.'

Mary nodded. 'She was religious. You said she prayed in hospital?'

'She muttered all the time, I assumed it was prayers,' I said, picking up the prayer book. 'But newly religious, I think, or remembering the religion of her childhood. These books and the crucifix are new.'

'Ah,' Mary said, spotting the desk in the corner of the room. It was a beautiful piece of marquetry with a lid that dropped down to make a writing area. It seemed out of place in that sparse room, like a duchess in a nunnery. 'Eureka.'

Mary opened the desk, and delved into various

pigeonholes. She glanced through a bundle of letters then held them out to me.

'References, I think,' she said. 'We're right: according to these letters she was a lady's maid.'

'A good one, these references say,' I said, as I read. 'They were all sorry to lose her.'

'Mrs Forrester, my last employer, said a good lady's maid was worth her weight in gold.'

'They can certainly earn a lot. She seems to have moved every two years, going up the social scale each time,' I said. 'What are you doing?'

Mary had pulled out some of the little drawers and was feeling around the back.

'Desks like these always have a secret compartment,' she explained, slightly breathlessly.

'Try the drawer on the left,' I suggested. 'I had one of these desks too.' Well, my mother did. She kept my father's love letters in the secret compartment. I used to love to curl up under the desk and unwrap the faded ribbon and strain to read the pale writing.

'Got it!' Mary said, as a piece of wood popped out of the side of the desk, and another drawer slid out. There were letters in there too. Mary picked up the first one.

'Well,' she said, reading it. 'That explains why she could afford an apartment like this.'

She held out the letter, and I read it. The handwriting was strong, but feminine.

Dear Miss Malone,

I am sorry to hear you are ill. I have arranged a bed for you in St Bartholomew's hospital. It is quite a private room, and you will only be sharing with a few other ladies, of great probity and high class.

'Well, most of them are like that. Emma Fordyce will be there. Remember her? We spent an entire summer years ago trying to puzzle out some of her secrets. She didn't spill a drop. Well, she's spilling now, pouring secrets like a waterfall. Get some for me, will you, dearest Sarah? Usual rates, of course.

Patrick West

'Him again,' Mary said, as I folded up the letter. 'For a blind man, he writes a lot.'

'He must have a secretary,' I said, glancing up at the crucifix. 'So all those years she was selling secrets to the gossip writers? Maybe she was feeling guilty at the very end. She must have turned to religion to save her.'

'You said she screamed,' Mary said, frowning, as she unfolded another letter. 'Some gossip selling hardly seems worth the eternal damnation of her soul, half the maids in London do it.'

She had a point. Sarah Malone had been certain something horrific was awaiting her on the other side. I made a remark about women trusting their lady's maids, but there was no reply. I looked up.

Mary was holding the other letter in her hand, and she

was shaking. She had gone as white as the paper she held and she stared down at the letter as if it burnt her.

'What? What's wrong?' I demanded. Wordlessly she handed the letter over to me.

I knew that handwriting. It made me feel sick to look at it. I had seen it so many times before. It was the handwriting of the blackmailer.

That man had destroyed people, mentally, socially, physically. He was a murderer. He was mad. He was supposed to be dead now. And yet here he was, still on paper, still threatening.

'It's dated two days before he died,' Mary said quietly. Two days before I . . . but I couldn't finish the thought. I daren't think it. I read the letter.

Malone,

I hear you are ill. You require hospital treatment. West has already arranged a bed for you. You know I know this.

Emma Fordyce is your quarry this time. Find out everything. Don't flinch in that way. Don't think I can't see you at all times. You used to enjoy this so much. Remember the power! Remember the joy in destroying these people.

I expect you to learn everything. Do not fail me. I hear you've found religion. All the crosses and Bibles and magic words in the world won't save you. I will come for you if you fail.

The letter was horrifying. What an awful fate, to be torn between fear for her soul and fear of this creature.

'That damned man,' I said softly. 'Will he never leave me?'

'No wonder she was terrified,' Mary said, sitting beside me. 'If I were dying and had spent my life serving him, I'd be scared he was coming too. I wonder what secret he knew about her, to make her work for him? That was always his way, secrets and threats.'

'It was all supposed to have ended,' I said, shaking, putting the letter down carefully, as if it would explode. 'Instead here he is again, rising from the grave.'

'"I tell you yet again, Banquo's buried; he cannot come out on's grave",' Mary quoted softly. I laughed, a short, bitter laugh.

'Did you just compare me to Macbeth?' I asked. Mary sprang forward and rummaged through the other letters.

'Don't be insulted, I quite like Macbeth,' she told me, glancing at them and stuffing them in her pockets. 'At least he did something. Not like that awful Hamlet, procrastinating all over the place. I always want to slap Hamlet over the back of his head and tell him to get on with it.'

I smiled. I couldn't help it.

'These are all letters he wrote asking her to gather information,' Mary said, as she put the last of them in her pocket, where they formed an unsightly lump. 'There're a few names I don't recognize. I'll write to them.'

Mary had taken it upon herself to write to the victims of the blackmailer telling them they were free.

'Sarah confessed,' I said suddenly. 'To Miranda Logan.'

'The young woman who wasn't sick at all?' Mary asked. 'The one with the interest in Emma?'

'That one,' I confirmed. 'I thought she was there to protect Emma, but what if she wasn't? What if she was there to make sure Emma didn't talk?' I stood up and began to pace around the room. 'But when she heard Sarah's confession, she realized that other people had been sent there to spy on Emma too. If Sarah was a spy, why not someone else as well? Surely it would be far easier just to shut Emma up?'

'It seems a bit extreme,' Mary said dubiously.

'It's all about Emma, I'm certain,' I insisted.

'But the other death, the shadows, the atmosphere in the ward . . .'

'Set-dressing!' I said triumphantly. 'There's no actual definitive proof anyone died before Emma. I could have imagined the whole incident in my drugged state. No witnesses, no tests, nothing more than a general feeling that something isn't quite right. Just like the giant footprints and the howling on the moor and the whole Baskerville legend are all simply diversions from the actual fact of one person killing another.'

'"Sound and fury, signifying nothing",' Mary quoted. 'Sorry, Macbeth really is my favourite play.'

'No, that's exactly right,' I said, excited, the blackmailer's letter forgotten, my fear dissipating. 'All of it, all of it means nothing except for the actual fact that Emma was murdered.'

'The attack on Nora . . .'

'She was investigating, too. It wouldn't have taken Sherlock to have spotted that – she wasn't subtle about asking questions.'

'So, we have a crime,' Mary said, taking the letter from me. 'At the heart of all the mystery there is an actual crime. But as for suspects . . .'

'I did a see a shape over Emma's bed,' I insisted. 'It wasn't one of the women, but I think one of them worked with whoever it was. I think he hit Nora, and killed Emma, on someone else's command. He had to be informed by one of the women, patient or nurse, in that room, because they knew Emma had changed beds.'

'So now we have suspects,' Mary said, far calmer than I, but smiling gently. It ought to be wrong to take such pleasure in crime, but I did love the joy of solving the puzzle.

'Betty Soland, Flo Bryson and Eleanor Langham were all patients on both occasions, Emma's death and the attack on Nora,' I said, counting them off on my finger. 'Sister Ruth Bey was present too – I know she was out of the room, but we've already established that is no bar.'

'And Miranda Logan,' Mary added. 'A patient the first time, a visitor the second. Why would she visit Flo anyway?'

'Emma talked to Flo a lot,' I explained, as we left the bedroom. 'She may have wanted to find out what Emma told Flo.'

I stopped as we reached the door. I had just had another thought, a memory really.

'What is it?' Mary asked.

'The shape that I saw that night,' I said to her. 'I know what it looked like. It was like a boy – a pale boy all in black.'

THE LAIR

Mary was lost in her own thoughts as we walked back down Henry Street. She only noticed I'd stopped when she walked past me a few yards. She came back to where I stood in front of the empty house I used to own.

'Feeling nostalgic?' she asked.

I shook my head. 'Not really,' I told her. 'I never lived here, just rented it out. It's just – something seems wrong about it.'

Mary looked around her.

'Isn't this the area where Wiggins and the boys thought the Pale Boys went to ground?' she asked. I nodded. The house was tall and pale, the paint peeling from the walls. It was bigger than all the other houses around it, the wings of the building spreading far apart. Once it had been gracious and elegant, the perfect rich man's London home, but it had fallen from grace from long ago. It was too big now, too chilly, too unfashionable. It suited nobody now. I walked forward, to the rust-encrusted gates, and tried to peer in. I could see nothing through the filthy windows. Just huge, empty, echoing rooms. It looked deserted. The garden was full of rotted leaves, the detritus of more than one autumn, piled up against the walls and . . . Ah, I saw it now.

'Why are the steps swept?' I asked. Mary turned sharply to look at the clean, brushed steps to the front door.

'To hide footprints,' Mary said, smiling slowly. 'There must be people in and out of there all the time, people who don't want anyone to know they're there. Let's go in.'

'We can't just break in,' I objected.

'Yes we can,' Mary replied. 'I've got my lock picks, remember?'

'That wasn't what I meant,' I muttered, as Mary pushed open the gate. It opened easily though rusty; the hinges were obviously oiled. She gave me a significant look. I followed her. It seemed that since becoming a detective, I was making a habit of breaking the law.

Oh well, at least it was in a good cause.

Mary was getting very skilled with her tools, and we were inside in a moment.

The house seemed empty. It felt too big, as if the rooms went on and on forever. The hall itself was filthy, covered with leaves that had blown in, and cobwebs heavy with dust. I thought I heard a rat scuttle away, the scratching echoing the deserted corridors. Before us rose the stairs, where once the hostess would have stood to welcome her distinguished visitors. No one welcomed us now. The walls, once brilliant white, were dingy, with the stains of old paintings long gone dotted here and there. The doors around the hall, cracked and pale, hung open, leading only to echoing empty rooms. The hall rose above high us, right up to a cracked and dark glass dome. It was freezing in here, the marble floor chilly underfoot. The windows were filthy, letting in only the haziest of light. It was the very definition of a once great house gone to rack and ruin.

Oddly though, it didn't smell disused. Empty houses smell of dust and dead animals. I could smell – pies. Pies wrapped in newspaper. I looked around. There was newspaper lying on the floor. The date was only a few days ago. I showed it to Mary.

'It could be a tramp,' I said.

'Look at the stairs,' she whispered. I don't know why she whispered, but I too did not want to disturb the silence. I looked.

The dust had not been cleared here. It lay heavily on the wooden stairs, and there were dozens of footprints left in it, none very large. Some were quite small indeed.

Children.

'We found it!' Mary whispered. 'This is their lair.'

'Lair?' I questioned. 'That's a bit over-dramatic. Mary . . .'

But it was too late. She was running up the stairs ahead of me, following the footprints. I followed her, more slowly. I didn't like this place. I felt like I didn't belong here. Nothing living did.

I had been over the house to clean it top to bottom each time I let it out. I knew the layout, and I saw that Mary was heading for the reception rooms on the first floor. She paused in the doorway to the old ballroom. It was a huge room, stretching back to the front of the building, and lit by windows running all along one side. On the other side lay a row of mattresses – at least ten.

'Who did you sell this to?' Mary asked in a low voice.

'I'm not sure: my solicitor sold it on my behalf.'

'He didn't tell you?'

'He thought women shouldn't have to bother their heads about such things,' I said, walking the length of the ballroom. There were some rooms at the other end, I knew. Small rooms for private meetings, for ladies to adjust their dress, and for gentlemen to have a quiet smoke. They led onto the first-floor balconies. 'I sacked him the third time he told me that.'

Mary followed me through the door at the far end into a corridor. The doors on this floor were mostly closed and warped shut. Mary tried a few, but they wouldn't open.

'I don't like this,' I admitted. 'I don't feel welcome here.'

'You've just had too many nightmares lately,' Mary told me, as she tried another door.

'You don't feel it?' I asked. 'Like we're not wanted?'

She turned to look at me.

'You only feel like that because we broke in,' she reassured me. But she didn't seem so certain herself now. The door she was trying opened suddenly under her hand, and she almost fell into the room. Then she gasped, and froze.

I walked in. It was just a small, square room. Nothing important. Nothing unusual – except the handprints on the wall. Dozens of handprints, all quite small, all over the wall, all red. Blood red.

'Mary, we have to leave,' I insisted.

'Wait, just a moment,' she said. She went up to the

handprints, pulling a handkerchief out of her pocket. She touched one, gingerly.

'It's dry, but I think it's blood,' she said quietly.

'I'm certain it is. We have to go,' I told her. I felt a cold draught down my back and turned to look, but nothing was there. Mary was scraping some of the blood onto her handkerchief.

'What are you doing?' I asked.

'I'm going to use Sherlock's blood test to see if it's human,' she told me. 'I've got enough, let's go.' She folded the handkerchief into her pocket. We turned to go, both thoroughly frightened by now, although we'd never admit it to each other. We walked back down the corridor to the ballroom. It was all so depressing here. These rooms had once been full of people, and laughter, and bright lights and hope, and now it was all returned to dust.

I shook myself. I was being ridiculous. My illness had left me weak and overly sensitive and it was time I got over it. I walked forward firmly towards the door to lead me back to the ballroom.

That was when the laughing started.

Children's laughter, high, but not kind, echoing through the walls, so it seemed they were above us, around us, behind all those closed doors. I couldn't tell where it came from. Was it behind that door, or the other? Below us, above us? We froze, then ran.

The door to the ballroom was shut. I could have sworn I left it open. Mary shook it, then bent down to the keyhole.

'It's locked, I can see the key.'

'Then pick it,' I demanded.

'I can't, not while the key's in there. Oh!' she said suddenly, standing up. 'Someone's turning the key. There's someone on the other side.'

Mr Holmes and Dr Watson would no doubt have pulled out their revolvers and waited for that person to come through. I decided discretion was definitely the better part of valour and ran in the opposite direction, trying to pull Mary after me. She was calling to them.

'We only want to help you,' she shouted, as I dragged her down the corridor. I remembered this house. I had shown prospective tenants round every corner. I knew where to go. 'We want to rescue you!'

They started hooting at that. I couldn't tell how many there were, the sounds echoed around the house, multiplying the calls and hoots and laughter.

'Mary, come on!' I insisted, trying to get her to run down the corridor. Was it really so long? It ran down the back of the ballroom to the other wing of the house, but it seemed to last the length of the whole street now.

'Let us save you!' Mary shouted, and for a moment, they fell silent. Were they thinking about it? Did they want her help? Then the banging started. I still saw nothing, but I heard them behind every door, the walls of the corridor. They were slapping the doors and the walls all around us. I saw one door shake as we ran past, and knew they were in there.

We reached the door at the end of the corridor finally, and I pushed Mary through, shutting it behind me.

We were in another reception room, coolly elegant, a perfect square, at the other end of the house from the ball-room. This was once designed to be a lady's drawing room, the ideal place to receive her visitors. I could hear the boys shouting behind us, and the slamming of doors as they came into the corridor. The door to our room, thankfully, had a bolt, and I shot it across, then looked round the room. One other door led out, on the same side of the room that we'd entered. It led to the stairs. The boys probably were expecting us to leave that way.

'I don't think they want to be saved,' I told Mary, looking around for what I knew was hidden in that room. Mary looked pale and shaken.

'Why?' she demanded. 'Why are they so vicious? They're like wild animals.'

'We have to leave right now,' I told her, feeling along the walls. It was here somewhere, but very well hidden.

'How? We're locked in, and we can't take the stairs, they'll be waiting.'

'There's a servants' door and staircase in the walls,' I told her. 'It was papered over, but I know it's here, if I just press in the right place – it's here!'

I ran my fingers over the damp and sagging wallpaper, and found the knot in the wood that opened the door set into the wall. None too soon, because the banging had moved to the door of the room we were in. I peered through the open door to the servants' stairs. A lot of the old houses had these. Corridors and stairs ran behind the walls of the home, making a secret network behind the public rooms. It meant the servants could move about and do their work without bumping into any of their betters on the stairs. It had been sealed off for ages as none of the tenants had felt comfortable with secret corridors in the walls – but they were still there, and I had found the entrance. This staircase was dim, lit only by a skylight high above, but I could see the dust on the floor. It was undisturbed – they didn't know about this. I got through the door and Mary followed me, closing it behind us.

It was very dark in there, with only the haziest trace of light, just enough to see our way. The dust was thick, and our dresses swept it up and into the air, choking us. We had to put our hands over our mouths so we didn't cough. We daren't run. It was too dark, and we'd fall. Besides, there was only a thin plaster wall between us and the boys. They'd hear us. We had to move slowly. We crept down that staircase, through the walls of the rooms, hearing the boys calling us, taunting us, laughing at us. We were as silent as the mice that ran over our feet, feeling our way down, waiting for the boys upstairs to break down the door and see the crack in the wallpaper and know where we were, and come after us, here, in the dark.

They banged on the walls, just an inch away from us, so close the noise rang in our ears, and I waited for them to come through. They must come through, they were so determined.

They had their quarry and they called and taunted us, screamed that we could not escape, that we had no way out. Yet we stayed silent, and crept down the steps, holding our breath, in case we coughed on the choking dust, and they would know we were there. Once my skirt caught on my heel, and I stumbled, just as Mary caught me. I fell against the wall, and we waited, utterly still, waited to see if they had heard us. But we had to go on.

We had to keep going down, not just to the floor below, where they would be waiting for us, but right down to the kitchen below that. They wouldn't expect us down there, hopefully.

Eventually there was no more staircase; we had reached the bottom. Ahead, Mary felt around until she found the catch that opened the door into the kitchen. We practically fell in, gasping for breath, leaning against the huge cracked wooden table. Light came in through a grubby basement window, and I could see the massive iron range, and old pots and pans still strung against the wall. But here too, no one had been. The range was cold, and dust lay everywhere.

We stopped and tensed, waiting for them to pounce on us. They still sounded so close. They were only children, but they sounded feral, and innumerable. But they didn't know this house as well as I did. They were still upstairs, still searching for us. The other door between the kitchen and the rest of the house was bolted, and the bolt was rusted in place.

The stair door slammed shut behind us before I could

catch it and we heard the children pause as they listened, and worked out where the noise had come from. I quickly bolted that door, but the bolts were feeble, and loose, and would break at the slightest pressure.

There was another door leading out into the garden. It was locked, and the lock was seized up, but the door was old and flimsy, and the frame warped. Mary shook it hard, and I could see the wood start to crumble. Then, as Mary fumbled with the back door, we heard them open the servants' door upstairs. They had found our escape route. We heard them run down the stairs, shouting their triumph, only to be stopped by the bolted door. Mary slammed her shoulder into the back door, once, twice – and then the wooden frame splintered. As they hammered on the kitchen door, we scrambled over the remains of the frame, and out into the garden, and back into the street.

I was shocked that everything was normal out here. I walked along, supported by Mary, each of us covered in dust, Mary's hands scratched where she had fumbled at the door, my hair falling from its pins, both of us gasping to catch our breath, feeling as if we had stumbled from an horrific hunt, and yet, London still continued calmly all around us. People strolled by as carelessly as if there were not a house full of murderous boys beside them.

Mary stood still, staring back at the house.

'We should go,' I told her.

'They won't come out now into the daylight,' she said, and she was right. She knew so much more about these boys than I did. How long had she been researching them? What stories had she heard?

'She's there, I know she is,' Mary hissed. I didn't need to ask who. She meant the woman who had taken them. The woman who controlled them. The woman who, I was more and more convinced, had made one of them kill Emma just feet away from me.

'Yes, she's there,' I said to Mary. 'She'll be watching us. Now she knows our faces.'

Silently, Mary turned and walked away with me.

A MOMENT'S REST

We walked away, trying not to draw attention to ourselves, and looking for a place to rest and clean up before we went back home. If either John or Grace caught sight of us in this state I doubted we'd be allowed to leave the house alone again. We washed briefly at a public fountain, and then found ourselves in Regent's Park, yet again. We were in a secluded spot, sheltered from the rest of the park by trees. We needed a moment to sit and think. Well, I did. Exhausted, I sank gratefully down on a bench under a great grey oak, stripped and bare. Mary pulled off her hat (a dark straw boater, as usual) and flung it onto the bench beside me. She walked – no, marched, up and down the path, hands alternately on her hips or running through her already disarranged hair. She was very upset or angry, I couldn't tell which. This case had touched Mary deeply, more deeply than I had realized. For all her lightheartedness and flippancy, Mary felt things down to her soul. I watched her as she walked up and down, trying to arrange the facts in her head. Occasionally she would stop still and I could see her mutter to herself. Her breathing slowed, and her march became a stroll as she calmed down. Eventually she came back to me, her face rueful.

'That was disturbing,' she admitted, reaching for her hat and pinning it back on.

'The house? Yes,' I agreed. 'Your hat's crooked, tip it to the left.'

'I thought they'd want to escape,' Mary admitted, straightening her hat. 'I thought it would be a daring rescue.'

Well, that was Mary all over. Always wanting to save someone. Just like her husband.

'They didn't seem to want to be saved,' I pointed out.

'Why not?' she pleaded. 'Why did they want to stay? Why did they hate us so much?'

Oh yes, there had been a lot of hate in that house.

'Why didn't they want to go back to their mothers?' she asked. We were both wondering it – was Mrs Turner's boy amongst them?

'Maybe they don't remember,' I suggested. 'Maybe she's managed to persuade them their mothers don't love them any more. I imagine she's quite persuasive.' Saving them was all very well, but what I wanted was answers, and a decent cup of tea.

'I suppose so,' Mary said, shrugging. 'Do you think we ought to tell the police?'

'That we were chased out of a house we broke into by some children we never saw?' I questioned. 'Besides, I expect the boys will move on. If I were her, I'd have more than one bolt hole. The Irregulars do.'

'If you were her . . .' Mary said, looking at me oddly. 'I

can't do that . . . I can't think like . . . like . . . someone like that.'

'You think I can?' I snapped, hurt. Although, I could. If I tried, I really could understand the way a woman like that thought. Collecting boys, children, for myself, making them love me, making them mine alone, replacing the boy I'd lost, hiding them away from the world – stop this. I won't become like this. I won't start to think like the monster of this piece. Not again.

'I didn't tell you how much this meant to me, did I?' Mary said.

'No, you did not,' I said softly. 'This is more than just curiosity; I can see that.'

'Do you remember when we found the Whitechapel Lady's body, and I was so angry?'

I did. Mary had been shaking with anger, white with it.

'I said the man who did this ought to burn. And then – well . . .'

'I was only there to save you!' I cried.

'I know, I know,' Mary said quickly, reaching out to me. 'I am grateful, and I understand. But that night, there was something about you, when you faced him. Something strong and dark and cold. Truth to tell, Martha, I was a little afraid of you that night.'

'Truth to tell,' I replied, 'I was a little afraid of me, too.'

I still was. I had been strong and fearless, which was not bad, but I had then become cold and ruthless, and it still haunted me. Had I meant it to happen? I still didn't know.

'Sorry,' Mary said quietly.

'It doesn't matter,' I told her. 'Well, it does, but not between us.'

It did matter. I hated her to think of me like that. I hated to think of myself like that. And yet, if I hadn't been like that, we'd both be dead now.

'No, it doesn't matter,' Mary said, slipping her arm through mine. 'Let's go, it's freezing. Besides I want to go home and test this blood, and look at the letters from Sarah's desk.'

We walked off talking of nothing more than the weather, and books, and Mr Holmes' Paris case. As we passed out of the gate, an urchin bumped into me, apologized, and ran off. Out of habit, I checked my pocket. He hadn't taken anything, but he had left something. Billy's first report.

BILLY'S REPORT

It was impossible to read the report immediately. We couldn't stand in the street and read it, and 221b seemed packed with people. In reality, it was only Mrs Turner and Grace, but they seemed to be everywhere I turned. Mary went home to do the tests and write to the women in the letters we had discovered at Sarah Malone's home. She would send me a telegram with her results. I went back to my kitchen and spent the afternoon making meat pies with Mrs Turner. They weren't up to my usual standard – I had kneaded the pastry too hard for too long – but she seemed to be impressed, telling me they were delicious. Grace, still hovering, wouldn't allow me to eat any, saying my stomach wasn't ready for such strong food yet. I wasn't about to tell her I'd had a very active morning, including a quite dramatic escape. I was certain I would get a stern telling off. I had gruel, with Valentines Meat Juice added. It was a poor substitute, though I was promised I could eat cake soon, 'sponge, not fruit, and only the lightest of sponges', Grace insisted.

I sent Mrs Turner home with another meat pie wrapped in a napkin. We hid it at the bottom of her basket, as she said anything nice or decent was bound to be stolen as she reached her room. I had tried to avoid thinking of her son all afternoon. Was he one of those that had terrified me and Mary in that house? If I had brought Mrs Turner there, would he have recognized her, and let himself be rescued? Probably not, I thought gloomily. They were all too far gone in villainy and subjection to their mistress.

In the evening darkness, I sat at the kitchen table. Grace sat by the range, darning socks (I don't know whose: there were no undarned socks in my home). By the light of one low gas lamp, I read the telegram from Mary.

Blood, not human.

Animal then. A ritual? A game? I put it aside and reached for Billy's report.

First of all, I am fine. Everyone is very kind. I'm being fed, and forced to wash my hands and face, and all that you do for me is being done, so don't worry.

Actually, this place is really interesting. All the servants are new, they've only come here in the past two years.

Here Billy named the servants, all fifteen of them.

They're well paid, but they don't like it. Like Wiggins said, I keep my mouth shut and my ears open. They like the master, Mr Langham, and the boys, but they can't stand her, Mrs Langham. They say she's nosy, and nasty with it. She reduced the parlour maid to tears the other day, teasing her about beaus. It sounds mild, but they say she can be really nasty about it. I wonder if she was always like this?

I haven't met the boys yet, and I know you think I shouldn't, but Wiggins says boys in houses like this like to hang about with boys like me, just to see what we're like. I haven't met their nurse yet, but I know she's sweet, Irish and sneaks cakes up to the boys when she's not supposed to. I think I'll try to get to know her – I know, I'll be clever!

Now for the interesting bit. You know how Mr Holmes can always tell where someone has been by the mud on their shoes? Well, being the boot boy, I clean everyone's shoes – and I get to see all the mud!

The servants' shoes are mostly dust and coal dust and tea leaves and stuff like that, although I think the cook occasionally sneaks out to a public house, judging by the drinks label I saw on her shoes. The butler buys a radical newspaper, and when he's read it, stuffs it in his shoes to keep the shape. The boys' shoes are always covered in mud from the park. The master's shoes are always clean, but they always have mud on the bottom too, the same mud from the park – but I never see him leave with the boys when they go out to play. As for the mistress – she's not supposed to be able to walk very far. She has a stick, and she gets carried downstairs and out to the carriage. But she's going out somewhere, at some time. She cleans her shoes very carefully before I get them, but as Mr Holmes

*says, you can't clean away every trace. I found leaf mould
on the buckle on her shoes. There's no leaf mould in the
garden, it's all swept away, so at some point, she's walked
through piles of rotting leaves.*

*I can see Micky outside, so I'm going to throw this out
of the window to him, wrapped round a bun. He looks
freezing. Once again, dear Mrs Hudson, don't worry.*

Well, I was worried. It was human nature. But also
intrigued. Leaf mould? Like the garden of the house on
Henry Street. The case against Mrs Langham was building.

Yet there had been other times when I was so very sure,
and turned out to be so very wrong. I'd be foolish to assume
leaf mould and a nasty character made her a murderer.

'Nora wants to see you,' Grace said suddenly. I'd almost
forgotten she was there.

'I'd like to see her,' I replied, folding the papers away.

'No, I mean, professionally,' Grace said, with a little sniff.
I was confused.

'In her capacity as a nurse?' I asked.

'No, in your capacity as a sort of unofficial detective,'
Grace said. 'She won't stop!' she cried out, suddenly bursting
the bonds of professional behaviour. 'Even though she was
hurt, she won't stop looking, and investigating and thinking.'

'Ah,' I said, understanding. 'She has the itch.'

'The itch?' Grace asked, quite angry by now.

'The urge to know the answer, and not stop until you
know, no matter the cost,' I told her gently. 'Mr Holmes

and Dr Watson both suffer from it, as apparently Mary and I do as well.'

'Well, it's not right,' Grace snapped. 'She was hurt, and yet she can't stop going on about Sister Bey and what could have happened, and how it could all fit together.'

Sister Bey? Well, she certainly was mysterious, with her two logbooks and her refusal to stir from her seat.

'I'll talk to her,' I said soothingly. Upstairs, someone knocked on the door. Mr Holmes must have returned from Paris, and forgotten his key again. He always had problems remembering the small, practical details of everyday life. 'Tomorrow. Can you arrange it?'

She nodded as I went into the hall and opened the heavy front door.

Ah. Not Mr Holmes.

'Good evening, Inspector Lestrade,' I said calmly, folding my hands in front of me. I had blocked this man's way into my house in April, when Mary was hurt in the kitchen, and I felt he remembered it every time I saw him. 'It's late for a call.'

'I was hoping for a word with Mr Holmes,' Lestrade said, his pinched face shadowed. 'I wanted to continue our discussions about the Richmond case.'

'The Richmond case?' I asked. I didn't need to ask. He meant the blackmailer.

'Yes, the dead man in Richmond. We discussed it quite extensively whilst we were in Dartmoor. The thing is, I've had a breakthrough in the case.'

INSPECTOR
LESTRADE'S MYSTERY

I was saved from having to reply by a familiar voice.

'Good evening Mrs Hudson, Lestrade.'

This time it really was Mr Holmes, walking up to the door of 221b.

'Good evening, sir,' I said, with a calmness I was far from feeling. I stepped back to let him and Lestrade into the house. 'Did you find Mademoiselle Carere?'

'I proved she wasn't dead, which was all the French police needed to clear Madame Montpensier,' Mr Holmes said, as I helped him off with his coat. 'I suspect she's gone to ground in America. It's where a great many people find they can lose their past. I shall set my agents onto it.' He handed me his Gladstone bag full of dirty shirts. I couldn't read anything from his expression. What had he discussed with Inspector Lestrade in Dartmoor? I hung his coat up on the rack on the wall as Mr Holmes turned to the inspector and questioned him.

'A breakthrough?' Mr Holmes said, when the inspector told him. 'I thought you'd given that case up entirely.'

'Almost, sir,' Lestrade said, as he headed up the stairs in Mr Holmes' wake. 'But I had the ground dug over one more time, and then I found it.'

'Very persistent of you,' Mr Holmes said. 'Mrs Hudson, we'll need tea!' he called as they walked into his rooms.

I went as quickly as I could into the kitchen. Luckily the kettle was just boiled (although a good housekeeper always keeps the kettle near the boil). I put together the tea things quickly, moving almost mechanically. After so long making tea for Mr Holmes, I didn't have to think about it. I could hear them talking through the air vent on the wall, the one that led to Mr Holmes' room.

'No Dr Watson tonight?' Lestrade was asking.

'No, after a few days away he felt an unaccountable urge to return to his wife immediately,' Mr Holmes told him. 'Why, do you feel tonight's conversation needs to be chronicled?' The voices drifted through the kitchen.

I threw the last of the shortbread onto a plate.

'You can hear every word they say,' Grace said, looking up at the air vent, scandalized, although she didn't move from her seat at the table.

'Really, can you?' I said quickly, pouring hot water over the tea leaves. There, I was ready. 'I can't hear a thing, I'm slightly deaf,' I lied. Nevertheless, I closed the vent with a snap before I slowly headed upstairs.

Grace told me the tea tray was too heavy for me, but I was adamant. I had been doing this for years, and I was well practised. Besides, I didn't like anybody else but me to carry tea to Mr Holmes. I caught up my skirt a little between the tray and my body so I didn't trip. I held out the tray at just the right angle to stop the plates spilling. I balanced the tray perfectly on my arm as I opened the door. But I was out of strength, and my arms were shaking by the time I set the tray down.

The fire had been burning low (I had ordered Mrs Turner to keep the rooms warm in anticipation of Mr Holmes' return at any time) and Mr Holmes was bent over it with the poker, vigorously stirring the fire into life. Inspector Lestrade was lighting the oil lamps on the table, and moved to one aside so I could set the tray down.

'So, what do you have?' Mr Holmes asked, as I poured the tea. Inspector Lestrade handed over a scrap of paper.

'Found it buried in the rubble,' he said. 'It must have been protected by the bricks in the flames.'

It was a scrap about an inch wide, and three inches long. Not much, but possibly enough. I handed a cup of tea over to the inspector (milky, one sugar) as Holmes read the writing on the paper.

'". . . do anything you ask, give you money, my body, my soul, do not tell my secr—" Well, we can imagine that last word is "secret",' he said, handing the paper back over. I gave him his tea (strong, only a splash of milk, three sugars). 'The man's clearly a blackmailer, then.'

'Still a murdered man, Mr Holmes,' Inspector Lestrade said. I held out the shortbread to him. He always loved my biscuits.

'You assume murder where I can only see a possible murder,' Mr Holmes snapped. 'It could also be an accident, or even suicide.' He took some of the shortbread.

'No man burns himself to death,' Inspector Lestrade insisted.

'I've known cases,' Mr Holmes said shortly. 'Cases where the man's guilt was so great he had to expiate it in the most painful way possible. Blackmail is vile. Blackmailers are the scum of the earth. If this man suddenly realized what he was, and felt the only way to pay for his crimes was to burn along with his papers, then I feel obliged to let him rest in whatever peace he can find.'

I ought to have left, but I dared not. I wanted to not just hear. I wanted to see them too. Men can say one thing, and mean another. Words would not be enough this time, I needed to see their thoughts on their faces. I placed myself in the background of the dim, dark room, and listened. Mr Holmes saw me, standing behind Inspector Lestrade, but did not say a word. If he had merely glanced my way, I would have left, but he studiously ignored me.

'And to be honest, if one of his victims had done the same to him,' Mr Holmes continued, 'I would not blame them, nor help you hunt them down.'

Inspector Lestrade laughed uneasily.

'That's not an attitude that would go down well at Scotland Yard,' he said.

'I don't work for Scotland Yard,' Mr Holmes said. They stood there, these two men, close to being friends, on either side of a huge divide. Inspector Lestrade gave in first.

'Well, well, we won't argue over this,' he said, handing the cup back to Mr Holmes, who handed it to me. 'I've got other leads to follow.'

'Follow them if you must,' Mr Holmes said. 'I think you'll find it's an accident in the end.'

'Maybe. I just need to satisfy my curiosity,' Lestrade said. 'As you said, always check the cabs.'

Cabs: I had taken a cab to the man's house. The cab driver had sworn secrecy, thinking we were working for Mr Holmes, but would he tell his secret if the police questioned him?

'Of course. Well, good night, Lestrade,' Mr Holmes said, holding out his hand. After a moment's hesitation, Lestrade shook it, then left before I had a chance to offer to see him out.

'Well, it seems Lestrade is finally learning the lessons I've been endeavouring to teach him,' Mr Holmes said dryly, before draining his tea cup. I set about replacing the crockery on the tray.

'It had to be for this particular case, didn't it,' I said bitterly. 'Maybe I . . .'

'No,' Mr Holmes as good as snarled. 'I am right, aren't I? He was a blackmailer?'

'I thought you already knew?'

'I knew some. Not all.' It was an old trick of his that I heard him use a hundred times before. He would pretend to know more than he did, and then people would talk freely. I hadn't quite fallen for it, I hoped.

'Yes,' I said softly. 'He was a blackmailer, and of the vilest sort. Not just money, but power, and control. And a murderer too.'

'Murder I can understand, usually. Blackmail never,' Mr Holmes said. 'Just to put my mind at ease, neither you nor Mrs Watson were . . .'

'Victims? No,' I reassured him. I smiled a little to myself. 'Mary says we were "vengeance".'

'There's a reason vengeance is always painted as a woman,' he said, looking at me curiously, as if seeing something new. I stirred uneasily.

'It was an accident, nothing more,' I said, picking up the tray. 'But I would rather not explain myself to Inspector Lestrade.'

'Of course,' Mr Holmes said, opening the door for me. 'But I shall do my best to make sure he does not have reason to question you.'

'That's kind of you,' I said.

'Not kind,' he said, snorting with a sudden burst of laughter. 'Self-preservation. If Lestrade investigates you, he might move onto me next, and God knows what he'd find then.'

So, you see, we both had our secrets.

A LITTLE BIT
OF GOSSIP

We'd arranged, via Grace, to meet Nora in a tea shop in the Strand that was supposed to have excellent cakes. All the way there I had sensed the same prickling on the back of my neck I had felt before. I saw no one follow me, yet I had the same uneasy awareness of my surroundings. It made me uncomfortable, and reminded me that people had died in this case. I had seen it. In fact, I remembered, I was possibly the only living witness, definitely the only reliable one, and certainly the only one currently out of hospital, and out on the streets daily. If this case had been Mr Holmes', he would have insisted I be protected. Eventually, I decided not to ignore that feeling. Sending a telegram to Wiggins was done in an instant (he didn't have an address, but all the telegram boys in Baker Street knew him) and only then was I able to judge properly the excellence of the cakes along with Nora's deductions.

The tea shop itself was a little crowded, but we found ourselves a secluded seat in the window. It was quite a charming little room, with red check curtains at the window, and bright, clean white tablecloths. The waitresses bustled about in mobcaps and print dresses – someone's idea of healthy country girls – and steam rose reassuringly from the floral tea pots. The cakes, on delicate silver stands, were small, but perfect, and there was a wide choice of them. I was reassured to see none of the cakes was too brightly coloured, which should mean their colouring was natural, not some harsh, possibly poisonous, dye. It was still morning, but the light outside was dim. The window ran with condensation, and it was difficult to see clearly who was on the street.

'Do you still think we're being followed?' Mary asked, as she perused the bill of fare whilst waiting for the sisters.

'I think so,' I told her. 'It's just a feeling really.'

'Well, I trust your feelings. Who do you think it is?'

'I've no idea,' I admitted. 'It could be anyone.'

I wiped the condensation away from the window so I could see outside. The Strand was, as usual, crowded with people of all kinds, businessmen marching to Charing Cross, ink-stained journalists hurrying to Fleet Street, harassed women shopping, running into tea shops to shelter from the cold, street children weaving in and out of the crowds, occasionally into people's pockets, stolid policemen strolling up and down. The tea room itself was full of women, from the very well-dressed, very loud sort ordering as many cakes as caught their eye to the quieter, poorer women spending carefully saved pennies on one cake and cup of tea for a treat.

'But I've telegraphed Wiggins,' I said. 'I have an idea.'

That was when Grace and Nora arrived, Grace supporting Nora. Both had changed out of their nurses' uniforms but were wearing plain grey almost like a uniform. Nora looked pale, with a bandage over her forehead.

Grace helped Nora sit opposite me and she herself sat anxiously beside her sister. Now they were together, I could see the difference. Not just that Nora was taller or Grace had slightly dissimilar eyes. It was the way they carried themselves: Nora, even now, with her head held high, ready to take on the world; Grace merely happy to take the world as it was.

A pot of tea and a plate of cakes arrived as I was asking Nora how she was, and she was assuring me that she was recovering nicely and would be back to work in a week. The hospital had investigated the incident and decided that it must have been one of the patients that attacked her, in a moment of disorientation.

'I've accepted that as it means I can go back to work, but I don't believe it,' Nora said, peering at the cakes. 'Oh, there's no lemon.'

'Martha can make you a lovely lemon cake,' Mary said, as she took a huge bite of a cream bun. 'Who do you think attacked you?' she asked, with her mouth full. Nora frowned, and took a slice of Victoria sponge.

'It wasn't the other night nurse, she was on her tea break on the other side of the hospital. I know it can't have been Sister Bey, because I saw her in the other ward just before I was attacked,' she said. 'And I asked the other staff, they didn't see her leave. But I do think that whoever attacked me had something to do with her.'

'Why is that?' I asked.

'Nora's never liked her, have you?' Grace said, pouring her sister's tea. 'She never does any of the work.'

'Well, that's not why I don't like her,' Nora qualified. 'I mean, she doesn't give medicine or straighten out beds or talk to patients or empty bedpans, but she's the sister, she doesn't have to do all that. I'm not sure why I don't like her, really. I just know I feel tense whenever she's around.'

'There'll be a reason,' I said to her. 'You just don't realize what it is. Something she says or does puts you on your guard.'

Nora thought for a minute.

'Maybe it's that second logbook,' she said. 'It's not the official one, it's personal, and she writes in it all the time.'

'Lots of nurses and Sisters keep a personal logbook,' Grace pointed out. 'Notes of experiences and things they've learnt and so on. Notes that aren't suitable for the official logbook but that they want to remember.'

'But we share those. No one's ever allowed to see Sister Bey's logbook,' Nora insisted. 'And of course, there's her past.'

'Her past?' I asked. Now we were getting somewhere.

'I shouldn't gossip,' Nora said.

'Please do,' I begged. Gossip was life and blood to a detective. 'It may be important.'

Nora looked around to make sure no one could overhear, then pulled her chair into the table and leaned over close to us.

'It was a few years ago,' she said, in a very low voice. 'She was a Sister on one of the day wards then. Bit of a rising star, they said. Could have been Matron in a few years.'

'What was she like, back then?' I asked, curious to know if she had always be the silent, closed-off woman I saw.

'Nice, people said,' Nora said, as if surprised. 'Shy, but trying hard not to be. Eager to learn.'

'What happened?' Mary asked.

'It was a dosage mistake,' Nora said. 'It could have happened to any of us. The decimal point was in the wrong place on the prescription, so she administered 30 instead of 0.3, something like that.'

'It's easily done,' Grace said. 'It's happened more times than doctors admit. The thing is, she shouldn't have been administering the drug at all. It should have been the doctor.'

'The doctor said he'd trusted Sister Bey to get it right,' Nora continued. 'The Sister said he'd written the dosage down wrong.'

'Who died?' Mary asked.

'A tramp,' Nora said. 'No one of any consequence or family, the hospital board said, which was lucky for both Sister Bey and the doctor. He was sent to Edinburgh. She stayed in the hospital, but as a night Sister now, on the understanding she'd never rise any further.'

'And never to administer medication again,' I added.

'Well, not without supervision,' Nora told me, sitting back now the worst of her story was done. 'But she's taken it further than that. No medication, no talking to the patients, no talking to the other staff except to give and take orders.'

'Why does she stay?' Mary asked. 'And how does the hospital let her stay?'

'I don't suppose she knows any other life,' Grace said. 'It's not just that hospital she stays in, it's that particular ward. She never allows herself to be moved.'

'Maybe she has some influence with a governor of the hospital,' Nora said. 'Or maybe she knows some scandal. Or maybe it's just easier to let her stay.'

'You think she knows something,' I said, peering at Nora's eyes over the rim of her tea cup as she sipped. 'Something about that ward?'

She put her tea cup down.

'I just don't like it there,' she said. 'I'm going to ask to be moved to one of the public wards. Soon.'

'But in the meantime, you think something odd is going on in your ward.'

Nora raised her hand to her head. She had gone even paler.

'Grace, you had better take Nora home,' Mary said. 'Head wounds aren't to be trifled with.'

Nora rose, supported by Grace. As she left, she leaned over and whispered to me, 'There're too many deaths on that ward.'

AMONGST THE
BACK STREETS

'Nora's well and truly smashed your theory about Emma's death being the only suspicious one, hasn't she?' Mary said, helping herself to another cake. 'These cakes aren't as nice as yours.'

'You've eaten five,' I pointed out. 'Nora hasn't quite smashed my theory; she's just shaken it a little.'

'Let me guess,' Mary said, wiping the crumbs from her hands. 'You believe Eleanor Langham, on behalf of Lord Howe or Richard Pembury or some other rich, powerful friend of hers, killed Emma Fordyce to keep her from telling her secrets about her past, using one of the Pale Boys gang which you believe she runs?'

'That's about right,' I admitted. 'On practically no evidence apart from a bit of leaf mould, a shape glimpsed in the shadows, and an awful lot of "feelings". Mr Holmes would be disgusted. What do you think?'

'Well, I think the stolen boys are the Pale Boys,' she said. 'I think perhaps they are connected to one of the women in the hospital and I think it's a mistake to theorize before you have all the data.'

'Stop quoting Mr Holmes to me,' I said. 'How will I know when I have all the data?'

'More importantly, how are we going to deal with whoever is following us?'

'Now there,' I said, 'I have a plan. Or rather, Wiggins does.'

I explained exactly what we were going to do next. She liked it.

'Oh, so that's the game, is it?' she said.

We paid the bill and went out into the street. It was one of those cold, damp November days where the chill seems to seep through your clothes and into your bones. The sky was a mass of thick grey clouds that felt oddly claustrophobic, as if it were only a few feet above our heads. I looked around and saw what I needed – a street boy wearing a red bandanna around his throat. He saw me looking and, without acknowledging me at all, darted down a side alley.

'That's him,' I said to Mary. 'We follow him.'

We walked down the alley at a slower pace, taking us into a mass of buildings and streets between the Strand and the Embankment.

Five people from the Strand followed us into the streets: two women wrapped in shawls, a dark, tall man in an ill-fitting sailor suit, another man in a deerstalker and tweed coat and a youth, not known to me.

I didn't stop to look at them. Wiggins' boys, far better at keeping invisible than they, would already be all over the streets, staring at them, assessing them, until the boys worked out who was following us.

The boy in the bandanna turned another corner, and another. He was our guide through this maze of streets. As we followed him, our route would get more convoluted. Hopefully it would winnow out those who had their own business down here from whoever was following us. It was a delicate game though. We had to look as if we had no idea we were being watched, and yet not move so fast we lost our pursuers.

Another twist, and one of the women veered off into a public house. Down to four.

'I never knew all this was down here,' Mary said. 'I thought it had all been cleared away when they created the Embankment.'

'It will be soon, I suspect,' I replied. We were amongst a row of arches, all of them huge and cavernous, dripping with damp. They were dark, but occupied, and men and woman inside shifted uneasily as we peered in. The boy we followed didn't pause, but ran through here. We went through, as the man in the deerstalker, looking around, went into one of the arches.

'What do you suppose he's doing?' I asked.

'Looking for someone he's lost,' Mary said. 'There's a few hiding places down here; John's tracked patients here occasionally.'

'Opium dens?' I asked. I had a hazy knowledge of the

darker parts of London streets, but I didn't expect to find them behind the Strand. Mary shook her head.

'Cheap lodging houses. Not as cheap as Whitechapel, but not pleasant. A lot of respectable people gone to the bad find themselves here.'

The youth now stopped, and stared at us for a moment. Then he shoved his hands in his pockets, turned on his heel, and walked away, whistling. Just another street boy. Two now. I was worried about the tall man in the sailor suit. He definitely had his eye on us. I wasn't sure if he was the person who'd been following us, or if he just wanted to rob us.

I turned another corner, but it must have been the wrong one, because I could see no sign of the boy in the red bandanna. I looked around frantically. We were almost at the river now – the Victoria Embankment was just over the iron fence – but I could see no way out. Then the tall man appeared at the end of the alley and moved purposefully towards us.

'Oh no,' Mary said. 'I think we played the game wrong.' She took a breath and straightened up, ready to face him, but at that moment something crashed somewhere, someone screamed, and a police whistle sounded. The tall man, obviously a street robber, took to his heels and ran.

'Oi!' a boy shouted. It was our guide. He was pointing towards a gate in the fence. We went through into the pleasant grounds of the Victoria Embankment; the boy didn't follow, he'd done his part.

Well, it's pleasant in summer. Now it was cold and bare, and the wind from the river cut through me so sharply it took my breath away.

That left the woman. We stepped down into an odd stone arch that had been left there, part of a fine estate that had once stood here, and waited.

It wasn't long. She came down to see where we were. She still hid herself well, but we knew who she was now. Before she could wander past, she was overwhelmed with boys springing out of nowhere, pushing her towards us. They didn't hurt her, but there was no escape.

'Stop them!' she called. 'Call them off!'

Wiggins whistled, and the boys stood back. She stood in front of me and Mary and Wiggins. Mary did the honours and ripped the dirty shawl from her head.

It was Miranda Logan.

THE TRUTH ABOUT
MIRANDA LOGAN

'Have you been following us all this time?' I asked. 'Since I came out of hospital?'

'Get rid of those boys,' she insisted.

'They won't hurt you none,' Wiggins said scornfully.

'I've seen them kill!' she insisted.

'No, these are the Baker Street Irregulars,' Mary said soothingly. 'Not the Pale Boys.'

'Oh, I see,' Miranda said, chastened. Wiggins called his boys and sent them home, but stayed himself.

'Nicely done,' I said to him. It had been an exercise I had heard him getting together with Mr Holmes one evening: how to weed out a follower from a crowd. They had practised it once or twice, but never done it with a live subject. When I realized I was being followed, I had suggested that Wiggins try it with me. He had been eager to accept, and I had sent him a telegram that morning to say I was being followed again. Luckily he had a boy – Jim – who knew the Strand streets well. As for the rest, it was just a matter of following and watching at a distance. The Irregulars were good at that.

Mary stood in front of Miranda.

'Who are you?'

'I am a private detective,' she answered.

'What, a female 'tec?' Wiggins objected. 'Never heard of the like.'

'Mary and I are detectives,' I said to him.

'Yeah, but you sort of fell into it,' he pointed out. 'Never seen one that got paid for it 'fore.'

'Shame, I'd love to get paid for it,' Mary sighed. 'Now, Miss Logan, I have some questions . . .'

'Which I'm not going to answer,' Miranda said, standing up straight against the wall.

Mary shrugged. 'Don't answer, then. Let's see what we can deduce,' she said, staring hard at Miranda. Wiggins and I took a seat on a nearby bench to watch. I had a feeling we were going to enjoy this.

'Martha, would you like to start?' Mary invited me. 'After all, you knew her in hospital.'

'Thank you. Your accent's very good, too perfect,' I said to Miranda. 'Not your original accent, and judging by the way you took Sarah Malone's confession, I imagine you are a Catholic.'

Miranda nodded, smiling a little.

'And you,' Miranda said, 'are no one's nanny. Could Mrs Bryson have been right about you? Are you Mr Holmes' housekeeper?'

'I am,' I admitted, 'but I am here for myself, not him.'

'You do lie well,' Miranda said softly, and admiringly.

Mary looked Miranda up and down. 'My turn,' she said. 'You know parts of London fairly well, if you've been

227

following us for a while, which Martha thinks you have. But not this part, not well enough to follow us from a distance; you had to stick close. Your clothes are from this country, your shoes are not.' Mary glanced at us. 'People rarely change their shoes when in disguise because they can't be adjusted for comfort,' she explained, quite in a Holmes-style manner. Wiggins winked at me in amusement. Mary turned back to Miranda. 'Judging by the shape, I'd say they were made in Spain – a friend of mine is writing a monograph on the peculiarity of the shapes of shoes across Europe – so you are Spanish.'

Miranda's eyes widened, then slowly she took a cigarette case out of her skirt pocket, took a thin black cigarette out and lit it.

'And so are your cigarettes, judging by that awful smell,' I said, waving the smoke away. Mr Holmes had tried every kind of cigarette and cigar and pipe tobacco he could get his hands on, for his monograph, and I had had the misfortune to air his rooms out afterwards.

'But working out your nationality is a parlour trick,' Mary continued. 'Let's see what I can find out about your relation to this case, shall we?'

Mary stepped back and stared at Miranda long enough to make the woman uncomfortable. The sun had come out and it wasn't unpleasant sitting on that bench. I was quite enjoying Mary and I working together.

'You were obviously in that hospital ward to watch over Emma Fordyce,' I murmured, apparently to myself, though everyone could hear me. 'To harm or protect? You were angry the morning after she died, so I believe you were hired to protect, or listen.'

Miranda said nothing, but she blew smoke in a very aggressive manner.

'Well, you failed at that,' Mary pointed out. 'So, hired by whom? Her publishers? No?' Mary said, as Miranda, seemingly bored, stared out over the river.

'Well, Emma didn't know you were there for her, did she?' I added. 'She barely spoke to you, and you took care not to speak to her. No, that was someone else's job, wasn't it, to get the secrets?'

Mary and I had gone beyond deduction now, into clever guessing. Miranda's reactions would tell us if she was right or not. I'd heard Mr Holmes do this a hundred times, but the two of us doing it ourselves was a whole new treat.

'Newspapers!' Mary cried, making Miranda jump. She was very tightly wound. 'A newspaper hired you to protect her – well, a newspaper reporter, hoping for a juicy story before it was printed in her book.'

Miranda glared at her, and sucked the smoke from the cigarette.

'But who? There're so many reporters who wanted that story,' Mary asked. Miranda merely smiled. 'You're going to make us work for it, aren't you? Luckily, I already have that answer. He had another creature on that ward.'

I stepped forward, and whispered in Miranda's ear, though Mary knew what I was saying.

'Patrick West,' I whispered.

Miranda's eyes opened wide as I pulled back to see the effect of my revelation.

'Ah, I see we're right,' Mary said, a little smugly.

'Is that what Sarah Malone confessed to you?' I asked. 'That she was working for Patrick West?'

'Confessionals are sacred,' Miranda said, and I had to respect that she, even as a detective, would not share that information.

'Not just Patrick West, but another man too? A horrific man, someone she was terrified of?' I persisted. 'Someone who'd persecuted others to their death based on the information she gave.'

Miranda nodded only slightly.

'That man is dead,' I told her.

'You are sure?' Miranda asked.

'She's sure,' Wiggins said shortly.

'So, back to Patrick West,' Mary said. Miranda looked at her, almost amused. 'Emma dead, no revelations, but you think she was murdered.'

Miranda shrugged.

'And her death was just a mite too convenient, wasn't it?' Mary pointed out. 'Well, maybe not for you, but for quite a few people with secrets to keep. So instead of earning your nice lovely fat fee from Patrick West to protect Emma Fordyce, you're going to earn it by bringing him the revelation of who killed her.'

Miranda was back to smoking again.

'Only first you have to find out who it is, and you have no idea, so you are following us because we're working on that case too,' I said.

'Which, quite frankly, is cheating,' Mary added indignantly.

'I am not cheating,' Miranda objected. 'I am following my suspicions.'

'Well, you can't possibly think Mrs Hudson is a suspect,' Mary said. 'She's Sherlock Holmes' housekeeper.'

'I once read 'bout a policeman's housekeeper wot poisoned a whole village,' Wiggins pointed out in a leisurely way, as if we were having a Sunday afternoon chat in the parlour.

'Where did you read about that?' I asked.

'Newspaper my chips came wrapped in,' he told me.

'Wiggins is right, of course, no one is above suspicion,' Mary said. 'But in this case, it's not Mrs Hudson. In fact,' she said, turning and walking away from Miranda, 'as we're all agreed it's Eleanor Langham, we can just get her arrested and . . .'

'Eleanor Langham!' Miranda cried out. 'What are you talking about?'

Mary innocently turned back to Miranda.

'Well, of course it's Eleanor Langham. She's far more mobile than she lets on, she watches everyone, she's distinctly nasty . . .'

'Yes, she's a bitch,' Miranda agreed. 'But she is not a killer! She's far too obvious! What makes you think she's mobile, as you put it?'

'Look, my theory is sound,' Mary insisted. 'We're agreed that the Pale Boys are somehow involved in the killing?'

'If that is what you call that strange group of boys I have seen on the streets outside the hospital,' Miranda conceded. 'I never see them come or go, they are just there one minute and gone the next. They are disturbing.'

'They're just boys,' I snapped. 'But yes, rather disturbing boys. But you see, we know they're connected to Eleanor Langham,' I continued inexorably, ignoring Miranda's rising anger. 'She has strange fancies, she is obsessed with her dead son, we have proof that she sneaks out at night . . .'

'Well, so does Florence Bryson!' Miranda countered, suddenly pushed into defending her theory.

'Florence Bryson is your suspect,' Mary said, smiling softly. 'Thank you so much for telling me.'

Miranda sagged as she realized she had been tricked. It had been very neatly done. Mr Holmes would have been proud. He always said people cannot help correcting others.

'So, Flo sneaks out of the hospital, does she?' I said. 'I understood she practically lived there.'

'I saw her twice,' Miranda admitted. 'She does it quite openly. She claims to be going home for an evening or two – but then she disappears into the streets.'

'She could be going home,' I pointed out. I had quite liked Flo, though I found her unsettling at times.

'She has no home I can find,' Miranda said.

'Maybe an hotel, then,' I said. 'Just to get away from the smell of the hospital.'

'It's not just the sneaking out that is suspicious,' Miranda said. 'I do have other questions, for her and for you.'

'Flo did talk to Emma a lot,' I said to Mary. 'They always had their heads together.'

'I never trusted that story about her dead son,' Miranda admitted. 'She talked about him all the time, but would never say how he died.'

'Maybe it was too painful for her,' I said. I still felt a sharp stab of pain when I talked about my boy.

'No, she endlessly discussed every tiny detail of his life and habits and his love for her. Only when it came to his end was she silent,' Miranda said, throwing her cigarette on the ground and grinding it out. 'And that's all I will tell you. Thank you,' she said, looking at Mary. 'This has been quite an education. You don't give anything away, do you? Either of you. You are quite unexpected.'

'A good detective needs to learn to make his face his mask,' Mary said. 'Or so I've heard.'

'I see,' Miranda said, turning to leave. Then she turned back, her face troubled.

'We are agreed the Pale Boys are mixed up in this,' she said, 'and you are investigating them.'

'We are,' Mary said, straightening up, suddenly defensive.

'Stay away from them,' Miranda warned. 'I have heard rumours of their part in deaths.'

'Why would they do that? They're just children,' Mary insisted.

'They are a secret society. In my part of the world, some

secret societies demand a sacrifice of blood from new members to show their loyalty. They have to kill for the society.'

'Yes, but this is England,' Mary said coolly. 'London. That sort of thing doesn't happen here. They play a few games with animal blood, but I refuse to believe they are actually dangerous.' Mary had forgotten or dismissed the fear she had felt in that house on Henry Street. She still wanted to save them.

'As you wish,' Miranda said, shrugging. 'I still think you should tell that woman to stay away from them.'

'What woman?' I asked.

'That pale woman all in grey and brown that lives in your home,' Miranda said. 'Mrs Turner, is it? I've seen her a few times. She goes out at night, looking for them. She sometimes leaves food and parcels for them, I've seen her do it. Maybe she even finds them, I don't know. She's difficult to follow, she fades into the background. But she is out there every night, on the same streets as the Pale Boys, leaving them messages and meat pies.'

AN UNEXPECTED
VISITOR

'She's just trying to find her boy,' Mary pleaded.

'Maybe she never lost him,' I replied. We were all three in a hansom cab heading back to Baker Street. Wiggins was very quiet. Mary and I had disagreed about Mrs Turner: I wanted to confront her right away, but Mary favoured a gentler approach.

'What about you?' I asked Wiggins. 'Have you seen Mrs Turner on the streets at night?'

'Yeah,' he admitted. 'Looking for her boy. She's been doing it for years. Ain't no harm in her. I thought you knew when she moved into 221b.'

'It's a perfect disguise,' I said, sitting back against the cushion. Quiet, harmless Mrs Turner and her loss. No one would question her being on the streets at night, the same streets as the Pale Boys. And if anyone ever saw her with them, she could claim just to be questioning them about her son.

Well, I'd started the day with one suspect, and now I had three. I wondered if Mr Holmes ever found his list of suspects getting out of hand?

Of course he did. How I felt now exactly explained those

evenings where he had sworn, long and volubly, sometimes in several languages, and stamped around his rooms all night throwing papers about and performing vile-smelling chemical experiments.

'By the way,' Wiggins said, 'got Billy's latest report here.' He handed me a filthy scrap of paper. 'Sorry 'bout that, he threw it out the window and it landed in mud. Anyway, he's fine, and he's made friends with the nurse. Let me out, will ya?'

Wiggins jumped out and the hansom carried on as I read Billy's report.

I've made friends with the Langham boys, he wrote. *It wasn't difficult. They're not allowed to see anyone but their nurse and their mother. Even their father is kept away. If he comes in to say hello, just for a minute, the nurse has to remind him of Mrs Langham's orders. Sometimes the nurse is kind and forgets, but Mrs Langham is very strict. They're not allowed to be alone together. Well, I fixed their toys and taught them to swear a little and now they tell me everything.*

They had an older brother, before they were born, who died of typhoid fever. He was ill in bed and Mrs Langham was with him all the time. Eventually Mr Langham persuaded her to go to her own room and rest, and that's when the boy died. So she blamed him, although she can't have blamed him right away, because they had two more children. I met her when I started and she was very strict on keeping the house locked up tight and not talking to strangers and not allowing the boys to talk to anyone they're not supposed to. She's a bit scary. I always feel like she's watching me, even when she's at the top of the house and I'm at the bottom. The others feel like that too. You can tell by the way they keep looking over their shoulder.

She hardly ever goes out, but she gets visitors. I don't see them, but they're important men, I know that. You can tell by the noisy way they walk, as if nothing is more important in the world than they are, not even peace.

Mrs Langham will probably have to go into hospital again soon, they say. She's always in and out. That's all I've got to report, except I miss your cakes. The cook here isn't a patch on you.

'What does he say?' Mary asked.

'He has indeed made friends with the boys,' I said, perusing the paper. 'Here, read it.' I handed it to her.

'Billy's got a gift for making friends,' Mary said, smiling.

'He's spoken to the boys too, though not for long. Eleanor doesn't like them talking to anyone,' I told her.

'Well, lots of mothers don't like their precious darlings talking to members of the lower classes,' Mary said, looking out of the window. 'Afraid they might get contaminated by poverty, or bad manners or something. Though Wiggins' boys have the nicest manners I've ever seen.'

'That's because I bribe them with cake,' I continued. 'No,

Billy says that they're not allowed to talk to anyone, not even other children. Just the mother, their tutor, who doesn't live in the home, and their nurse.'

'What, no one?' Mary asked, turning to look at me. 'Why ever not?'

'I know their older brother died,' I said. 'Perhaps she's afraid of losing them? Perhaps she's afraid they'll catch something?'

'Well, they'll have to talk to someone eventually,' Mary pointed out. 'Children can't grow up speaking to just their parents and their nurse.'

'Not parents,' I said, reading the letter again. 'Just mother. They're not allowed to spend time with their father either. Not alone. He tries to meet them in the park but . . .'

'But Eleanor can see them with her telescope,' Mary finished. 'That's sad. Why . . . you don't think . . .' She turned to me, her face full of dread at what she had just imagined. We knew more than ordinary men and women did. Thanks to Wiggins, and Mr Holmes, we knew some of the horrors on the streets for unwary children. We knew about the men and women who tried to lure them away into dark corners, we knew about the houses of children for men with a certain taste. We knew the worst that could happen.

'No, I don't think anything of the sort,' I said firmly, folding the letter away into my handbag. 'Do you think I'd allow Billy to stay there if I thought he was in danger of being molested in some way?'

And yet I felt distinctly uncomfortable about leaving Billy

at Eleanor Langham's house. He was so proud of being able to help, and his information was useful, and he wasn't alone, but I wanted him out and at home with me. Although I also recognized that Billy was growing up fast, and he might never forgive me if I swooped down and swept him away like an over-protective mother hen. Besides, he had Wiggins to keep him safe.

We were on Baker Street now, and we pulled up outside 221b to find Mrs Turner on the doorstep, obviously waiting for us. I had a few questions for her, but she stopped me.

'You've got a visitor,' she said breathlessly. 'Down in the kitchen.'

We went down. There, in the dim light of my kitchen (that suddenly seemed scruffy and dowdy) stood a vision. A woman with black hair swept off her face, under a daring purple hat. A purple velvet ribbon round her throat set off startling green eyes. Her dress swept the floor in swathes of startling pink silk. She shimmered – no, glowed – in that room.

'Lillian Rose,' Mary breathed.

Lillian Rose. Last time I saw her (apart from that brief glimpse previously) she had been dressed cheaply, shaking with fear, still earning her living as a prostitute. She had run away to Scotland to hide from the blackmailer. Now she stood in my kitchen, and she looked glorious. It had only been a few months, yet she was a completely different woman – but I had always suspected Lillian Rose had a gift for transformation.

'I didn't know you were back in London,' I said, rather meekly.

'Was I supposed to keep you apprised of my movements?' she snapped. The old Whitechapel accent had gone. Her voice was cultured now, though her temper seemed to be the same.

'But we sent you to Edinburgh,' Mary said, confused. 'We wanted to keep you safe.'

'I came back,' Lillian told her. 'Did you think I would let my life rot away in Edinburgh? I belong in London.'

'You're . . . very different,' Mary said, gesturing at Lillian's clothes, her hair, her very presence. Mind you, she wasn't that different in demeanour from the proud, clever prostitute we'd met in Whitechapel – but she had transformed her appearance utterly.

'I should hope so,' Lillian said, mollified. 'I've put quite a lot of work into becoming a new woman.'

'You've succeeded,' I told her. 'Though I thought I saw you the other day.'

'Quite possibly; I've been here for a while.'

'And earning a lot, too,' Mary said, with more than a trace of admiration. 'That dress must have cost a fortune.'

'Not that much,' Lillian said, but Mrs Turner had been walking round her, frankly appraising it.

'Finest silk and velvet, hand-made, very well fitted, I'd say around thirty guineas,' Mrs Turner said, then blushed as Lillian glared at her.

'Who are you?' she demanded.

'No one,' Mrs Turner said quietly, retiring to the corner of the room where she could gaze at the dress quietly.

'How did you get so much money?' Mary asked.

'I earned it. And not on my back neither!' Lillian said quickly. 'I've been helping a journalist. He can't write for himself, nor read any more, so I assist him. Between us we earn a great deal of money. He is teaching me.'

'Can't read or write,' I said softly. 'Is he blind?'

'Patrick West,' Mary realized. 'You work for him?' she said to Lillian, with a moue of distaste.

'Yes, I do,' Lillian said calmly. 'What of it?'

'But he's a gossip writer,' Mary said. 'The nastiest kind of gossip. I mean, he writes these awful columns hinting at all kinds of things, and dredges up all these secrets.'

'So?' Lillian said, one hand on her hip.

'Well, it's not that different to what you were doing for *him*, is it?' Mary snapped back, meaning the blackmailer. Lillian's hand shot to her throat. The blackmailer had slit her throat once, leaving her for dead. When she survived, he had made her his creature, forcing her to collect secrets for him.

'I'm getting paid now!' she said. 'Good money, and it's my choice. No one's holding a knife to my throat! And besides, I was good at it,' she said, with an odd sort of pride. 'I succeeded where others failed. I could always find the secrets. Why shouldn't I use those skills?'

'But . . .' Mary said, but Lillian interrupted her.

'Would you rather I was back on the streets, in men's

beds?' Lillian said, with scorn. 'Or even better, starving to death in a garret somewhere, cold and hungry but at least with my honour?' she went on, mocking Mary. 'To hell with honour. To hell with everyone else. I survived, and I intend to go right on surviving.'

'I have no doubt you will,' I said to her. I couldn't say I blamed her. What else was a clever woman to do? 'What do you want from us?'

'You never had illusions about me, did you?' Lillian said, turning to me. 'Never thought I could be saved.'

'You're alive, and he's dead. That's saved enough for me,' I told her, sitting down at the table. 'He did die, you know, in the end.'

'Yes. That's why I came back. Did it hurt him?' she asked.

'Oh yes. It hurt,' I told her. Him and me both.

'Good,' she said viciously. 'I'd ask who killed him, but you wouldn't tell me, would you?'

'No,' Mary said shortly. 'What do you want?'

'Patrick wants to see you,' Lillian said. 'Right now.'

'We may not want to see him,' Mary said, sitting down. 'Cheap little gossip writer.'

'Oh yes you do,' Lillian said triumphantly, pulling on her gloves. 'You think we don't know you've been investigating Emma's death? And everything else, too. We know you want to talk.'

'We're not selling him our story,' I said quickly.

'Think of it as more of an exchange of information,' Lillian said. 'Oh, and Patrick said to tell you something else. He said he hasn't always been a gossip writer. He used to cover the crime stories too.'

'Why would he tell us that?' Mary asked. 'Oh, I see, he's going to tell us a few crime stories too.'

Mary and I glanced at each other. There were a few questions I wanted to ask. Sometimes crime reporters knew more than the police, thanks to their network of informers. A lot of what they knew was never printed. Patrick West could be a mine of information. But what would I have to give up in return?

We decided, with not a word spoken but in silent agreement, to go with Lillian.

'Lead the way,' Mary said, and the two of them left.

'But what about Mr Holmes?' Mrs Turner asked. 'What if he wants something?' She was genuinely nervous. I found it hard to believe she had anything to do with the Pale Boys other than searching for her son, but I had been fooled before.

'Well, give it to him,' I told her. 'He probably won't disturb you; he's cataloguing his newspaper archive.'

'What if he asks where you are?'

'Tell him I'm hunting my Hound,' I told her, as I followed Mary and Lillian. I only hoped I wasn't following it into my own personal Grimpen Mire. I was going to have to tread carefully with Lillian Rose and Patrick West.

DARK AS INK

Patrick West's home was in a tiny court off Fleet Street. Fleet Street itself was always noisy, packed and filthy. It was a street of ink, papers and books. Men and women rushed by, weaving expertly in and out of the crowd, fingers and faces and clothes smeared black with printer's ink and writer's ink and newspaper ink. Between them ran clerks, all in black too, and telegraph boys bolting up and down the street. Newspaper boys hauled piles of papers as big as they were to their jealously guarded spots, trying to outshout each other. Meek and frightened men and women waited shyly outside the Courts of Justice, avoiding the gaze of the cocky, careless habitués of the place. This street was never silent. The great presses underneath it thumped day and night. Fleet Street was a constant, turbulent flow of people, echoing the filthy river beneath it.

Patrick West had previously lived in Kensal Rise, but, missing the smell of print, and the excitement on the streets around the presses, had moved to one of the numerous courts off Fleet Street. The houses were of black-encrusted red brick, with tall, narrow windows. The court was lined with black railings, and gas lamps, but seemed shabby, covered in dried leaves blown in and caught in the corners. The fierce roar of Fleet Street was subdued to a whisper here.

I had tried to talk to Lillian on the way there. I asked her how long she had been with Patrick West, and she said three months. I told her she had changed quite a bit in that time, and she said she was used to changing herself to suit other people, and now she was changing to suit herself. More than that she wouldn't say.

Patrick West saw us in a large, dusty room, lined with books – not novels, but biographies, not all of them flattering. He sat in a large red leather armchair before a spluttering fire. He looked old now, his hair white and standing up all over. He wasn't thin, his cheeks were plump, but he gave the impression he was recovering from an illness. His eyes were milky with blindness. He wore a frogged purple smoking jacket, and his hand rested on a stick held upright by his chair.

He was pleasant and polite, but back in his day this man had a reputation for seeking out secrets – not for his own amusement like Sherlock's friend Langdale Pike, or even for blackmail, but to print. His god was circulation figures, and his had once been the highest. Great men and women of the Empire had alternately avoided and courted him, hoping for a secret concealed or a kind word of praise. He treated them both the same, and always told the truth, no matter who it hurt. His truth, however, was tinged with hints and assumptions that could lend a green tinge of suspicion to the most innocent remark.

Lillian sat behind him on a stool, a pad and pencil in hand, ready to take notes. I took the seat opposite him. Mary disdained to sit, and instead wandered about the room, peering at the bookshelves and leafing through the books.

'I have information, and questions, and so do you,' Patrick West said, in a cultured voice that sounded like it belonged in a drawing room of fifty years ago. 'Shall we make a deal? I answer a question, and then I ask one. If you want the next answer, you must answer my question.'

'Very well,' I agreed. 'Who do you think killed Emma Fordyce?'

'Straight to the point,' he said. 'Good. I am not sure Emma Fordyce was murdered. Miranda Logan, who I believe you've questioned already, insisted on it, but I cannot see how a woman can be murdered in the middle of an English hospital. My turn. What were you doing in that ward?'

'I was ill, and I was rushed in for surgery,' I said calmly. He looked sceptical. Well, so be it. I don't think either of us was telling the full truth at that moment. 'I have the scars, if you wish to see them.'

'Quite a coincidence, Sherlock Holmes' housekeeper in the same ward as an allegedly murdered woman,' he said.

'Was that a question?' Mary said sharply, turning from the bookshelf.

'No, my dear, merely an observation,' he said politely. 'Your turn.'

'Why did you hire Miranda Logan?'

'I believed Emma to be in some danger,' he said softly.

'Please understand, I knew the exact nature of the secrets Emma held. I knew the price some would pay to stop those secrets being revealed.'

'And it would be wonderful publicity,' Mary said, pushing a book firmly back onto the shelf. 'Former courtesan whose secrets are so dangerous she must be kept under guard, speaks exclusively to Patrick West. Except she didn't, did she? She didn't like you.'

'Is that a question?' Patrick asked, his blind eyes turning towards her.

'No, merely an observation,' she said sweetly, turning back to the books.

'Why do you believe she was murdered?' Mr West asked me. Very well then, truth for truth.

'I saw it,' I said. Lillian looked up suddenly and met my eyes. 'I woke up and saw a shadow by her bed. The shadow bent down and suffocated her. She fought, and scratched him. There was blood on her bed the next day. To save you a question, I didn't tell anyone because it was a ridiculous story. A shadow by a bed. I was drugged and ill and no one would have believed me.'

'Who do you think did it?'

'A boy, working for someone else. I'm not sure who,' I replied.

'That's two questions,' Lillian Rose pointed out. Mary looked at her in surprise. Lillian refused to look back.

'So it is,' Mr West agreed, with no malice. 'We must be fair. Ask away.'

'Did you hire Sarah Malone?' I asked.

'I did,' he said regretfully. 'I had no idea she really was very ill. She had been working for me for years, ever since she was a lady's maid. We had pulled the hospital trick before. People talk to anyone in hospital, just to relieve the boredom. And your second question?'

'Were you aware you weren't Sarah's only employer?' I asked. It was a dangerous question to ask, but I had to know if he knew about the blackmailer. They were, after all, both in the same profession: the acquisition of secrets, even if they had different outcomes.

'No,' he said, and his surprise seemed genuine. 'Who else was she working for?'

'We don't know,' I said. 'We found letters in her room to someone else.'

Patrick West leaned forward, one hand on his stick. He couldn't see me, I knew, but I felt as if he watched me.

'Is she lying?' he asked Lillian Rose. She looked at me, peering at me, watching me for a twitch or a blink. I looked back with the impassive face twenty years of housekeeping has taught me. I thought of telling her, just for a second, that Sarah had been trapped just like her, but I didn't want to reveal her past in front of Patrick West. She had, after all, managed to escape. Besides, it was my secret to tell when I chose.

'I honestly don't know,' Lillian said. 'She's very good.'

Patrick West sat back, and I thanked my lucky stars they hadn't had to test Mary. She never could lie.

'My turn,' I said. 'Emma talked almost exclusively to Florence Bryson while in hospital. What do you know of her?'

'Nothing,' he said, aggrieved. 'Miss Logan mentioned her name to me too, and I regret to say I can find nothing about her in previous newspapers. Her family must have been very private. Nor can I remember anyone with that name, and I have a prodigious memory. What is it like living with Sherlock Holmes?'

Ah. The questioning had taken a different tack. Well, I expected this.

'I really don't have much to do with him,' I said. 'I cook his meals, send his shirts to the laundry and dust his rooms. That's all.'

'My husband's book gives a far fuller picture,' Mary said, turning back to us. 'And he will be publishing some stories in the *Strand Magazine* very soon for everyone to read.'

'Oh, of course, you're Mary Morstan,' Lillian said.

'How do you know?' Mary asked. 'John hasn't published that account yet.'

'We don't have to wait for the news to be published to read it. Tell me, will they ever retrieve the Agra treasure from the bottom of the Thames?'

'If they do, I shall send it back to India,' Mary said promptly. 'I have all I need.'

'You are not involved in Mr Holmes' cases, Mrs Hudson?' Patrick said, disbelieving.

'I am not,' I said firmly. 'And he has nothing to do with this current investigation of mine.'

'Well, he doesn't like women, according to Dr Watson,' Lillian said. 'Is that true?'

'Quite true,' Mary said. 'Not even the clever ones.' Mary moved to the next bookcase. It might look as if she was just randomly looking at the books, but I knew differently. We had known houses where vaults had been hidden in a secret cupboard behind bookcases. Mary was secretly hoping to 'accidentally' stumble across a similar arrangement here.

'What about Ruth Bey?' I asked Patrick West. He shook his head.

'Florence and Ruth . . .' Lillian said slowly. I turned to look at her.

'No,' she said, shaking her head. 'I thought that meant something, but no. It must have been a book I read.'

I turned back to Mr West.

'Eleanor Langham?'

He started to shake his head, but Lillian whispered to him, 'Crime.'

'Ah, of course!' he cried. 'I occasionally did crime reporting, under a different name, of course. I find it so grubby. Lillian, would you find the relevant cuttings, please?'

Lillian swept out of the room, followed by Mary. I walked over to the window to look out into the courtyard. It was quiet down there, but through the entrance I could see men and women hurrying down Fleet Street.

'I do miss that life,' Mr West said wistfully. 'Reporting, I mean. Finding out stories. But when I went blind, I had to give it up.'

'But then you found Lillian,' I said. 'And she became your secretary.'

'So much more,' Patrick said. 'Oh, not my lover! Far closer. My apprentice. She is very skilled. She is already earning far more than I pay her.'

'How did you find her?' I asked disingenuously.

'Don't play innocent with me,' he said softly. 'I know what she was before and I know you knew her. She won't tell me what happened.'

'Neither will I.'

'I can accept that,' he said. 'She came to me. She told me she knew how to find secrets, and I knew how to make money from it. And so a partnership was born. She's actually a very good reporter. It wouldn't surprise me if she moved on from the gossip columns one day.'

'She's changed a great deal since I knew her,' I said. 'Not just her clothes. Her voice, her bearing – everything, in just a few months.'

'Oh, you and I both know how clever she is,' he said softly. 'She always had a gift for altering herself to fit the situation. I've known her play the innocent and the whore in barely an hour, merely by altering her voice and her walk. She has an unrivalled gift for transformation. It is a prostitute's gift, is it not, to be exactly what the client requires? All the best can change at will to suit.'

'Lillian is no longer a prostitute,' I said. 'Who is she suiting now?'

'Herself, I think,' he said, mildly surprised. 'Believe me, all I require from her is her mind and her writing skills. The rest she is discovering for herself.'

Mary and Lillian returned with a few yellowing old papers.

'There's a room full of them, back there,' Mary said to me.

'I keep all my old papers,' Patrick West said. 'Not just the cuttings, I like to keep my stories in context. Ah yes, Eleanor Langham. Well, there's quite a story here. In fact, it requires quite a story in return. Tell me, why didn't Sherlock Holmes hunt down Jack the Ripper?'

That was a heart-stopping question. Lillian audibly gasped. She, of course, had been a prostitute in Whitechapel as Jack hunted. Mary, standing by the bookcase, froze. She and John had been on honeymoon then, leaving Mr Holmes alone for the first time in years. As I sat back down on my chair and arranged my skirts, I thought: lie or tell the truth? Deny everything or tell them what he did?

'You cannot print this,' I said.

'I won't,' Mr West said. 'Not now, anyway. But someone will ask, in fact everyone asks, and at some point in the future I would like an answer.'

'He tried,' I said slowly. 'He was down in Whitechapel every night, and all over London during the day. He did not sleep, or eat. He would spend the day riding the trains to work out timetables, or visiting butchers and surgeons to work out how the cuts were done. At night he would walk the streets watching every man that passed him by, trying to see if he was the one, or him, or him. Yet Jack slipped by him, as he did the entire police force. Mr Holmes never spoke of it,' I said, and yet he had. He had sat in my kitchen and asked how he could hunt a man who had no rhyme or reason to his actions. How could he use logic to track down a creature that had no logic whatsoever? 'He could push himself hard, but even a man like Mr Holmes has his limits. He collapsed, and was confined to bed. While he slept, Mary Kelly was murdered.'

Mary gasped.

'We never knew,' she whispered.

'I was never to tell you,' I told her. 'Don't tell him you know.'

'Did he go back to Whitechapel?' Lillian asked, her face pale. I nodded.

'He sent the Irregulars through Whitechapel every night looking for suspicious men. But, it's Whitechapel, it's full of suspicious men, and women too. They came in and told him about Mary Kelly. He left, and didn't come back for three days. Then he came in, very early one morning, unshaven for the one and only time in his life that I've seen, and said, "It's over", and it was. I don't know if Holmes caught him, or if he knew the Ripper had finished. He never told me.'

And I'd never tell about the blood I washed out of his shirt that night, the one and only time I washed his shirt rather than send it to the laundry.

'I see,' Mr West said. Lillian sat back in her chair, her emotions exhausted. 'Well, when they ask, I can say he tried.'

'Now tell me about Eleanor Langham,' I insisted.

Lillian opened the papers and said, 'Mrs Langham had a son that died, at the age of sixteen, about ten years ago.'

'We know,' Mary said shortly.

'It was supposed to be of illness,' Lillian continued, ignoring her, 'but . . .'

'Ah yes, I remember!' said Patrick West. 'She became quite hysterical at the funeral. She accused all and sundry of murdering her boy. The father, the nurse, the doctor, even herself. She screamed that he had been poisoned, or suffocated, or anything. Everyone put it down to her grief – until another boy from the same street disappeared.'

'From his front garden?' Mary said insistently. 'While playing? I know that case. I mentioned it to you, Martha, in hospital, didn't I?'

She had mentioned so many cases she'd heard of whilst researching the lost boys.

'That's right. It was a hot sunny day, he was in the garden, there one minute and gone the next. He was never found, poor thing,' Mary continued.

'I believe this was next door to Eleanor Langham, is that right?' I asked.

'Yes, the very next house,' Patrick said.

'No, wait,' Mary objected. 'It was a different street . . .'

'People move,' Patrick West pointed out. 'Especially after an event like that. But at the time, after that incident, there was a lot of hysteria, and suddenly a lot of stories of boys going missing.'

'How many?' Mary demanded.

'Not that many, in the end,' Mr West told her. 'For a while, every boy that went off for an afternoon was reported lost. In the end, though, it was just the boy in the garden.'

'And Eleanor Langham's son died,' I said.

'And Eleanor Langham's son died,' Patrick West agreed. 'She became more and more convinced he'd been murdered, and given the lost boy, the authorities agreed to exhume him.'

'What did they find?' I asked.

'Nothing,' Lillian said, reading from the newspapers. 'It was a death by natural causes. Gastritis – well, they put typhoid down, but it was basically gastric symptoms. All pretty much the same in the end.'

'Mind you, many poisons can look like gastritis, and fade from the body after death,' Mr West said. 'On the other hand, genuine gastritis can look like poison.'

'So she was wrong,' Mary said. Downstairs someone banged on the door and Lillian went to answer it.

'Probably,' Patrick West said. 'There was no proof either way. But why kill the boy? No one gained from it.'

Cui bono, Mr Holmes always said. Who profits? That was one of the reasons he'd had trouble with Jack the Ripper – no one seemed to profit from it.

'But Eleanor Langham would not be convinced,' Mr West continued. 'She was in an asylum for a while . . .'

He was interrupted as a small boy burst in.

'Micky?' Mary asked. It was one of Wiggins' boys, panting and worn out.

'I bin all over town looking for yer!' he cried out. 'If I 'adn't found the cab you took . . .' He bent over, hands on his knees, trying to catch his breath.

'Well, you found us,' Mary said. 'What's wrong?'

'Yer gotta come to the park,' he said. 'I gotta cab. Hurry.'

'Why?' I said, standing up, suddenly cold. Billy . . .

'Dr Watson sent for you,' he said. ''E wouldn't let me see, but 'e says there's bodies. More than one. And it's your case, 'e said.'

THE BOYS ON
THE ISLAND

He took us to Regent's Park, yet again. So much of this case led us there. It was damp and misty, the rain hanging in the air and soaking through our clothes, and the park was empty. We got into a small rowing boat with a police constable, and he took it over to the island at the centre of the boating lake. It was cold, and foggy, and all we could see were the tops of trees above the white mist. The only sound was the oars dipping in and out of the water, and faint voices, coming from who knows where. It all felt unreal. Once we landed, we made our way through the trees to the centre of the island. There, we found policemen gathered around holes in the ground – five of them. Beside the holes stood John Watson, stolid and reassuring in his tweeds and huge greatcoat. Beside him stood Inspector Gregson, talking in a low voice. When they saw us, they came over.

'When I saw what I was dealing with, I came to ask Dr Watson for an opinion,' Inspector Gregson said, once the greetings were over. 'As Mr Holmes was there, I asked if he'd like to join us. He said no, that this was your case, Mrs Watson. I don't understand?' He looked unhappy about her involvement.

'I've been investigating several missing boys in the area,' she said, staring at the graves. Her face was white and strained, but her voice was strong. 'I believe they're connected to the Pale Boys.'

'Yes, I've heard of them,' the inspector said. He was a large man, with intelligent eyes and a gentle voice. He grasped his hat, too polite to wear it in the presence of a lady, though his blond hair was damp. 'Mr Holmes said he would only take over the case if you failed.'

'Which she won't,' John said firmly. 'It would do Sherlock good to have someone else solve a case for a change,' he told Mary. She smiled and nodded.

'What happened? How did you find them?' I asked.

'The park keeper noticed a patch of dead grass,' the inspector explained. 'He dug down and noticed the soil was loose, and then he found the edge of a body. He called us, and we brought in the dogs. They found more bodies. We've been digging all night.'

'May I see?' Mary asked.

'Are you sure?' John asked gently. 'It's a very upsetting sight.'

'I know,' she told him, equally gently. 'I'm ready for that. But I cannot help unless I can see. I have to close the books and look at the reality eventually.'

'I could tell you . . .'

'You can probably tell so much more than I can,' she agreed. 'But I feel I owe it to them. I spent so much time looking for them when alive, I can't abandon them now. I'm not as fragile as you think I am, my darling.'

He looked at her, very closely, and then nodded. He took off his greatcoat and wrapped it round her, murmuring that it was freezing. Then he took her hand and led her to the graves.

Mary hesitated for a brief second, then knelt down beside one of the graves and looked in.

I walked closer, so I could hear, but did not look. I didn't want to see. Beside me, Inspector Gregson stirred uneasily.

'A sad business, Mrs Hudson,' he said. 'I wish Mr Holmes had come.'

'Mrs Watson's been searching for these boys,' I told him, as I watched Mary kneel down by the grave. 'She wished to help them.'

'A very worthy cause,' he said. 'And yet I'm not happy with this,' he admitted, waving a hand at Mary, now crouched over the grave and gently touching something inside. 'Women being involved, I mean. This sort of thing isn't fit for women.'

I turned to him in a flash of anger.

'Not fit for women?' I snapped, though keeping my voice low. 'Women gave birth to those boys, nurtured them, fed them, comforted them when they cried. Women lost them and grieved for them. Don't you dare say that now they're dead women aren't fit to look after them.'

He looked at me, surprised, and then nodded slowly.

'You're quite right,' he said. 'I apologize.'

'Thank you,' I said. 'And for goodness' sake put your hat back on.'

'What do you see?' John asked Mary.

'Just bones,' Mary replied. 'Not disturbed. Been here a while, years, I'd say. Thin – bad nutrition?'

John nodded.

'By the shape of the pelvis, a boy. And by the skull, around fifteen, sixteen?'

'It's a fair enough assumption, given the height,' John agreed. They were both businesslike now. They didn't lack respect for the remains in front of them, but the bones were a puzzle to be solved.

'Some old, healed breakages,' Mary mused. 'But not healed well.'

'Well spotted,' John said. 'Caused by falls, perhaps.'

'So, poor, and perhaps ill-treated,' Mary said.

'Deduction, not known facts,' John warned. Mary nodded.

'What's this?' she asked, pulling a scrap of material out of the grave. 'What's left of the clothing, perhaps? It's black.'

'Rotted?' John asked, putting the scrap into an envelope and handing it to Gregson.

'No, dyed black,' Mary said.

'Dyed black cloth is expensive,' I called out. Black dye washed out very easily. Mary nodded. 'Can you tell exactly how long he's been here?' I asked.

'Hard to tell,' John replied. 'The second grave is the same, just bones. The next two are worse.'

The wind changed for a moment, and a stench of

putrefaction wafted over the site. I put my hand over my nose, and Mary stood still a moment. Then she dropped to her knees beside the next grave and started to examine the remains.

'Nearly totally decayed,' she said, and only the slightest catch in her throat betrayed her reaction to the stench. 'Dead less than a year?'

'Six months, I'd say,' John said, standing beside her and looking down at her with a mixture of respect and affection.

'What do you know about the missing boys?' I asked Inspector Gregson, as Mary gently touched the body in the grave.

'Nothing, really,' he said, shrugging. 'I know that Mr Holmes mentioned it to Lestrade, who mentioned it to me. I thought it was a fool's errand, something to keep Mrs Watson occupied.' He looked around him, as if searching for answers. 'It seems I was wrong.'

I told him about the house on Henry Street and our experience there, about the rumoured deaths attributed to the Pale Boys, and the woman. I told him what Wiggins had said about the stories, and I told him what Mrs Turner had said about her son (though without mentioning her name).

I didn't mention the hospital, or the deaths, or Emma.

'Is that all?' Inspector Gregson asked. He wasn't stupid.

'All that is definite,' I said.

'I see,' he said. 'Well, when you have something definite, will you come and find me? I will be at Scotland Yard.' He stared at the graves. 'I will not have this going on in my city,' he said forcefully, but quietly. He was very angry. He walked back to join John and Mary.

'No obvious marks of violence – but with the body in this state, how could you tell?' Mary murmured to herself in a way reminiscent of Mr Holmes. 'There's black cloth again – different materials, but always dyed black.'

'But worn,' John pointed out. 'Look, you can see where the material has just started to rub away under the arms. This wasn't newly put on before he died.'

'So, he wore black habitually,' Mary said. Just like the Pale Boys. Mary moved to the last grave, and looked up at John in surprise.

'This can't be more than . . .'

'Three months,' John said grimly. 'Perhaps less, exacerbated by the unusually warm weather.'

'No bruises,' Mary said, puzzled. 'No breakages. Clean. Wearing a complete suit, all in black, even the shirt. How did he die?'

'Look at the last one,' John said. Mary did, and then looked up at me, horrified.

'What is it?' I said quickly. 'Not someone we know?'

'No, no one we know,' she said quickly. 'But Martha . . .'

'Freshly dug, freshly killed,' John said. 'Dead no more than a week. He's killing faster.'

'She,' Mary corrected. 'And we didn't know she was killing the boys at all.'

A PEACEFUL
DEATH

Oh, we should have suspected it. All of those boys disappearing, never to be found again? Some had to die. They couldn't remain Pale Boys all their lives. But we had hoped. In much the same way a child is told a favourite dog has been sent to the country, we had hoped the older boys had escaped in some way. But now we had the proof in front of us. Dead boys. They didn't escape. They died.

But why did the others stay? Did they know? We couldn't ask them, they wouldn't even let us see them, let alone talk to us.

'I'll need to know everything you know about the Pale Boys,' Inspector Gregson said calmly.

'I'll write it all down, if that will do,' I told him.

'It will,' he said grimly. 'It seems women can also kill. Good day, Mrs Hudson.'

He called some orders out to his men and marched off. He wasn't needed here, not until the boys were dug up, and besides, he was angry.

'Are you sure it's not one of the boys you've been looking for?' I called out to Mary.

'None of them had red hair,' she said softly. 'He can't have been more than fourteen.'

'He was underfed once, I'd say,' John said. 'But not lately.'

'A suit of black clothes?' I asked.

'Yes, but no labels or laundry marks that I can see. Hand-made.'

Hand-made? Well, that opened up a certain possibility. But then I remembered, I had hand-made my boy's clothes; he had grown so fast, I had to. Suddenly I had to turn away. I had to turn my back on those graves and catch my breath and swallow, and not cry, please don't cry, not here in front of John and Mary.

That's when I saw two things. The wind blew the mist aside, just for a moment, and I saw a woman standing on the other bank of the boating lake, watching us. The other was a flash of light, as if what little sun there was caught a telescope lens, up in Eleanor Langham's house. She could see the whole grave site.

Mary and John were discussing the cause of death. There were no marks, and no bruising. Suffocation often left marks round the mouth, and apparently in the eyes, but there was none here. John said the police surgeon would have to examine the bodies more carefully. Strictly speaking, he was only there to certify death; the police surgeon was supposed to do the examination.

'You've learnt a lot,' I heard John say to Mary. I don't think I was meant to hear, but I couldn't help it.

'I need to, if I'm to help,' she replied.

'I meant to keep you safe from all the horrors of the world,' he told her.

'I love you for that, but I cannot live in a fairy-tale castle,' she told him. 'If there are horrors, I'd rather face them, and stop them.'

I saw him smile, and reach out to pull one golden curl through his fingers.

'You are a thoroughly modern woman, Mrs Watson,' he said proudly, and a little sadly. I think he wanted to play the knight and save his queen, but Mary was no helpless victim. Then they both turned back to examining the body.

It was Mary who found it. She had remarked that the hands were unscratched, that the boy hadn't fought for his life. As she put the hand back in place, she had in a moment of tenderness pushed aside the boy's hair. Then she suddenly saw something, and called John's attention to it.

'What? What is it?' I called out.

'Needle marks,' John called out. 'Just one, in the neck.'

'It is poison then,' Mary said, as John helped her up.

'No signs of struggle, no rictus, no convulsive marks, perhaps laudanum or opium,' John said. 'Injected straight into the vein, it would have been a very peaceful death.'

'So he just slept?' I asked, as Mary walked towards me, wiping her hands on John's handkerchief.

'Yes,' John said, as the wooden boxes for transporting the bodies arrived.

'Murdered, but gently murdered,' Mary said. She started

to take off John's greatcoat to hand back to him, but he shook his head.

'I'm going back to 221b,' he said. 'I'll tell Holmes you're on it. Make sure you solve it, won't you?' He kissed Mary quickly. 'It's good for him to have rivals.'

She nodded, and he walked off.

'Look,' I said to Mary, pointing towards the boating lake. The mist had lifted completely now and we could see the woman clearly. 'Look who's been watching.'

It was Mrs Turner.

By the time we reached her it was obvious she was in great distress. She clutched her thin shawl to herself and she was shaking.

'What are you doing here?' I demanded.

'I heard, through the air vent,' she cried. Damn it, I'd forgotten I'd reopened it. 'Inspector Gregson said the boys . . . he said they were dead . . . he came for Doctor Watson. I should have gone, but I knew the doctor had sent for you before they left. Is it my boy, is Stephen there, is it my boy?' she begged.

Lie, I told myself. You lie so well, lie now, tell her no!

'I don't know,' I said. They were all the right age. We didn't know what four of them looked like. 'Perhaps.'

She crumpled to the ground, sobbing. We knelt beside her, Mary throwing John's coat around her.

'I'm sorry, I'm so sorry,' I repeated. No words had helped

after my son had died, but I could think of nothing else to do.

'Mrs Turner, you have to help us now,' Mary said gently, lifting the woman's face to us. 'You have to help us find who did it.'

'It's too late,' she whispered.

'Maybe not; we don't know who those boys are,' I said.

'And besides, there are other boys. Other mothers,' Mary said firmly. Mrs Turner nodded.

'You've been seen with the Pale Boys. Talking to them, even leaving food for them.'

She nodded, weeping quietly.

'I thought if I was nice to them, they'd help me,' she said, almost in a whisper. 'They'd tell me where Stephen was, or if he was safe. I hoped one day it'd be Stephen that'd come to me. I'd bring them food and tell them who was looking for them. I tried to help. But they just mocked me, and laughed at me and told me I was stupid.'

'Where did you take the food to them?' I asked. 'Here, in the park?'

'Yes, but they don't live here,' she said quietly. 'They live in these empty houses, all over London. Those big houses no one likes any more. They've got dozens of them. If someone finds them, they move on. They only hunt in the park.'

Hunt?

'Why did you keep helping them?' Mary asked.

'I had to!' Mrs Turner cried. 'Just in case, one day, they

took me to Stephen. Just the slightest chance. I gave them all my money and they said they'd bring him, but they never did.'

'Did you ever see the woman?' Mary asked. Mrs Turner shook her head.

'You made their clothes for them, didn't you?' I asked. It was a guess, but I was right.

'Yes. They left the materials at my house, and I was to make up the suits and leave the packages. They collected them from my house.'

'How did you know what size to make?' Mary asked.

'She can size up a person by looking at them, can't you?' I said.

'Even a photograph will do, if there's something in it for scale,' she told me. Mary and I looked at each other. She had photographs?

'We need to see those pictures,' I said gently.

'They took them back,' she said, rising, calmer now. 'But I still have one. The last one they gave me.'

'Why didn't you tell me all this?' Mary demanded. 'You know I've been looking for your boy. This is all helpful.'

'They said they'd kill him if I told,' Mrs Turner told her. 'I don't know how they found out I'd been talking to you, but they did, and they said I had to keep quiet, and tell me everything you did, or they'd cut Stephen up and put his head on my doorstep.' She looked out over the park to where the graves were. 'I don't know if that's true or not now.' She seemed certain in her belief that Stephen was one of the boys in the graves.

'Go home,' I said. 'Collect the photograph, and your things. You're moving into 221b,' I continued firmly. 'You'll be safe there. Because, quite frankly, I don't think you're safe in your home.'

I called a constable over, one of the ones that knew Mr Holmes, and asked him to escort Mrs Turner home and then to 221b, and to let Mr Gregson know we had some information. Then I looked over to the edge of the park, to Eleanor Langham's home.

Wiggins lounged there, beside the park gate. It was his turn to watch over Billy today. Perfect.

'You know what we must do now?' I said to Mary.

'Oh yes,' she said. 'We're going to get Billy.'

THE WRONG
PATH

We gave Wiggins a brief precis of what we had found in the park, and told him we were getting Billy out right now.

'He's not safe in there, I'm convinced of that,' I told him. 'Besides, I have questions for Eleanor Langham.'

'Yeah, I reckon you're right,' Wiggins said. 'You go in; I'll wait out here for you. Lucky there's a park full of rozzers right behind me, innit?'

As soon as the dignified but slow butler opened the door, Mary shot past him and up the stairs. I followed more sedately, as befitted my status (and my still-sore stomach wound). As I passed him, I requested the butler bring the boot boy to Mrs Langham's rooms.

'The boot boy?' the butler queried.

'The boot boy,' I confirmed, as if surprised he questioned me. Mr Holmes always said that if you acted like you expected everyone to do exactly what you asked, most of the time they did.

I arrived at Eleanor's rooms just in time to hear Mary accuse her.

'You saw, I know you saw!' she cried. 'You saw those graves in the park.'

Eleanor looked distressed, but not by Mary. Her hair was wild, her hands grasping each other convulsively. The blanket on her knees had slipped halfway down. The telescope was pointed directly at the park. Up here, we were above the mist.

'Saw what? I saw nothing,' Eleanor said, but her voice was querulous.

'The graves,' Mary insisted. 'The boys in the graves. They were found this morning. I know you saw.'

'You see everything, I think,' I said calmly. I wonder what impression I made in Eleanor's mind, coming in like that, all in black, so wonderfully still next to Mary's anger, making that statement? Because Eleanor saw me, and confessed.

'I saw,' she snarled. 'I saw them dead and buried and rotting. Just like my boy. Just like the boy next door. He killed them all, you know. I kept his secret, but he can't stop himself, he can't help it, he has to rip their tiny innocent bodies apart, bit by bit, tear them from limb from limb, dripping with blood.' She'd lost her sanity. Her mouth dripped drool as she outlined the horrors the dead boys must have gone through.

'But they weren't—' Mary started to say.

'Who?' I asked, stopping Mary before she could say the boys weren't torn at all. Maybe it was cruel of me, but Eleanor had her story, and we had to let her tell it in its entirety.

'Him,' she cried, throwing out her arm in a gesture. 'Can't you see it? Everyone else can. He's evil. He kills boys. They haunt me.'

'She means me,' said a weary voice from the door. I turned

to see Mr Langham standing there. He was still tall, still with that military air about him, but now he leaned a little, his hand resting on Billy's shoulder.

Billy. Thank goodness. Was he different? Was he safe? I looked at him, and he shook his head a little. He wasn't afraid of Mr Langham. He wanted to be his support at this time.

'Forgive me, sir,' I asked. 'But do you mean she thinks you killed the boys?'

'I'm afraid she does,' he said. He went to Eleanor, and with infinite tenderness straightened the blanket on her knees. 'I'm sorry you had to see her like this.'

Billy came and stood beside me. He looked very serious, but I could not restrain myself from grasping his hand just slightly, and squeezing it.

'Billy told me who you are,' Mr Langham said, straightening up. 'Just now, in the kitchen.'

'I asked too many questions,' Billy admitted. 'I gave myself away.'

'Did Mr Holmes arrange all this?' Mr Langham asked. I looked at Billy, who looked a little shame-faced.

'I mentioned Mr Holmes' name and he just assumed . . .'

'It's all right,' I said. It wouldn't be the first or the last time I shielded myself with Mr Holmes' name. 'What were you asking questions about?'

'The room upstairs,' Mr Langham said. 'The room where my son died.'

'Where you killed him,' Eleanor insisted. He only touched her shoulder. He loved her still.

'He had been ill for a while; vomiting up everything he ate, when he could eat, terrible bloody diarrhoea,' he explained. 'She had been caring for him for days. I made her get some rest while I stayed with him. It was only for an hour, but in that hour, he died.'

'He poisoned him,' Eleanor said. 'The bottles are still there; you can test them.'

'They have been tested,' he said, 'three times. My child was given a post-mortem. He was even exhumed and tested again. There was no poison. It came on so slow,' he said, looking at Eleanor and I understood he was talking about her instability, not his son's death. 'She wasn't like this at first. She was sad and broken-hearted, but accepted the death of our boy as God's will. We took comfort in each other. We even had other sons.'

'They're still alive because I watch,' Eleanor said, shrinking away from him.

'That is when this started,' Mr Langham said. 'When the boys were born. She wouldn't let me be alone with them. She wouldn't let me play with them, or go into the park with them, and after a while, she tried to stop me seeing them at all.' The old soldier's voice cracked.

'She suspected you of killing your boy,' I said. 'And now she suspects you of killing the boys in the park.'

He looked puzzled, and Mary gestured towards the

window. He peered out for a moment, then, sadly, he turned the telescope away from the graves.

'I didn't hurt anyone,' he said softly.

'Children don't just die,' Eleanor cried.

'Mine did,' I told her. 'He just lay down and died. I did blame myself for a while but . . .'

'Oh, you and Florence Bryson, glorying in your dead sons,' Eleanor said, and I swear she enjoyed her cruelty. 'They don't hold a candle to mine.'

'You're mad,' Mary breathed into the heavy silence.

'She is unstable,' Mr Langham replied. 'She'll need to go back into hospital for a while. Please tell Mr Holmes there never was anything to the rumours.'

I looked at him, and I believed him. He was just a sorrowful man.

'You follow other boys,' Eleanor said. 'You follow our sons into the park. I know. I followed you.' Well, that explained the leaf mould on her shoes.

'They're my sons, Eleanor,' he said. 'I know you don't like me spending time with them, but they are mine too. Please believe I would never hurt them.'

'I didn't think you could walk far,' Mary said.

'No. I made sure you all thought that,' Eleanor said triumphantly. 'They think I can't follow them either, but I will, one day.'

'Who?' I asked.

'The dead boys,' she said. 'The ones he killed. They walk past the house at night. I see them.'

'That's only in your imagination, my love,' Mr Langham said. He was in tears. It was time for us to leave. There was a great sorrow here, and a shadow of death, but not murder.

Mr Langham showed us out, pausing in the hall.

'She was wonderful once,' he told us, needing to explain, though I felt guilty I had ever intruded. 'Such a bright woman, always inquisitive, always asking questions. She wanted to know about everyone. I used to love that about her. Now it's become twisted, as if she has ice in her eye, like the fairy tale.'

Wiggins met us outside, and he and Billy walked behind us, conferring in low voices. Mary and I were silent.

'I feel awful,' Mary said eventually.

'Me too,' I admitted. 'I was so sure it was her, and all the time . . .'

'She was insane,' Mary said, 'and blaming her husband too.'

'He still loves her. That's utterly heartbreaking.'

We walked on a few steps before Mary began, 'What she said, about the ghost boys.'

'What about it?' I asked.

'Pale boys all in black, out at night – wouldn't that suggest ghost boys to you?'

'It would,' I said. 'I have to admit, it's strange how her name kept popping up in this investigation. It seems every path led to her.'

'When every path goes one way, try another way,' Wiggins

called from behind me. "Cos someone's trying to lead you on.'

'Is that one of Mr Holmes' rules?' Mary asked.

'Nah, it's one of mine,' Wiggins said. 'Now, you gotta go back to the beginning and see where you took the wrong path.'

'Back to the hospital,' I said wearily. 'But tomorrow. I'm so tired now.'

It's very demoralizing when you take the wrong path. But tomorrow, we would find the right way. We had to, before the silent death of another boy.

THE PHOTOGRAPH

John was just leaving as we arrived at 221b. He saw Mary's misery – she was very upset at the scene at the Langham's – and insisted she come home. She didn't argue. I saw them standing in the hall, as he adjusted her hat, and though they talked of nothing more than what to have for dinner, they looked as if they spoke words of deep, passionate love to each other. I turned away, a little lonely and a little envious, but happy for them. If any two people deserved love, it was John and Mary.

I offered Wiggins a bed for the night, but he refused, as I knew he would. He had to go back to the Irregulars.

'We got somewhere warm to sleep,' he said, when I objected that it was freezing.

'Where?' I demanded, but he merely tapped the side of his nose and disappeared into the mist. It was twilight already by then, and the gas lamps were just a pale glow.

Grace and Mrs Turner were in the kitchen. Mrs Turner slept in the chair by the range.

'Let her sleep,' Grace whispered. 'She needs it. She's been very upset. Goodness knows what happened today,' she said,

looking at me sternly. I nodded, and prepared Mr Holmes'
tea.

I felt at peace for the first time that day as I carried it up
to him. This was what I knew how to do – not just the tea,
but dealing with Mr Holmes. Be he angry, happy, busy or
in a drug-induced haze, I knew what to do, and he knew
what I would do. It was something solid in a world that was
changing fast – and Mr Holmes didn't always deal well
with change.

I had listened through the air vent while cooking and
heard nothing but the rustling of papers and the crackling
of the fire. That meant he was sorting through his clippings,
and would likely forget to eat. There was no point making
him something hot – it'd cool down by the time he got to
it. Instead, I made a pile of mutton sandwiches.

He was on the floor – scissors in hand, a yellowing newspaper in the other, surrounded by all sorts of papers – when
I got in there.

'I'm busy, get out,' he said, almost automatically. I ignored
him, laid the tray on a table and went to close the blinds.
It would rain later, that heavy black rain London seemed
to specialize in, and even the street lights were just a dim
glow.

'I brought you some sandwiches,' I said to him. The room
was lit only by the fire, and I lit the oil lamps on the table.

'Take them away, I'm not hungry.' He was in one of his
contrary moods. I was used to that.

'They'll keep,' I told him calmly. 'I also need to tell you Mrs Turner is staying.'

'Who?' he asked impatiently, flinging the cutting over his shoulder and riffling through the pile of papers beside him. I knew he was listening, though he gave the impression he was not.

'The woman who's been helping me since I came back from the hospital,' I told him. 'I know you've seen her. You see everything.'

'What, that pale, grey woman?' he said, a little bit flattered by my praise, as I knew he would be. 'Why is she staying?'

'To help me clean and look after this house, and do the things I don't want to do any more, such as lay your fire every morning,' I told him. I had just planned to ask her to move in to keep her safe from the Pale Boys, and herself, but the more I thought of it, the better the idea seemed. Mr Holmes glanced at the fire as if it had never occurred to him that someone had to spend half an hour raking it out and rebuilding it, and getting thoroughly filthy in the process, every morning.

'Can she be trusted?' he asked, sitting back on his heels and looking at me. 'You know the kind of cases I take on. They cannot be discussed in the street by kitchen gossips.'

'As if anyone in this house would,' I replied, not quite snapping, but firmly. 'She can keep a secret; you can take my word on that. And I suspect she would be rather good at mending knife cuts in suits.'

'Hmm, well, yes, then,' he said, as if I needed his approval.

He went back to his papers. 'I suppose you have better things to do now.'

I nodded and left him to it, but as I reached the door, he said, in a quite different tone of voice, 'Lestrade was questioning all the cab drivers in the street today.'

I did not turn around.

'Did he discover anything?' I asked, as if it were only of minor interest to me.

'Judging by his walk, I would guess not,' Mr Holmes said, concentrating on an old paper. 'His gait alters quite significantly when he is frustrated.'

'He didn't find the right driver,' I said, turning round.

'Or no one would speak,' Mr Holmes said, quite unconcerned. 'I tip well; the cab drivers would prefer not to lose my custom.'

'So is that it? Is it over?' I asked. Mr Holmes looked up again at me.

'I fear he will keep looking. Perhaps question the people in the houses that overlook the street, to see if anyone saw someone get into a cab that night.'

'At that time of night?' I said.

'This is London,' Mr Holmes observed. 'Somebody sees everything.'

I went down to the kitchen determined not to think about it. I would not think about the blackmailer, or Eleanor Langham, or the Pale Boys, or the hospital. I needed a break.

But when I got down there, Mrs Turner was awake, and

clutching a photograph. It was the picture she'd promised: the last boy she'd been asked to make a black suit for.

'Would you like to stay?' I said abruptly to her. 'Not just tonight, but for good. Well, as long you want to.'

'To do what?' Grace asked. She seemed to have taken a protective interest in Mrs Turner.

'Much as you do now,' I said to Mrs Turner. 'Clean, wash, the usual, except the cooking. I will always do the cooking.'

'And she'll be paid?' Grace asked. 'More than now?'

'Of course,' I said, taking the photograph Mrs Turner held out to me. 'Well, will you?'

'Yes, please,' she said quietly, standing there as if waiting for orders.

'Do you have your things?' I asked her. She nodded. There was a pathetically small bundle by her feet. 'Rest today,' I told her. 'You can sleep in the bedroom next to mine.'

I looked at the picture. It was a boy, I'd say around ten, with blond hair that fell over his eyes. He wore a torn suit of what looked like brown or grey tweed. He didn't look afraid, or wary. He looked as if he couldn't quite believe such wonderful things were happening to him. I suppose that was how they all started. They were taken in by this woman who fed them and clothed them, and gave them somewhere warm to sleep. If they had anyone who loved them, she must have persuaded the boy they were long gone, and only she loved them now. And now that she had done all this, they owed her everything. What would they do to repay her? How would they prove their loyalty?

I threw the photograph back on the table. I didn't want to think about it, not tonight.

'The urn in the background is exactly four feet,' Mrs Turner said, gesturing. 'And I knew the measurements of all the carvings on it. That's how I got the measurements for the boys.'

I had noted the urn. I'd show Mary the photograph tomorrow.

'Mrs Langham will be returning to hospital,' I told Grace.

'Ah, has she had a relapse?' Grace asked.

'Of sorts,' I replied, keeping my own role quiet. 'But the problem is in her mind again, rather than her chest.'

Of course I was using Mr Holmes' trick again. I knew a lot less than I made her think I knew, but it was another way to make her talk. Grace had revealed, as she chatted to me, that whilst Eleanor Langham did indeed suffer from a heart problem for which she needed treatment, her real illness was in her mind. However, it had become clear that her instability lessened when she was in hospital, away from her husband, and her boys.

I tied my apron on. All these mysteries could wait. Now I wanted to make Banbury cakes.

A HOUSE OF SECRETS

Banbury cakes are finicky to make, and I had to do at least three batches before I was satisfied. It felt good to have my hands covered in flour again, to smooth together the butter and sugar, to measure to an exactness the right amount of allspice needed. I felt like I had achieved something at the end. I had cakes to show for my efforts, and not just a morass of information I did not know what to do with, or how to progress.

It was ten o'clock at night and pouring with rain by the time I finished. It beat hard on the window, and I felt sorry for anyone caught in it. Mrs Turner had long since gone to bed, and Grace had gone home (as she had been doing at night several times now), on the strict understanding that I took my medicine, changed my dressing and ate none of the cakes. She said I wouldn't really need her from now on anyway.

I sat at the kitchen table, and tried not to look at the photograph. I ought to have taken it to Mary, I knew, but it could wait. She had had a hard day, looking at those bodies of the boys she thought she could rescue. In fact, the whole case of the Pale Boys seemed to have shaken her somewhat.

She could become obsessed; I knew that from April, when she had deliberately walked into traps. She had only escaped with her life because I played the game and solved the puzzle.

In the middle of my ruminations I heard a knock at the door.

Inspector Lestrade stood on the doorstep, soaked to the skin. I took a breath. So this was it, then: he must be close to the truth now.

'I'll see if Mr Holmes is home,' I said, in the well-known code for 'check if he wants to see you'.

'Thank you – no, wait,' he said suddenly. 'I'm not sure . . .' For a man who was normally so certain of himself it seemed odd to see him vacillate. He glanced back at the street, and then back to me, and then up the stairs.

'I came to tell him I found an eyewitness,' he said. 'Someone saw someone take the cab to Richmond.' He had succeeded, but he didn't look happy about it. He looked miserable and exhausted.

'Would you like to come in and have a sandwich?' I asked. His face lit up. I doubt he had eaten all day.

'I would,' he said. 'I would like that very much.'

I led him to my kitchen table, placing his hat and coat on the chair before the kitchen range to dry. He sat down, slightly shyly. He had never been to my kitchen before.

I had put the photograph in my pocket before I invited him in, so the table was bare. He put his hands on it, as I often did, liking to feel something so old and solid beneath my hands. I watched him as I poured a steaming cup of tea, and cut him a thick beef and mustard sandwich. I watched him still as he bit into the sandwich with an expression of bliss, and all the time I held myself back from demanding who was seen, what did he know?

'It was a woman,' he said, as if reading my thoughts.

'What did she look like?' I asked, joining him at the kitchen table. He sat at the end, and I sat across the corner, so I could see his face. I expected triumph, not this misery.

'They didn't see much. Just a glimpse of a middle-aged woman all in black, asking the driver to take her to Richmond.'

'Well, that describes half the women in London,' I said. 'It could even apply to me.'

He smiled thinly at my joke, putting the sandwich down and taking a long drink of tea.

'I didn't expect it to be a woman,' he admitted.

'Does that make a difference?' I asked.

He paused a while, then continued, 'I tracked down the scrap of paper I found at the burnt-out home. I remembered Mr Holmes is always looking at watermarks and so on, so I did the same. There was enough left to find out the paper was bespoke, made for a very fine family. I was quite proud of myself for that. I went to visit the family. That was when I found out the woman who wrote that note killed herself.'

'I'm sorry,' I said gently. He'd obviously been affected by this woman's death.

'I wasn't so proud then,' he said. 'Do you mind me telling

you this? Mrs Lestrade doesn't like it. Well, I wouldn't want to tell her. All this stops when I close my own front door. But I need to tell someone, and you're very easy to talk to.'

'I don't mind. Tell me.'

'I expect you hear worse from Mr Holmes. Well,' he said, fiddling with the remains of his sandwich, 'it appears she was being blackmailed. The family were very polite to me. I wouldn't have been, not if I was them. But they let me read her letters. I think they wanted me to know she'd done it out of a sense of honour. Does that make sense to you?'

I nodded. Who was she, this woman? There had been so many the blackmailer had blithely destroyed. I was eager to ask, but dared not.

'I saw the letters that man sent her. They were horrific. I shan't tell you what they said. No woman should hear that language. I found reference to another woman too – did you ever hear of the Whitechapel Lady?'

'I did,' I said. She too had once been a fine lady. The blackmailer had ruined her, but she had found a life of sorts helping the people of Whitechapel, until he murdered her. Officially, her murder remained unsolved.

'I met her a few times,' Lestrade said. 'I liked her. I wanted to investigate her murder, but Abberline took it on as he thought the Ripper had killed her. That man,' and he spat out the word, 'that man who burnt had blackmailed her too.'

'How many more?' I asked, pouring more tea into his cup.

He shrugged. 'I've no idea,' he admitted. 'But now I think the woman who killed him must have been a victim.'

'So they were taking the law into their own hands,' I said softly.

'But people can't do that,' he said earnestly. He truly believed in the law. 'The law is the law, and it must be obeyed, whatever the provocation. If we allow people to kill for this reason, how long before people kill for political differences, or personal dislike? It'd be anarchy.'

'Yes, I see that,' I said. I did, I really did. The first death was difficult, but after that, a small voice would whisper 'you've already done it once'.

'But if I caught this woman, and took her to court,' the inspector continued, 'all those secrets that lady died to keep would be revealed and then he would have won, even from beyond the grave. And what about those women still living, keeping secrets?' He was agonized. The battle between the law and what he felt to be right was tearing him apart.

'What would happen to the woman who killed him?' I asked. 'Would she get the death penalty?' I put more sugar into his tea, though he didn't need it, just to keep my hands steady.

'I'd do my damnedest to make sure she didn't,' he said quickly. 'I'd speak up in her defence. And I am sure no jury of good Englishmen would convict a woman for this. Yet the law is strict, and some judges have no mercy.'

His voice trailed off as he stared into the dark corners of the kitchen.

'Why didn't they come to the police?' he asked softly.

'They were afraid,' I said, before I could think. He looked at me sharply, then nodded. He could understand the fear of officialdom and mistakes and setting into process something that could not be stopped.

'Then that is our failure, as the police,' he said. 'My failure.'

'No . . .' I said, trying to reassure him, but he had made his choice.

'I'm going to stop,' he said firmly. 'I'm going to stop looking for this woman.'

'Are you sure?' I asked.

'No,' he said, then drained his tea. 'But I will not condemn her for doing what the law ought to have done. I should have protected her – all of them – from a man like that.'

He stood up, and then looked at me.

'Don't tell Mr Holmes, will you?'

I glanced up at the open air vent. Possibly he already knew.

'Why not?' I asked, as he took up his hat. 'If he thinks you failed to find the murderer, he'll crow over you.'

'I know,' he said, as I took his coat and held it out for him.

'He'd understand your reasons,' I said. 'He'd done the same, once or twice.'

'No,' the inspector said, shrugging his coat on. 'I like to think Mr Holmes and I are friends, especially after Dartmoor. But more than that, I am Inspector Lestrade of the Yard. I am the living embodiment of the law. I cannot, and must not, be seen to bend or break the law. Especially not by Mr Holmes, who has a tendency to see law as elastic at the best of times.'

'I won't tell,' I said, as I showed him out of the front door. After all, as I've remarked before, this was a house of secrets.

I took my time clearing up, wondering if Mr Holmes would come down to talk to me. He didn't, and I went to bed. Mrs Turner was at the top of the stairs when I reached the second-floor landing. She was wrapped in her shawl, staring anxiously at me.

'They're here,' she said quietly, 'outside, watching me. What should I do?'

'Close the curtains and go to bed,' I said firmly. 'They can't get in here.'

To my relief, and surprise, she nodded and returned to her room. I went into mine and walked over to the window.

I had been slightly afraid she was imagining things, but no, there they stood. Three boys, all in black, standing in the mist, staring at my house. One was blond, and his hair glittered in the gaslight. I thought maybe he was the boy from the photograph. The other two had dark hair, and their faces were pale white. They couldn't have been more than fourteen, one no more than ten. They were silent, and still, and it was very eerie. They had come to scare us, and it was succeeding. I looked at those boys, all alone in the dark. Had they killed? Had they chased us through that house?

Could they really get through locked doors, and disappear into the night? I was afraid, for a moment.

But there, if I looked closer, the little one was shivering in the cold. The older one had fallen, and had mud on his knee. They were just boys after all. Just children, not shadows or demons. They weren't supernatural, and probably not even that dangerous, not without their mistress to guide them. And as for me – well, tonight I felt fearless. I flung up the window.

'I've seen you,' I called out, cheerily. 'You've made your point, you can go now.'

They didn't move.

'Look,' I said. 'It's freezing cold, and very late. You might want to hang around and catch your death of cold, but I don't. Go home and go to bed.'

And with that, I closed the window, pulled across the red velvet curtains, and got ready for bed.

By the time I'd undone my buttons, I heard them walk away, their footsteps echoing in the empty streets. Sound drifted so far at night-time.

Just boys, after all. The real villain was the woman who used them.

BACK TO WHITECHAPEL

I got up early, went down to the kitchen, and started to cook. First breakfast for Mr Holmes, but once that was out of the way, baking. I always think better when I bake. There's something about the action of smoothing flour or cream or eggs between my fingers that concentrates my mind. But more than that, I felt like I wanted to be busy. I had spent weeks sitting back, feeling ill and worried and haunted. That was no way for a housekeeper – especially Mr Holmes' housekeeper – to behave. So, I set to work. When Mrs Turner got up, I chivvied Mr Holmes out of his rooms, telling him he needed fresh air, and set her to work dusting there, and picking up all his discarded, torn and battered clothes. Mr Holmes liked his shirts to be pristinely white, but usually forgot he had to give them to me to be cleaned. I even set Grace to work when she arrived for the day (as she said, I didn't need her nursing skills any more) putting together the boxes I used for the cakes I sold at the bakery. By the time Mary arrived, the house smelled of freshly baking bread, and the kitchen table was covered in cakes cooling.

'Good grief,' Mary said, looking at the evidence of my hard work. 'I can see you've had quite the morning.'

'I suddenly feel much better,' I told her. 'You can have any cake you like, except for lemon: that's for Grace and Nora.'

Grace smiled in thanks, and said she was going to check on Mrs Turner. Since I no longer needed her, she had devoted herself to Mrs Turner until her job ran out at the end of the week. She quietly accompanied her around the house, helping her, talking softly to her, trying to soothe the woman's shattered nerves. I think Grace helped her a great deal.

I handed Mary the photograph of the boy Mrs Turner had given me.

'It looks familiar,' Mary said.

'The boy?' I questioned. 'He was outside 221b last night, trying to intimidate me and Mrs Turner – what is her first name, by the way? As she's going to stay I can't keep calling her Mrs Turner.'

'Harriet,' Mary said, peering at the photograph, then looking up. 'Oh, she's staying? Wonderful. Wait a minute; the boys were outside your house?'

'Standing in the gaslight and the fog, trying to frighten us,' I explained. 'It was really far too cold for them to be out that late at night. I sent them home.'

Mary laughed.

'Now I understand all this,' she said, sweeping her arm to indicate the cakes. 'You're like the chatelaine of the castle standing on the battlements telling the attackers they can stay all they like, they'll never break the siege.'

'Well, thank you – I think.' I smiled. It was quite an

attractive image, and rather glamorous compared to the reality of a dumpy middle-aged housekeeper. 'So you said you recognize the boy? From where?'

'Not the boy, the urn,' she said. 'I've seen it. Let me think.'

'It's just a standard urn found in any photographer's studio . . .' I said, but Mary held up a hand to stop me. She sat down at the table, closed her eyes, and started to think.

Ten minutes later, she jumped up.

'Got it!' she cried. 'I know where I saw the urn before. It was in Robert Sheldon's studio!'

We sat in the cab going to Whitechapel. That part of London was bright and cold that morning, and almost deserted. The few people on the street huddled around a chestnut seller's brazier. Robert Sheldon was a very ordinary man, but an excellent photographer – of pornography. Mary and I had met him when the blackmailer had tasked him to follow me. He had been afraid of the blackmailer and also, for some reason, of me.

Perhaps it was because he was a photographer: he looked at people and saw them clearly. Perhaps he could look at me and see something no one else – not Mary, nor Mr Holmes – could see.

I wondered what he'd see now?

The warehouse where he had his studio was on the edge of Whitechapel. We knew our way, and pushed open the door.

'What the hell do you want . . . oh,' Robert Sheldon said,

recognizing us. He stood behind his camera as usual, looking very unnoticeable. The room was softly lit with the grey morning light this time, though he had a different backdrop arranged. This time he had a complete lady's dressing room set up, painted and gilded to look very expensive. On the red velvet stool a young woman sat still, pouting as she removed her stocking, frozen in position.

'Ruby,' Mary called to her, 'how lovely to see you.' Mary meant it. She and the model had found lots to talk about last time they met. Mary went over to join her.

'Good morning, Mr Sheldon,' I said, stepping forward. Was it my imagination, or did he flinch a little? Somewhere the bells struck twelve. 'Good afternoon, now,' I added.

'What do you want?' he demanded, glaring at me from behind the camera.

'Only information,' I said, holding out the photograph. 'Just that.'

'Why should I?' he snarled at me.

'Why should you not?' I replied, very softly. 'It's in the public interest.'

He snatched the photograph, glanced at it, then handed it back to me.

'I don't know nothing about it,' he said, sniffing. He was a Whitechapel man, used to death and danger, and yet somehow he saw something in me that scared him. Me! I don't know what it was, but I was determined to use it.

'Liar,' I told him. 'I can see the urn across the room. I know these boys were photographed here.'

'Just like that,' he insisted. 'Fully clothed, always in front of the damn urn. No funny business!'

'I didn't think there would be,' I replied. 'Who asked you to take the pictures?'

'I'm not telling,' he insisted. 'Now get out, before I call—'

'Call who?' Mary demanded. 'Your friend? Your superior? The blackmailing evil bastard that ruined lives with your help?'

He spun to face her, his face white, shaking on his feet.

'You can't,' she told him. 'He died.'

She stood up and walked towards him. He held onto the camera, shaking so much it rattled. She came right up to him, and said:

'He burnt.'

He turned to look at me.

'Truly?' he asked.

'Truly,' I promised. This time his knees did buckle, and he sank to the floor, head in hands. Ruby rushed to his side, but he didn't need help.

'Thank God,' he murmured, and it was a prayer. 'Thank God.' He looked at me. 'Finally met his match, did he?' he said bitterly.

I stayed silent. I didn't know what to say. To claim a victory seemed wrong, considering what it had cost, but I had set this man free of an intolerable burden, it seemed.

'Might have known it'd be you,' he said, as Mary and Ruby helped him back up. 'Let me look at that picture again.'

I gave it to him, and he studied it.

'Yeah, I took a few of these,' he said. 'Been doing it about five years.'

'How many?' Mary asked. He shrugged.

'Dunno. Lady always took the plates with her. But about every six months, I reckon.'

That made perhaps ten boys. How many had she taken? I guessed Robert Sheldon was not the only photographer.

'Did you get her name?' Mary persisted. 'Can you describe her?'

'Oldish,' he said. 'Pretending to be older than she was, do you understand? Walking slow and bending over when I reckon she could move fast enough if she wanted to. She wore a veil, and put on an accent, but definitely from London, a posh part.'

'Why you?' I asked.

'Because I don't advertise,' he said. 'I don't keep the pictures to show my skill to other clients. I don't keep anything, and I don't tell. I'm a photographer for those people who like things nice and private. Mistresses and illegitimate children and things like that. It is what I'm known for, really.' His voice trailed off. Of course, all those pictures ended up in the blackmailer's hands – but not any more. He could change now.

'Were they scared, the boys?' Mary asked. He thought for a moment.

'Not scared, but silent,' he said eventually. 'Like they daren't even breathe until she gave them permission. It's not like she hit them, she loved them, I reckon, but like they belonged to her. Like dolls.'

'She never left a name?'

'Never. Though she dropped a letter. She picked it up quick, but I saw the address. It was a hospital ward, in St Barts.'

Mary and I looked at each other. It fitted the facts. We made our thanks and left.

'You,' he called out to me. 'Whatever you call yourself, I owe you. Whatever you want from me, any favour, you just ask, all right?'

I nodded and left.

Back to the hospital then: back to where it began.

THE DEATH BED

Mary was all for going to the hospital right away, but I wanted to wait until six, when the night shift came on duty. The night shift had, after all, been when it all began. I got home to find that Billy had gone out to Regent's Park to find Inspector Gregson, who was searching the area for clues and witnesses. I baked bread all afternoon, and refused to think about why Robert Sheldon was afraid of me – and how I had used it.

We decided to take Grace with us to see Nora. It would give us an excuse to come in the evening, rather than standard visiting hours. As we left, I had that feeling again, that I was being watched. Miranda Logan must still be on the case.

Once we got to the hospital, Grace led the way to the ward. She held a package of sandwiches and a huge slice of lemon cake for Nora, which was our excuse for visiting her. It was odd to be back here. I didn't like it, and I wanted to get away as fast as I could. It was the smell that hit me first, that mixture of sharpness and decay. Bleach and death. It almost turned my stomach, and for a moment I felt as weak as I had when I left. How anyone could stand to work here, or voluntarily be a patient over and over again, I could not understand.

And yet Nora was happy enough. She grasped the point of our deception quickly and asked if I'd like to say hello to my old ward companions. She checked with Sister Bey to see if it was all right. Sister looked up at us with dark, angry eyes.

'I suppose anything is acceptable for the wife and patient of Dr Watson,' she said bitterly, and returned to her logbook.

'How charming of you,' Mary said, without the least hint of sarcasm. 'I know you must be very busy. My husband is very proud of the work done in this ward.'

Sister Bey refused to rise to the flattery. I suppose some people must be immune to charm, but Mary would not be stopped. She stood in front of Sister Bey's desk, and chattered inconsequentially of her duties – which effectively screened me from the Sister.

Eleanor Langham was there, in her usual bed at the end. She scowled when she saw me. There was no hope of conversation there, although she looked calmer than when I last saw her. I merely nodded, and turned to Florence Bryson.

'I am sorry to see you still here,' I said to her. 'I hoped to see you recovered.'

'Oh, I like it here,' she said. 'They take such good care of me.'

'That's very kind of them,' I said.

'He pays them well for it,' she said, laughing.

'Who?' I asked, but she didn't answer. She looked to the bed next to hers that had been Emma's. Now it was occupied by an extremely large woman, wheezing more than breathing. She nodded and smiled, but I doubted she'd be capable of sustained conversation.

'You must miss Emma very much,' I said to Flo, walking closer to her bed. 'The two of you had such long talks.'

'She told me wonderful things,' Flo said, her gaze far away, beyond me. 'Parties and flowers and jewels and lovers. She had such a colourful life. Not like mine. Her life was all red and gold. Mine was all black and grey.'

I stepped a little closer. Was she medicated? It was difficult to tell. Had her eyes always been this unfocused? Had she always been this dreamy? I couldn't remember. I had been in no state to notice when I was here.

'We talked about my son,' Flo said. 'My boy. He was so precious to me. He was the only joy in my life. I was the joy of his life too. He would have done anything for me, he proved that. No one else has ever loved me like he did. He's been dead so long, but sometimes, it's like he's in the room, standing beside me. I can see him.'

I shuddered a little, remembering the boy who had come into this room, and killed, on someone's orders. I didn't think it could be hers. She seemed so vague, and she truly missed Emma, I felt.

'It was a shame she died,' I said, in a low voice. Flo sniffed. Yes, those were tears in her eyes.

'I was so upset that it was her time,' she said to me. 'But it had to happen.'

'Her time?'

'Everyone has a time to die. Doesn't it say that in the Bible?' she said to me. 'She used to have so many visitors, important young men with briefcases, asking all kinds of questions. She just told them it would all be in the book, and sent them away. But then they asked me. I pretended I was stupid, but I'm not. She told me everything.'

'What did she tell you?' I asked.

'Oh, secrets and stories,' Flo said. 'About men we knew. Old men, long dead. But they were so alive, so many years ago.'

'They're not all dead,' I said.

'No, that's what I said.'

'To who?'

'Miranda Logan,' Flo said, as if surprised I had asked. 'She came to visit me. She wanted to know what Emma talked about too.'

'Did you tell her?' I asked.

Flo pulled a face. 'No, I didn't,' she said. She seemed almost childlike in her dislike of Miranda. 'She has an evil face with hard eyes. I didn't like her. She talked to *her* instead.' She gestured towards the end of the room.

'Eleanor?' I asked.

'No, Betty,' Flo said. 'Remember Betty, in the bed by the door over there? She had come back in – her leg wasn't healing properly. They talked for ages. I asked what about later, but Betty kept her mouth shut.'

'She looked smug,' Eleanor called out. 'Like she knew something. Sitting there, knitting, like a good little wife,' she said scornfully.

'Where is she now?' I asked Eleanor.

'She died last night,' she told me triumphantly. 'I suppose you think that's suspicious? You and your suspicious filthy little mind. I suppose you get that from Mr Holmes, always seeing the worst in people.' It had been Eleanor who had the suspicious mind, Eleanor who saw the worst, but as so often with people who don't want to see the worst in themselves, she gifted her worst faults to me. I stepped towards Betty's bed.

'People die in hospital all the time,' I said to myself. 'And she was ill.' How annoying that she should die now, though.

'Oh, she didn't die in that bed,' Eleanor announced. 'She kept complaining that the opening and closing of the bathroom door kept her awake all night. She was moved. She died in that bed over there, by Flo. Pay what little respects you have to that bed.' She pointed, and I turned to look.

She was pointing at the end bed, the one where Emma had died. The one where the woman had died on the first night I was there. The implication hit me and my knees buckled.

Mary rushed over to me, as I whispered, 'Oh God, you were right. It's not about Emma. It never was.'

302

SEEING IT ALL
FROM A DIFFERENT ANGLE

I felt sick. I know I went pale. As I stumbled, I fell against the Sister's desk. She looked up, startled, and I saw she had been writing in her own private logbook. I saw the book open before me, I saw what she had been writing, I saw it all in the glare of her lamp in that brief moment. Then she slammed the book closed as Mary held me up, and guided to me towards the bed.

'Not there!' I whispered urgently. She took me outside, to the corridor, and sat me on a chair there.

'I'll be all right,' I insisted.

'You're not as well as you think you are,' Nora said, following us. 'You're faint; put your head between your knees.'

'I have no intention of doing something so undignified,' I protested.

'She just needs some air,' Mary said, crouching in front of me. 'Just some peace and quiet.'

Nora looked at me, nodded, and went back into the ward. Mary looked up at me.

'I heard,' she said softly. 'I heard what Eleanor said about where Betty died. This changes everything, doesn't it?'

I nodded. Mary, bless her, understood. She shifted to a

more comfortable position, though still on the floor, and continued to talk in a low tone.

'We've been assuming that Emma was the target all along, a planned murder, for appropriate reasons.'

'It seemed logical,' I agreed.

'But now, it seems far more likely that Emma's death was just one of many. That the targets were just whoever was in that bed, regardless of who they actually were.'

'Totally illogical,' I said, 'which makes this impossible to solve.'

'What do you mean?' Mary asked.

I got up and began to walk up and down. I felt I needed to move.

'What I'm about to tell you, you mustn't tell John,' I insisted. 'He wouldn't want John knowing.'

'Who wouldn't want him knowing?'

'Mr Holmes,' I said, 'and his search for the Ripper.'

It had been two days after the double event, the deaths of Catherine Eddows and Elizabeth Stride on the same night. Mr Holmes had gone out as soon as he heard the news. He had combed Whitechapel. He had even seen the mysterious inscription above Catherine Eddows' body before it was washed off. He had seen all the clues. He had hunted down everyone. He and every other amateur and professional detective in London had saturated Whitechapel, and yet they had found nothing.

He had come home tired, cold and hungry. It was the one and only time I saw him unshaven. I had insisted that instead of going up to his room, where I knew he would brood, he come to the kitchen and eat. He had hesitated in the doorway, as if unsure, but I had hurried him in and sat him down, and placed beef sandwiches before him, and a large treacle tart. Heart-warming food. He ate, and then began to talk. Not to me, really, but just out loud. I might have been the sideboard for all the notice he took of me.

'There is no logic to it,' he said. 'No reason for these particular women, seemingly no motive behind it, except for pleasure in the act.'

'Surely a man like that is obvious to all,' I said. I might be a sideboard, but that was no reason to be silent. I felt I had the right to take on John's role, just this once.

He shook his head.

'A man – or a woman – can find it very easy to hide their perverted pleasures by day as they hunt at night. Stevenson was right about that. Everyone assumes a man like this must be a gibbering idiot, or a butcher, or a surgeon. I think him to be a very ordinary man, unassuming, meek even. How else could he get close to these women when they are terrified of every man?'

'There are no clues?'

'Oh, there are plenty of clues!' he cried. 'Mysterious chalk marks, the peculiarity in the way the bodies are cut, the eyewitnesses seeing men in top hats, or carrying black bags, here, there and everywhere. But none of the clues leads anywhere!'

'So the only way to catch him would be . . .'

'To catch him in the act. Which is inevitable. His actions take a long time, and the streets are packed. He must be seen by someone. And yet he slips by us, again and again.'

He looked at me and saw me then.

'I fear I may fail,' he said. He would never have said that to John.

'You have failed before,' I reminded him.

'But it has never mattered so much before. To fail in the case of fraud or robbery is one thing – to fail to find such a horror as this . . . this is unforgivable.'

'You may succeed.'

He looked up at me with haunted eyes.

'I cannot. I rely on logic. One action must follow another, and all actions have a reason and thus I am led to the correct solution. But there is no logic here. There is no sane reason. How can I catch a killer who has no logic?'

I finished telling my story to Mary.

'John doesn't know he hunted for the Ripper,' Mary said.

'I know. Please don't tell him,' I asked. 'I don't think Mr Holmes wants him to know. I don't know why. He only asked me never to tell John.'

'I won't. Thank you for telling me.'

'It's the same, do you see?' I asked. 'There is no logic here. When we thought Emma died because of secrets she knew, that made sense. We had a path to follow. Even the woman looking after the Pale Boys made sense – she was using them as assassins. But now – dying because of the bed you sleep in? And using the boys for what? There is no sense.'

I sat down again, peering into the ward.

'Not necessarily,' Mary said. 'You're assuming their logic is the same as yours. They have reasons, just not the same reasons we would have. That particular bed has certain qualities. It's in shadow. It's near a door.'

'I wonder if whoever planned it liked it because they could see that bed clearly?'

'They liked to watch it done, you mean?' Mary asked, looking up at me. 'Why?'

'Proof of something: loyalty, love.'

'You'd think someone would notice all the deaths in that bed,' Mary said, standing up.

'Someone did,' I pointed out. 'Nora.'

As if in answer to her name, Nora came out.

'Are you well?' she asked me.

'Quite well,' I replied. 'Tell me, how long have you noticed the deaths in that bed?'

'There haven't been that many,' she said. 'Statistically, it's not that high a discrepancy. It was more of a feeling than actual numbers. I was foolish to be disturbed by them.'

'You weren't foolish,' Mary insisted.

'Well then, there have been about five in the last year, before Emma Fordyce's death. That number is not high on a ward like this . . .'

'But high for one bed,' Mary finished for her.

'How long has Florence Bryson been a patient here?' I asked.

'Flo?' Nora questioned, frowning. 'Well, she's in and out, so about a couple of years, all told. The same as Eleanor Langham.'

'What about Sister Bey?' Mary asked. 'She's not a nice woman. She wouldn't let me anywhere near that logbook of hers.'

'A few years,' Nora said. 'But she's not the one who hit me.'

'No, it was probably a boy,' I said. 'I'll explain later.'

Nora left, puzzled.

'We can't discount Miranda Logan,' I said. 'She was here yesterday. She could quite easily sneak in and out of hospital.'

'I suppose so, but why would she?' Mary asked, but I wasn't listening. I was staring through the open door of the ward. The lights were on, shining full on everyone's faces. Flo was bent over the newspaper in her hand. In front of her, Ruth Bey was bent over the logbook on her desk. I had seen what Ruth wrote, all night, every night. Not notes, or thoughts. Gibberish. Not even words, but just shapes and lines and circles. Utterly meaningless. Her logbook was full of nonsensical shapes.

'Look,' I said to Mary. I hadn't seen it before. Their colouring was different – but perhaps Flo too had once had black hair. But now, in the same attitude, highlighted by the gaslight, I could see they had exactly the same nose and mouth and throat and ears. Exactly the same profile. Mary looked back at me.

308

Not one, but two. Two could do this together. Two bound together by blood. By family.

'I think I could swear,' she said, 'that Florence Bryson and Ruth Bey are mother and daughter.'

AN OLD STORY

'Why are we going to Fleet Street?' I asked, as the cab hurried along, as fast as it could. It was dark now, and damp, and it seemed very late at night, though it could only be seven, at the latest. London nights drop fast in the winter. I looked through the window at the gas lamps, and saw the first of the Christmas lights were beginning to appear in shop windows. Christmas: I'd have to start planning for that soon. I should have started earlier, it wasn't long to go now.

'Lillian Rose said something about the combination of the names Florence and Ruth,' Mary said. 'Don't you remember?'

'Vaguely,' I said. I was quite tired now, but unable to stop just yet. 'You think it was something in Patrick West's archives?'

'I think she's been through the whole thing, learning the master's style,' Mary said. 'I know the names are probably different, but if we mention Florence, and a daughter Ruth, and a dead son . . .'

'About twenty years ago,' I said. 'Making Ruth about thirteen or fourteen.'

'Then maybe that's enough to trigger a memory for Mr West,' Mary said eagerly. 'I bet it's one of his crime reports.'

I sat back. There was no stopping Mary when she was like this. I had tried before and she had merely thrown herself into deeper danger. We'd have to go on; I had no choice. I couldn't stop Mary now, or let her go on alone.

Which was a blatant excuse. I was as eager to find out the facts as Mary was. I looked out of the window and started to hum Christmas carols under my breath.

We pulled up outside the alley that led to the court where Patrick West lived. As we did, I felt rather than saw someone brush by us.

'Miranda?' I said quickly, but the figure had disappeared into the crowds.

'What's wrong?' Mary asked.

'I think Miranda Logan is following us,' I said to her, as we walked into the court. It was pitch-dark, lit by a single fading lamp, and we felt our way as much as saw it.

'Good, she may be useful later on,' Mary said. 'Which door was it?'

'The blue one. Look, Mary,' I insisted, 'if we discover the truth, we go straight to the police with it. Inspector Gregson, at the Yard.'

'All right,' Mary said, as she pulled at the doorbell, but she didn't look at me.

'No, Mary, I mean it,' I said, turning her to face me. 'This can't be like last time.'

'It wasn't so bad . . .' she started to say.

'Really! Have you actually forgotten what happened?' I snapped, just as the door opened.

Lillian Rose stood there, and she had obviously heard what I said. I waited for her to pass a remark, but she smiled an odd smile and stood aside to let us up the stairs.

'I promise,' Mary whispered. 'Straight down the Strand to the Yard, I promise.'

Patrick West sat in his chair, hand on his stick, waiting for us to enter. The room was lit by a flickering fire. It seemed unreal, a room from a ghost story, waiting for the horror to start. Lillian came in behind us and closed the door.

'Mrs Hudson. Mrs Watson,' Patrick West said. 'More information?'

Mary stepped forward eagerly.

'This could save a life,' she said, 'many lives. And solve a mystery.'

Mr West merely waved his hand.

'You know my price,' he said. 'Information for information. What have you to give me?'

Nothing. I had nothing that I wished to tell him. No secret would be safe with him. It would be told, sooner or later, with that dark little twist of his that made every action suspect.

'I owe them,' Lillian said from behind me. She didn't say anything else, but Mr West moved his hand towards her.

'Then we must pay our debts,' he said. 'Ask.'

'About twenty years ago,' Mary said, looking at me for confirmation that she was right, 'I think there was a case where a boy died. He would have been between ten and sixteen.'

This was the age of the boys that were being taken.

'I'm not sure of the names, but I think the mother was called Florence, and there was a daughter, Ruth.'

I still wasn't sure either was guilty, but it was that combination of names that had triggered Lillian's memory last time.

'That's it?' Mr West asked.

'I remember something,' Lillian said slowly. 'Florence, and Ruth, and a boy. There was something, when I was going through your crime archives.'

Mr West waved his stick.

'Your memory is quite exceptional,' he said. 'How very useful. Very well, take them to it.'

There was a dark panelled room, uncarpeted and dusty, groaning with the weight of newspaper, the air thick and choking and sharp with the scent of ink. For a moment I hesitated, remembering the room full of secrets at the blackmailer's house, but Lillian swept in. She was dressed in dark red now, and she looked prosperous and confident. Not a trace of the Whitechapel prostitute was left, not even in her voice. She had reinvented herself utterly in such a short while. It was an enviable skill.

'Down here,' she said, sinking to her knees in front of a pile of yellowed newspapers. 'Help me look.'

There were hundreds of papers, every article Patrick West

had ever written, in chronological order, but with no index. That was apparently one of Lillian's tasks, to catalogue his articles, crime and gossip and whatever else he'd written. Mr West appeared to have spent most of his life as a Grub Street hack, being paid by the word, and so turning out thousands of them.

We read of long-ago scandals of people, some dead, some alive and respectable, the past forgotten. Sir Richard's name was there, in passing, and I could see the clues to his true nature. Lord Howe was there, too, angry and determined, striding across the pages of the past. And here was Emma, flittering in the papers, tempting and delicious, the only woman (or man) that Patrick West treated kindly.

But that was just gossip. We needed the crime. Patrick West had an eye for a secret, and he seemed to find them when the police failed. Murders were his speciality, especially poison. The quiet, secretive deaths, suspected but never proved. He found them all, and side-stepped the laws of libel neatly, always hinting, never saying for certain. There were other deaths, too: dramatic trials, courtroom revelations, deathbed confessions. He wrote well, I had to admit, and I wanted to sit for hours and just read. We were lost in that dim little room, surrounded by the stories of decades of murder and death and lies and secrets. How would we ever find our one case?

But Lillian had a good memory. The blackmailer had relied on her to go into people's houses and sift through their papers and read and remember what she saw, very quickly. It was a skill she had honed to perfection. And luckily for us, the paper we needed was one she had already read. It only took us an hour to find it.

'Here,' Lillian said, handing over a paper to Mary. Mary was covered in dust, and sneezed as she took it. Lillian had somehow remained spotless.

Mary tipped the article towards the faint light and began to read.

'This is a different name,' she said. 'Nabour, not Bryson.'

Lillian shrugged.

'Names change,' she said carelessly. 'Do you think I was born Lillian Rose?'

Mary nodded, and turned back to the paper, reading through for other clues.

'Look at the address, and the ages, and the physical description,' I said to her. 'Well?' I demanded, as she read. 'Is it them?'

Mary's eyes grew wide as she read, and she looked up at me.

'Florence's son . . .' she said.

'Is he not dead?' I asked, reaching out for the paper.

'No, he's dead,' she said. 'He died in prison. He was a murderer.'

THE PALE BOY

No wonder Lillian remembered the case. Over the next hour, we pieced together the story from various articles and court reports, and it was a twisted, disturbing story.

Florence Nabour had two children, Ruth and Edward. Her husband had died soon after Edward was born, and Florence had devoted all her energies into raising her children – or rather, raising Edward. Ruth was neglected and left to run wild, as Edward grew into his mother's darling. They were very close, and barely left each other's side. She kept him indoors, fearful of the dangers of the outside world, and dressed him in perpetual mourning for his father. He was always in black, which looked well on him. She was his pole star, and he hers. She taught him, and nursed him, and cosseted him, and there were even stories that he slept in her bed long past the age he should have had his own.

But of course, such rumours could not be ignored. The local vicar visited, and tried to point out the error of her ways. He took the family under his wing, seeing it as his parish duty, not out of any sense of friendship. By all accounts, he disliked both mother and son heartily, but felt it incumbent upon him to see they lived a 'proper' life. He tried to force her to send Edward to school, to 'make a man of him', in his phrase. He often called, and stayed the night, as their house was remote. One night he argued with her, and brought up the allegations of Florence and Edward's unnatural closeness. He even hinted at incest, and said that he would contact Edward's father's family. He clearly meant it, and he threatened to split them up. But he saw only fear and disobedience in the family. He didn't see the anger. He wasn't afraid. He slept under their roof that night, feeling as safe as he would in his own home.

In the morning, he was dead. The doctor was called, and Florence said the vicar had just had a seizure in his sleep. But the doctor was suspicious, and sent the body for a post-mortem. The verdict was murder by suffocation.

Florence was under suspicion at first, but the boy had been seen sneaking out of his room by a housemaid late at night, and had scratches on his face. He was arrested, and tried.

Florence was devastated, but Edward didn't seem to understand what he had done was wrong. Separated from his mother, he confessed easily. The vicar had been trying to split them up, and so he had killed the vicar. He could see no wrong in what he had done. It was the natural outcome, as he saw it, of someone trying to take him away from his mother.

The case went to trial, where Ruth caused a scene by trying to take the blame. Her own mother had mocked her in court, saying that Ruth would never have had the strength and courage to kill anyone for her sake, and that Ruth had never really loved her.

That was enough. The boy was found guilty. No one wanted to hang a sixteen-year-old boy, though, so he was sent to prison. There were whispers that Florence had talked him into it, and the boy himself, bewildered by the world, inspired some pity. But in that environment, and alone, he soon died.

For a while, Florence and Ruth stayed in the house. But Ruth left, presumably to become a nurse, and Florence was alone. She was known to visit homes where boys had died recently, and tell the grieving mother her own sad story. She saw no guilt in what her son had done. It was only what any boy would do for his mother, she asserted. Eventually, after being chased away from another funeral, she left the area and changed her name, and disappeared into London.

'Quite a story,' I said, once we had worked all this out.

'I bet she never stopped visiting bereaved mothers,' Mary said. 'Suppose she visited Eleanor Langham after she read about the death of her son in the papers, maybe doing nothing more than standing outside the house?'

'And saw the boy in the garden next door?' I asked. 'Perhaps she reminded him of her own boy. She can't have been sane by then.'

'If she ever was,' Mary added.

'I read up on that case,' Lillian said. 'He was seen walking away with a woman all in black. He was wearing black too, out of respect for Mrs Langham's son.'

'So she takes him,' I said, working it out, 'on the spur of the moment. A son all in black to replace her own. But he has a mother he loves, and he wants to go home.'

'He's disloyal,' Mary said. 'He doesn't love Flo. At least, she sees it as disloyalty.'

'And he dies,' I said softly. 'Perhaps it's an accident. Perhaps she was just trying to stop him crying.'

'Perhaps she murdered him, because she's plainly mad,' Lillian said, standing up and smoothing down her skirt. 'But she wants a replacement boy, and one who no one will notice is gone.'

'Street boys,' Mary said. 'Boys from the workhouse. Boys with no parents – or at least, she thinks they have no parents.'

'So she collects her replacements, and makes them her sons,' I said. 'She gives them a home and warmth and food and love, and in turn all they have to do is love her.'

'Prove they love her,' Mary corrected. 'Just like her son did.'

'Perhaps it started with animals,' I said, remembering the blood in the house. 'A sacrifice, just like in the Bible. Abraham and his son, and so on. But then she moved on from the animals. She needed real proof they loved her. Always in front of her, so she could see their love.'

'No one noticed?' Mary asked.

'Of course not,' Lillian said scornfully. 'How many people do you think die on those streets? And if all she's doing is suffocating them, who's going to look closely at that? They'll just think someone died in their sleep, that's all, sell the body to the surgeons and the clothes to the pawn shop and that's done with. No one cares if someone poor and ugly dies. There were always stories about the Pale Boys, don't get caught on the street with them, they'll suck your blood, they'll steal your soul, but not about them being ordinary murderers. No one noticed. It's just another death on the street, and another gang.'

'She's right,' I said. 'No one noticed until Flo was in hospital, and her victims had to be in that bed next to her, where she could see them. Only when it was middle-class women dying did anyone notice.'

'Do you think Ruth knew?' Mary asked.

'I think Ruth has been protecting her mother for years. I think she's even given up on her career to look after her mother. I think maybe she's even been the one arranging for her mother to be housed in her own hospital ward.'

'Why?' Lillian asked. 'Her mother abandoned her and mocked her.'

'Mother's love,' Mary said gently. Mary's mother had died when she was very young. 'It makes people desperate. They'll do anything to earn it.'

'It's supposed to be given, not earned,' I said, as I stood up. 'Do you think it's too late to go to the Yard?'

'Wait – why kill the boys?' Mary asked. 'She killed them with love, so she wasn't angry, but why?'

'How old were the boys who died?' Lillian asked.

'Fifteen, sixteen, roughly around that age' Mary replied.

Lillian smiled, a crooked half-smile. 'Well, there's a good reason,' she said. 'What do boys do at that age?'

We shrugged.

'Notice girls,' Lillian said, as if we were idiots. 'She stopped being the centre of their world the minute a pretty girl smiled at them. That's why she killed them. They loved someone else.'

A MOTHER'S GLORY

Lillian let us out, reminding us that we were now even. Mr West called after us that if we ever had an interesting story to tell, we should come to him.

We were still dizzy with discovery when we reached the street. Fleet Street was crowded and noisy. The street was packed with cabs and carriages, head to tail, none moving more than a few inches. An omnibus was halted in front of us, the windows steamed up, a pile of dung steaming gently behind the horse. It had obviously been there for a while. Dogs nipped between the exhausted horses, snatching at bits of dropped food. Men hurried down the street, too busy to step round Mary and me, knocking us aside. It was a cacophony of noise and smells and people, but that was London for you.

'It's not much,' Mary objected, when I insisted we go to the Yard. 'Really, it's only a theory.'

'It's a very workable theory that could easily be proved,' I said, looking around for a cab. 'I suspect that, confronted, either Florence or Ruth would confess. They are not exactly stable. Where are all the empty cabs?'

'It's the fog,' Mary said. The day had been cold and damp,

and now night-time was here, the fog had settled all around us. It was a true pea-souper, thick and choking, winding tendrils settling around the gas lamps, other people nothing but shapes that loomed out at us and then disappeared. 'It'll be quicker to walk to the Yard. Will you be all right to walk all that way?'

Well, no, I wanted to say. It had been a long day, I was very tired, my stomach hurt, I was hungry, my legs felt weak and I just wanted to go home. It could wait until tomorrow. I didn't need to go to the Yard tonight. I could just plead illness, and catch the train home.

'I shall be fine,' I said.

I didn't mind the fog. Mary and I were hardened Londoners, and the fog was just a fact of life for us. Scotland Yard was within walking distance from here, and we set off – only to run headlong into someone.

'Wiggins!' I cried. 'What are you doing here?'

'I brought him here,' Billy said, coming out of the fog. 'I figured you were either at the hospital or here.'

'Lucky guess,' Mary said, smiling at the boys. Wiggins looked very serious.

'Deduction,' Billy said, smiling back.

'Do you know?' Wiggins asked earnestly. 'Who's been killing the boys?'

Street boys, boys he might have known, boys he could have looked after. Boys he'd dismissed as a fairy tale.

'Yes,' I told him. 'We're going to the Yard to speak to Inspector Gregson now.'

'Well, tell me on the way,' Wiggins said. ''Cos I need to know.'

We set off, Mary telling the story to the boys on the way. I followed slightly more slowly, tired now. The work was done, the excitement was draining away, and I just wanted to be in front of a warm fire with a cup of tea.

A couple of times I looked back to see if Miranda Logan was still following us. I wish she'd make herself known. I could tell her she was right. I wanted to know why she suspected Flo.

It took a long time to tell the boys, and we were on the Strand and almost at Charing Cross before we realized our way was blocked. Several carts and carriages had run into each other in the fog, and boxes of apples and barrels of fish had split open and spilled over the street and pavement. A harassed police constable was trying to impose order as people darted to and fro snatching up the food. It was chaos. We couldn't go any further.

'Down 'ere.' Wiggins gestured. 'We'll go by the river and up White'all.'

It was a perfectly ordinary street leading down to the river, well lit and well used – Villiers Street. I knew it. But in the fog, London becomes a strange city, every sound deadened, every light dimmed. Even those of us who are used to it can feel unsettled. I felt unaccountably nervous as we walked down the street until we reached the Embankment. I could hear the river lapping up against the high stone wall, though I could not see it. The fog was dispersing a little now, and I could just see a few feet in front of me. And there it was again, that prickling sensation in the back of my neck.

'We are being followed,' I insisted. 'I keep seeing someone behind us. Come out, Miranda!'

Instead of Miranda Logan, a boy stepped out of the mist. He was tall and slim, all in black, and his blond hair lay damply against his head. He didn't speak; he just smiled, and waited.

The Pale Boys did not travel alone. I had been so careful. I had insisted that Mary make no rash moves, I had insisted we go to the police, but here we were, trapped again, facing the villain again, no way to escape, yet again.

Beside me, Mary looked round, trying to peer into the fog. Wiggins stepped in front of me, curling his hands into fists.

'Billy,' I said quietly. 'Can you find Scotland Yard from here?'

'I can,' he confirmed. Another boy stepped out, younger, stockier, with thick black hair. He didn't smile.

'Then run, as fast as you can, find Inspector Gregson or Lestrade or anyone and get them here.'

Billy looked quickly at Wiggins, who nodded. Billy, always a fast runner, darted between the two boys. The blond one merely watched him go, but the black-haired one grabbed for him. Wiggins pulled the boy round before he could catch Billy and thumped him across the face. The boy back-handedly slapped him, as Billy ran away into the fog.

'Wiggins, no,' I called. 'You can't fight all of them.' He grunted, wiping the blood from his mouth, and ran back to me. We took advantage of the disturbance and ran ourselves, along the Embankment, down the river, anywhere, away from these boys.

But I couldn't run. My breath came fast and sharp and I felt the wound in my belly tear and rip and the blood come. Deep inside something twisted and hurt. I felt the dampness spread across my belly. I gasped, and held my hand up to my dress. I was bleeding – but my dress was black, and it was dark. No one would know. I could not run – but I would be damned if I would let them know that. I stopped, held my head up, and walked back to the boys.

'Run!' I hissed at Mary. But she and Wiggins turned back to me.

'You stay, we stay,' Mary insisted.

'Even if it is a bloody stupid idea,' Wiggins added. As he spoke, three more boys came out of the fog around us. We wouldn't have been able to run very far, just enough to make the chase interesting for them.

Just five boys. Small, slim boys.

Boys who weren't quite normal. Boys whose minds had been twisted and damaged. Boys who had killed. Boys who were proud of their killing.

Boys who carried knives. The knives didn't shine. They were already stained with blood. Someone else had already died tonight, and now they were here for us.

They teased us, like cats taunting mice. They darted

forward and waved a knife, then laughed when we winced. They blocked our path, and left another one open. They were herding us.

'If they want you, they have to come through me,' Wiggins said. 'No matter 'ow many there are.'

'Oh, they will,' she said, walking towards us. Florence Bryson. Not the chatty, vague, friendly woman in the hospital bed now. She walked tall and proud, her head high. I could see her boot-button black eyes, like a doll's eyes, almost lifeless, disturbing in their glee.

'My boys don't let anyone stop them,' she cooed. 'My boys do as they're told, and they like to do it. They'll do anything I want for me, won't you?'

She looked round at them. They nodded, some eagerly. The smallest one stepped closer to her and smiled shyly at her. The tallest one, the blond, never took his eyes off me.

'You are going to die,' she asserted. 'All of you, because that is what I want. Unless you want to come with me?' she asked, holding her hand out to Wiggins. The boys accompanied her as she came closer and stationed themselves around us. By the river here, no one could see us, or disturb us. There was no one to rescue us until Billy got to Scotland Yard. 'I can give you such a good life,' she said to Wiggins. 'Warm bed, warm food, and a mother.'

'No, thanks,' Wiggins said shortly. 'Got all I want.'

She looked at me, and smiled. One boy flashed forward with his knife, and caught Mary's skirt. Wiggins growled at him, but the boy just laughed. Another pulled at Wiggins' sleeve, but he didn't make the mistake of letting himself be drawn away. He stepped back, in front of me, panting, afraid, but never leaving his post.

'You've failed,' Flo said to me. 'I just want you to know that, before you die. You thought it was Eleanor Langham, didn't you?' she asked, as if inviting my praise.

'You've been directing me that way,' I said. Little hints dropped here and there, the trail left for me.

She shrugged. 'It could have been her,' she said. 'She fits the bill, as they say, but then again, so do you. Once they knew it wasn't her, I'd have blamed you next. Why do you think I rented your old house? That was quite a useful little find. You could have made such a convincing killer.'

That hit a little too close to the mark for me.

They had started to hum, a low sound, barely there, just enough to unnerve us. One laughed, and the other wiped his knife on his sleeve. They were pressing closer, surrounding us, and we had no escape. They were tense themselves now, blood lust up, waiting to be let off the leash and take their prey. Their knives didn't hang by their sides any more, they held them up, in front of us, waiting, five knives for one boy and two women, one of whom was already bleeding. The blond boy glanced at Flo and frowned. He was ready to kill us. He wanted to. He stepped closer. He might not wait. Mary made a grab for the boy closest to her, the youngest, but he stepped back quickly. The other four moved in, flashing their knives at Mary, slashing at her skirts, and her bodice, but never actually touching her. She spun round and round, trying to shake them off, but they darted forward, catching the blades in her clothes, dodging Wiggins as he tried to stop them.

'Enough. You can have her in a moment,' Flo said gently. 'I just need them to understand first. Understanding is very important.'

'Understand what?' I snapped.

'I don't normally do this outside,' she explained, as if making arrangements for tea.

'No, you do murder in empty houses and hospital beds,' Mary retorted. When Mary was afraid, she became angry. 'Why Emma? You liked her.'

'She was in the right bed,' Flo explained. She stroked the cheek of the boy next to her. 'I like to see it done. It makes me feel special, and in that bed, I could see every little struggle. I could see every twitch of everyone who died in that bed. She fought, didn't she? Well, she was strong, not like you, Mrs Hudson. You'll fall at the first stab. Don't think I don't know you're bleeding. I can smell it.'

She did sniff the air, tracing the scent. All those nights she had lain in that bed, unable to get to her boys, so brought the boys to her, to prove themselves.

'And it was that boy's turn,' she continued. 'Tonight two more have their turn. They've passed all my other little tests. They've shown their loyalty. They just have to do one last little thing, and I'll be their mother forever.'

'Kill us,' Mary said scornfully. 'In the street, like thugs.'

'Kill you,' Flo said, her voice still cooing and soft. It was oddly hypnotic. 'I know what you've been trying to do. You've been trying to separate my darling boys from me. You've been trying to take them away from their mother.'

'You are not their mother!' Mary shouted out, almost pushing past Wiggins in her anger at Flo. He pushed her back. 'Their mothers looked for them and cried for them and wanted them back.'

'That's not true,' Flo insisted. 'Their mothers abandoned them and forgot them.'

'There is one in my home who has been searching for her boy!' Mary insisted. 'You stole her son.'

One of the boys wavered and looked around. Flo smiled gently at him.

'See the lies they'll tell? Just to get you away from me,' she said sweetly. 'But I won't let them.'

The littlest one stared at Mary, but the tall blond one put his hand on his shoulder, and squeezed. The little one winced, but stepped back to Flo.

'These are not your sons,' I told her. 'Your son is dead. These are just substitutes you've gathered together. You'll kill them. You make them kill to prove their love, and then one day, they'll look away from you and you'll decide they've failed and you'll kill them too. You like it, don't you? All that death around you? All this death just to replace your dead son.'

'You'd know all about that, wouldn't you?' Flo said, her voice suddenly becoming biting. 'You lost your son, and now you've got your little band of Irregulars. You're doing just the same as me.'

'She in't,' Wiggins said fiercely. 'She in't ever told us lies, or made us do what we don't want to do. She never made us kill for her. Look at you,' he said, appealing to boys. 'Look what she got you doing. This in't what a mother should be doing. She's treating you like puppets. I bet you daren't even breathe without her permission.' One of the boys lashed out and the blade slashed across Wiggins' face. He gasped, and pressed his hand to the cut. The blood oozed through. He would have gone for the boy that slashed him, but I grabbed him and pulled him back to me. All those blades. All that blood. It had to stop.

I had a weapon of my own.

'They are my sons . . .' Flo insisted.

'Your son died,' I persisted. 'You didn't need to replace him, you have a daughter.'

'Her?' Flo said, with scorn. 'That mewling, whimpering thing? Always begging me to love her and want her. Always pushing my boy aside, thinking I'd want her. Why would I want her when I had my son? When I have sons? She's just a girl. Boys are clever and strong and brave. You must know, Mrs Hudson, a mother's glory lies in her sons.'

We had been followed, I knew that. And not by the boys. I had seen a woman's shape in the fog. Only I had been wrong about which woman it was.

'Did you hear that, Ruth?' I called.

Ruth Bey stepped out of the fog.

A DAUGHTER'S DUTY

Flo did not look disturbed by the sudden appearance of her daughter. She merely looked at her, and then looked away. The boys stared at Ruth. They obviously had no idea who she was, though I guessed they had seen her before. Flo went to the tall boy, and whispered in his ear. He pulled the boy next to him round, and there we were again, faced by the row of knives. There was no way past. The momentary distraction of Ruth's appearance was not enough.

I was losing too much blood. My knees felt weak. Any moment now I'd fall, and then they would be on me. I could show no weakness now, but how long could I hold on? I tried not to show I was leaning on Wiggins.

'Clever and strong and brave, Mother?' Ruth quoted, full of bitterness. 'Was I not all that for you? Think of the things I did for you.'

'It was your duty, as my daughter,' Flo said. She could not look at Ruth, or would not. She only looked at me.

'What did you do?' I asked.

'I hid her,' Ruth said, and now I could hear the tears in her voice. 'She developed this obsession for a new son, lots of new sons, who would be just like my brother, even down

332

to what they'd do for her, and I didn't stop her. I helped her. I hid her and the boys. I found places for her. I brought them food when she could not. I covered her tracks, I even kept my back turned whilst she made her boys kill, God help me; I never stopped her.'

'If you had been a little more convincing in court, they would have believed you killed the vicar,' Flo said to her. 'Then your brother would never have died.'

'I tried,' Ruth sobbed, breaking down and stumbling forward to her mother. Flo merely sniffed in contempt. 'Mother, I tried.'

'Not hard enough,' Flo told her. The boys moved closer to me, unsure of what to do, but ready for orders. Were they beginning to question the lives they had been living? I saw the metal in their hands. How could we stop them? We couldn't. Not by strength alone.

'See!' Mary cried. 'This is how she treats her children,' she said, gesturing towards Ruth, slumped to her knees, sobbing. The boys looked at her, and I could see uncertainty on some of their faces.

'I don't love her,' Flo said, in her cooing voice. 'I love my boys.' The youngest one was looking at Ruth and I could see him wavering, but the tallest boy was still watching us, and I could swear he was enjoying himself. He still wanted our blood. I wondered what he was like before Ruth took him. He seemed the most like her dead son.

'Really?' Mary said scornfully. 'Then where are the older ones?'

Flo froze. That mask of supreme certainty was shaken.

The blond boy stepped towards us. He wasn't going to wait for orders. I felt Wiggins tense beneath my hands, and I felt myself become a little weaker, as more blood dripped from me.

'Older ones?' Flo asked.

'We know you've been doing this for ten years,' I said. 'Where are the boys over sixteen? The boys who became men?'

The older boy stopped. He looked at Mary with an odd expression on his face. He was intelligent, I could see that. Had he wondered that himself? He held out his hand to stop the others.

''Adn't asked that question, 'ad you?' Wiggins jeered. 'Well, go on, ask it now. Where did they go?'

'They went to the country,' Flo said, regaining her self-composure, 'when they grew up.'

'When they started noticing girls, you mean,' Mary said. 'When you realized they weren't going to love you forever. Soon they'd want a wife, not a mother.'

'They went to the country . . .' Flo repeated, as the tall boy turned to look at her. He looked back at me. He was thinking it through.

'Did you see the graves in the park?' I asked him gently. 'Did you hear about the dead boys all in black?'

He spoke for the first time, and it was a shock to hear his voice had not yet broken.

'Why would she do that?' he said to me. 'She is our mother.'

'Why? Is there a girl you like?' I asked him. 'Someone you smile at, and talk to? Has she seen you talking to her? Did she tell you that you could love only her? That you had to stay with her forever?'

He was silent, but I could see on his face that she had. This time, he had agreed.

'Ask 'er,' Wiggins demanded of the boy. 'Go on, ask 'er where the others went.'

The boy turned to Flo.

'Where did the older boys go?' he asked.

'I told you, the country,' she insisted.

'Where?' Wiggins persisted. 'Is this the same "country" that sick dogs go to?'

'They're in the park,' Mary told them. 'Go and see for yourself. It'll be in all the newspapers tomorrow!'

'I love you,' Flo said to the boy, pleading. 'More than anyone else ever could. I'd never hurt you. I didn't hurt them!'

'No, she didn't hurt them,' Mary said, magnificent in her anger. 'It was very painless when she killed them.'

The boy swung round, his knife still in his hand.

'They're dead,' I told him. 'There are five bodies in the graves in Regent's Park.'

'Goodness knows how many elsewhere,' Mary finished. The boy stepped back. The others, uncertain now, followed his lead.

'It's not true,' the boy insisted.

'It is true,' Ruth said, getting to her feet wearily, as if every bone ached. 'I dug the graves.'

335

Ruth looked at her mother with a sense of wonderment, as if finally coming to her senses and realizing what the woman was.

'You never once said you loved me,' she said. Flo ignored her. She only looked at the boys.

'It's not true . . .' Flo said, reaching out to the tallest boy – but he pushed aside her hand.

'You told me I was going to the country soon,' he snarled. 'Was I next?'

'I remember my mother,' the smallest boy said suddenly. 'She sang to me, when she was drunk.'

'She lied to you,' the older boy said. 'She's been lying all along.'

'Yeah, she 'as,' Wiggins agreed. 'You still going to keep doing what she tells you? 'Cos whether she kills you, or you end up swinging at the end of a rope for what she made you do, you're still dead.'

The boy looked at Wiggins, and me, and Ruth, still gazing at her mother with a curiously blank expression. He stared at us, and then Flo. His grip tightened on his knife, and I braced myself.

Then he just left, simply walking away. He didn't speak. He brushed by Flo, as she reached out to him, but he ignored her. He disappeared into the fog.

The other boys looked around at him, and us, and Flo.

'We had mothers?' the little one said. 'Mothers that loved us?'

'I love you!' Flo cried.

'You did,' I told him. The boys looked at each other, then one by one, the boys followed the oldest into the fog.

'No,' Flo begged, as they walked away. 'No, don't leave me, not alone!'

'You're not alone. Your daughter's here,' I pointed out.

'Yes, I'm here, Mother,' Ruth said, in a curiously dead tone. Flo didn't even look at her. She merely stared at me, her black eyes full of hatred.

'You . . . you . . . bitch,' she whispered. 'You stole my sons!' She flung herself at me, fingers crooked into claws, eyes wild. Truth to tell she couldn't have done much harm, even in my weakened state, but before she laid a finger on me, Ruth had grabbed her and pushed her up against the wall, over the river, her fingers wrapped around her mother's throat, squeezing hard.

'No, don't!' I cried out. Wiggins and Mary grabbed her, trying to pull her off, but her grip was too strong.

'You never loved me!' Ruth howled.

'Ruth, this is not the way!' I shouted at her. Her mother choked and scrabbled at Ruth's hands, but she wouldn't let go. 'You'll regret it.'

'I won't,' Ruth insisted, squeezing tighter.

'You will,' I told her. 'It'll haunt you, you'll dream of it; it'll be there everywhere you turn, even if it's the right thing to do, you'll be sorry every second of your life.'

'She should die for what she's done,' Ruth insisted.

'But not here!' I cried, as her mother leaned further and further over the wall. Strangulation or drowning, either would finish her. 'Not by you. It'd destroy your life too! Believe me, I know.'

Ruth looked at me, saw I meant it, then loosened her grip. She let go, and stepped away. Wiggins and Mary pulled Flo back onto the ground. She crumpled into a heap, all the fire and passion gone from her. She was just an old woman now. Ruth looked at her, sobbing and choking.

'Your mother . . .' I started to say.

'I no longer have a mother,' she said. 'I'll tell the police what they need to know.'

'Where are they?' Flo sobbed. 'Where are my boys?'

'Gone,' Mary said. 'You're all alone now.'

In the distance, I heard the police coming towards us.

EPILOGUE

Mrs Turner placed the flowers, small posies of hothouse daisies, on the five graves. The sod had been replaced now, and you could barely tell anyone had ever been buried here, but we would always know.

She turned to me.

'I know they can't tell me if Stephen was one of those boys, or even if he's alive,' she said. Stephen would have been sixteen, and there was no trace of him. 'But this is as close to him as I reckon I'm going to get now.'

'It's good to know someone's thinking of them,' I told her. Some would have had mothers like her. Some of those boys would have had cruel mothers, or mothers who sold them. Some of them would never have known a mother, or only known Flo Bryson's twisted version of motherhood. But Harriet Turner would remember them all.

She smiled and nodded, and walked away. I stayed by the graves. I hadn't visited my boy's grave in years. He wasn't there in the ground. He was in my memory, and if I closed my eyes, I could see him.

Robert: his name was Robert. I couldn't save him, but we had saved others. That mattered.

I opened my eyes. In the distance I could see Mary, who I knew had been to see Inspector Gregson.

'Ruth told them everything,' she said, striding up to me. She took my arm and led me away from the graves.

'How many more boys died?'

'They've found four more,' she said, her face grave. 'They're buried in the gardens of the empty houses they used. There could be more.'

'And how many people did they kill?'

Mary frowned.

'Ruth isn't sure,' she said. The mild winter sunlight shone onto the lake and its single duck. 'She was never around for that part. She says the victims were chosen at random. She thinks they killed mostly street sleepers, and who would notice if they died?'

'It would be easy. Bring them inside on a cold winter night,' I said, imagining the scene. The nice lady, the friendly boys, the invitation to share some soup. 'Then suffocate them, so there's no marks, and dump them on the street again. People would think they died of cold.'

'So why switch to the hospital?' Mary asked. 'It was more dangerous there.'

'Because that's where she was,' I said. 'She had to see the proof, all the time. She couldn't wait. It was the best way to maintain control.'

'Talking to Ruth is odd,' Mary said. 'There's no emotion in her at all now. It's like it all burned away that night by the river. She just recites the facts, like she's repeating a catechism. I don't think she cares about the boys at all, living or dead. I don't think she ever did. Not even her brother.'

'What were the other tests they had to go through?' I asked. We crossed the bridge over the lake, and paused. Somewhere a barrel organ was playing 'Hark the Herald Angels Sing'. It felt very peaceful here now.

'Stealing, at first,' Mary said. 'Most of them were used to that, they were street boys, but she made it into a sort of ritual to prove themselves. They didn't steal for food, or money. Inspector Gregson found a whole pile of trinkets in one of the houses. Then robbery, killing an animal, that sort of thing. That must be what we saw in the house, the remains of an animal-killing ritual.'

The boys had gone back onto the streets. They were survivors, they knew how to hide. They stood out now, their pale faces in black clothes, but their faces would be dirty in a day or two, their clothes torn and ragged in a week or two, and by the time Christmas was over they'd look like any other street boy. Perhaps the lucky few would try to find their mothers. Most likely they'd use the skills Florence had taught them to scrape a living. I could only hope none of them had learnt to like killing. That tall blond boy had a dangerous look in his eyes when he left us.

'I saw Miranda Logan,' I said. She had been waiting outside 221b that morning. I had explained the whole thing to her, and she had nodded and taken notes. She had suspected Flo out of instinct, nothing else, and seemed shaken to find it was not a conspiracy to kill Emma, but something far worse. 'She still won't say who she was working for.'

'Ruth won't speak now,' Mary said. 'She said she's told her tale, and that's the last of it. They think she'll end up in an asylum.'

'And Flo?' I said, looking towards the graves.

'Inspector Gregson wants her to hang,' Mary said. 'His superiors aren't so sure. They think hanging an old, mad woman might not look decent.'

We stood in silence a little while longer, enjoying the feeling of having nothing we needed to do, right now.

'I never knew you felt like that,' Mary said softly. 'What you said to Ruth, about regret, about it eating away at you.'

'There was nothing else I could do at that point,' I said firmly. 'He had to die, and I have to live with the consequences. It's a small enough price to pay.'

For Mary's life. For all those secrets. For myself. I could live with that. The price was high, but the price of failure at that moment would have been higher.

I looked over at Eleanor's house. Was she there? Were Lord Howe and Sir Richard there? They had been lucky. Their nasty, awkward little secrets had been kept, and they were spotlessly clean again. No trace of blame.

'Mad . . .' I said softly.

'What?' Mary asked, surprised.

'I'm thinking about Emma,' I told her. 'If Florence's choice of who died was purely random, anyone who slept in that bed, isn't it convenient that one of her victims was someone so many people wanted silent?'

'I thought that, too,' Mary replied grimly. 'She could choose the time she wanted. She chose us. We weren't random. We were in the way.'

'I swear that I saw Flo knock that drink over Emma's bed,' I said.

'Meaning she was moved to the death bed,' Mary agreed, 'making her a chosen victim. Are you saying Flo wasn't mad?'

'I'm saying maybe someone guided her,' I said slowly. 'Someone influenced her choices, perhaps. My house too. What led her to my old house? Just like the blackmailer.' I bit my lip. I was working my way towards something, but what I could not quite grasp.

'Like the blackmailer?' Mary questioned. 'Are you saying the same hand guided them both?'

'I think I'm saying,' I answered slowly, as I thought it out, 'that through these two cases, and one or two others I've heard about, there is a fine thread, and if we were to follow the thread, we'd find they were all tied together in one knot, and that knot is gently pulling and tugging at a thousand other threads.'

'Yet if we were to grasp the thread, it would snap,' Mary said softly. 'That's quite an image.'

It was, chilling and yet illuminating. It reminded me of something I'd thought before, but couldn't remember when. Twice now I had felt the hand of someone else behind these crimes, and yet perhaps it was my imagination. Perhaps I merely did not want to think that people could be that mad or that evil all by themselves.

'It's just an idea,' I said, shaking myself. 'It really doesn't mean anything. Let's go.' I took Mary's arm in mine, walking towards the park gate.

'Go where?' Mary said, thinking we were off on a grand adventure. Which, in a way, we were. We just didn't know it yet.

'Back home,' I replied. 'Back to 221b Baker Street.'

AUTHOR'S NOTE

This book started in hospital. In May 2013 I was rushed into hospital with terrible stomach pains, vomiting and malnutrition, and was diagnosed with ulcerative colitis. I had to stay in hospital for two weeks for treatment.

I wasn't used to hospital. I don't like sleeping in the same room as other people, I don't like being ill in front of strangers (or friends either, really) and I don't like staying inside all the time. I found the whole experience very difficult, and to deal with it, I asked my friend to bring my paper and pens – I was going to write my way out of this.

I had a lot of time to just lie there and think. I also had a lot of time to get to know the other women in the ward. Some were interesting, some had stories, and some were very annoying. Lying there, I started to think how a murder in a hospital would go practically unnoticed – after all, people are expected to die in hospitals, especially Victorian hospitals. But how would it be done? And who would do it?

I was still in the middle of writing *The House at Baker Street* at the time, but I didn't work on that. I wanted to write about where I was, what I was seeing every day. This was a unique opportunity to see a scene and situation I hadn't seen before. If I was stuck here, I was going to make the most of it.

A hospital ward is an enclosed environment, and one that is always overlooked. People were in and out, administering various medicines, closing curtains, always watching each other. A murder here would be a challenge (and thinking like that is why I'm a crime author).

So I wrote, and as I wrote, I recovered. I came home, and carried on writing, both *The House at Baker Street* and this book. Over the next few years, as I went in and out of hospital and had various treatments, I coped by escaping into the world of Mrs Hudson and Mary Watson. I had their puzzles to solve, whilst the doctors were trying to cure me.

The book was finally completed as I had what I hope is my final treatment for ulcerative colitis (an ileostomy and J-pouch, for the information of my fellow sufferers). Writing this was very cathartic. I hope you enjoy reading it.

ACKNOWLEDGEMENTS

The second book turns out to be just as much hard work as the first! So, thanks are due to the following;

First, my agent Jane, for continuing faith and much-needed support.

My editor Catherine, who really knows her Sherlock Holmes.

Everyone at Pan Macmillan, who are so enthusiastic.

To all my friends, for putting up with my constant drifting away into daydreams when I'm supposed to be talking to them.

The St Bartholomew's Hospital Museum. It's a fantastic place, tiny yet crammed full of knowledge – and the most beautiful Hogarth paintings I've ever seen.

Arthur Conan Doyle himself, of course, for giving me Mary and Martha to play with.

And finally as always, the librarians, teachers and book-sellers. They started this.

THE HOUSE AT BAKER STREET

Behind every detective stands a great woman . . .

When Sherlock Holmes turns down the case of persecuted Laura Shirley, Mrs Hudson – the landlady of Baker Street – and Mary Watson – the wife of Dr Watson – resolve to take on the investigation themselves. From the kitchen of 221b, the two women begin their inquiries and enlist the assistance of the Baker Street Irregulars and the infamous Irene Adler.

A trail of clues leads them to the darkest corners of Whitechapel, where the fearsome Ripper supposedly still stalks. They soon discover Laura Shirley is not the only woman at risk – the lives of many others are in danger too.

As Mrs Hudson and Mary Watson put together the pieces of an increasingly complex puzzle, the investigation becomes bigger than either of them could ever have imagined. Can they solve the case or are they just pawns in a much larger game?

Turn the page to read an extract from Mrs Hudson and Mary Watson's first adventure . . .

FAREWELLS
AND GREETINGS

April 1889, London

If you have read John Watson's thrilling stories, and I am sure you have, you know me best as housekeeper and land-lady to the Great Detective, Sherlock Holmes.

Such a short sentence to write, and yet, oh my, what a wealth of information is there. Such adventures, such stories, such people. And as for me – I did so much more than bustle in and out with the tea. Although to be fair, I did bustle, and there was an awful lot of tea consumed by everyone. And I feel you should know John did make a few mistakes in his stories. He claimed artistic licence, though I feel it was faulty memory. But what people don't know about me is that I had adventures of my own, with Mary Watson, and sometimes other friends and acquaintances, and the occasional enemy, of Mr Holmes. So now it's time I told a few stories of my own . . .

Believe it or not, I was a young woman once. For the first nineteen years of my life, I was Miss Martha Grey: sweet, innocent, and ever so slightly bored. Then, one particularly dull evening, I met Hector Hudson, and I wasn't bored any more. I loved him on sight. He was a soldier, so tall and handsome in his uniform, with dark blond hair, and a special smile just for me that made the lines around his grey-blue eyes wrinkle in a fascinating way. To my delight, he loved me on sight too. He proposed just a week later, and I said yes before he had even finished asking.

We were a love story come true, but unlike most love stories, it did not end with a happy marriage.

It ended with his death.

He was a soldier and we were at war. Six months after our marriage, he died alone, on a blood-soaked battlefield, in some place I had never heard of, leaving me only with his child growing inside me.

But he didn't leave me destitute, like so many other poor widows of the war; Hector provided me with the rent from several properties he had owned in London, which were now mine. Including, of course, 221b Baker Street.

But I didn't go to London then. I stayed in the country with my son. He grew strong and clever and adventurous. He would stride out in the morning and not return till tea, full of tales of what he had done and seen, his pockets stuffed with treasures that he laid on my lap with pride. I know I should have tried to keep him indoors, keep him at his lessons, but he would not be shut up. He would escape into the world, and I did not have the heart to stop him. He looked at me with his father's eyes, full of wonder and joy, and I knew he would grow up to be a great explorer, or writer, or something thrilling and exciting.

Except that he didn't grow up. One day he was tired and stayed indoors, quietly watching me do my work. Poor fool me, I was glad of his company. One week later, he died – his last, great adventure – leaving me behind, as his father had done on that godforsaken battlefield.

I don't want to talk about what my boy's death did to me. Not yet. Not now. I will just say that I could not stay there, where every object, every sound, just the light in the trees, reminded me of what I had lost. I moved to London then. I became a landlady and looked after my properties efficiently, all those rooms in all those houses. All those bright young men and lovely hopeful young women in my rooms became ill and old and bitter. London can do that to some people, when they are alone, and poor, and lose all hope. It's not kind to everyone. London can be cruel. I did not find friends. I did not find love. I did not find my place.

However, I did learn to balance account books and make agreements with tradesmen and haggle for the best prices and everything else that came with running a business. I learnt how to appraise a maid or a tenant on sight, and how to get rid of them too. I learnt how to offset loss with profit, and what was a good investment, and what bad. Whilst Parliament argued over whether women had the mental ability even to own their own clothes, I quietly administered an empire – and no one noticed.

I also discovered cooking. As Hector's wife I'd had

nothing to do except tell the servants what to do for me. As the landlady of all of these properties, I had to be capable of doing any work required, at any time. Therefore, I learnt to do every job of every servant. Cleaning bored me, laundry I loathed, but cooking I loved. Taking the ingredients one by one, all looking so simple, and then combining them and cooking them and using all kinds of secrets to make them into something delicious, I felt to be a form of magic. With all these discoveries about myself I changed and grew and became not Martha Hudson, grieving widow, but Mrs Hudson, formidable housekeeper and successful landlady.

As I got older, I gradually sold all my properties and moved into what I was sure would be my final home: 221b Baker Street. It was a very elegant new building, rising several storeys above the busy street, with a smart black door edged in white woodwork and red brick. There was room for me, and a suite of rooms for a pair of gentlemen, and I settled down for my long and inevitable slide into old age.

The first few men who rented my rooms were nice and polite. They had reasonable hours and required only breakfast and the occasional cup of tea, and kept themselves to themselves. They were the perfect tenants. Other landladies envied me.

But I was so bored.

They didn't need me, they needed an automaton. I did not need them. We were perfect strangers living under one roof.

Then *he* came. On a rainy night in September, he rang my bell and asked if my rooms were still vacant.

He was so tall and thin that at first I thought he was quite elderly. Then he stepped into the light and I saw his face was young and lean, with restless dark eyes. He looked around then smiled and raised his hand, but oddly, as if he was remembering he was supposed to be polite. Those hands were covered in sticking plaster, and his jacket was strangely stained.

He was soaked to the skin, so I invited him in and said I would bring him tea and, in the meantime, he could pop upstairs and view the rooms.

I knew he'd like them. They were nice rooms, though I say so myself. Comfortable, but not shabby, well furnished, with plenty of space for my gentlemen to keep their books and suchlike, with two large bedrooms and all conveniently situated near the centre of London. The question was: would I like him?

When I brought in his tea, I found him standing in the middle of the carpet – the exact middle – looking around curiously, with a certain intensity. I felt sorry for him then. There he was on a rainy cold night, all alone, nowhere to go, wet through, searching for a home. He turned to me as I entered, and took the tea and drank it gratefully. I felt he too had looked at me and studied me and come to his conclusions.

'You keep a very clean house, Mrs Hudson,' he said. I liked his voice. It was low, but expressive and strong.

'I do, and a very private one,' I assured him. He struck me as a man who treasured his privacy. 'I will supply your meals and do your washing and clean your rooms, of course, but I won't impose or interfere.'

He nodded.

'I may have many visitors, Mrs Hudson, in connection with my profession. Will that be an inconvenience?'

'Not at all,' I told him. Though I would regret that in years to come, running up and down those stairs to show in some very odd visitors, at all hours of the day and night. 'May I ask . . . ?'

'A consulting detective. The *only* consulting detective,' he said, with a touch of pride.

'How interesting,' I said politely, as my heart stirred inside me. A detective! The things that could happen in those rooms, what I might see and hear, the kind of people who would visit – the lost, the lonely, the curious, even the dangerous . . .

Excitement, of a sort, even just second-hand – but still, excitement!

'I work with the police, but not for them, so discretion must be guaranteed,' he warned.

'I understand.'

'I have odd habits,' he admitted. He almost seemed to be warning me against allowing him into my home. 'I keep strange hours. I can be very messy. I do chemical experiments that always seem to smell,' he said ruefully. 'There may be noise . . .'

I raised a hand to stop him.

'None of that will be a problem,' I assured him. Oh, how I longed for noise and mess in my pristine home!

'Other landladies have found me difficult,' he warned. 'In fact, I have been thrown out of my rooms three times – the latest just two hours ago.'

'Why?'

He took a breath, determined to admit it all.

'I poisoned her cat. It was entirely accidental . . .'

I burst out laughing. I couldn't help it. His contrite face, his bizarre admission – it was all so ridiculous! He stared at me, and then smiled. I looked up at him, this man tramping the streets searching for a room. He seemed to have no family, no friends to turn to in his hour of need, nowhere to go, never quite fitting in anywhere, no place he belonged to, and my heart just went out to him. He was a lost soul, just like me.

'I don't have a cat,' I told him. 'Do as you will, sir, as long as you pay for any damages.' I was not a soft touch, after all. He nodded, serious again.

'The rent . . .' he started to say. His coat was patched, his bag worn. Consulting detectives were, I imagined, paid by results, and how many results had there been so far?

'There are two bedrooms. I would have no objections to your bringing a companion to share the rooms and the rent.'

'I have no companions,' he said, his face turning from me towards the windows. 'I have not that nature.'

'You can have the rooms half-rent for a month whilst you

find one,' I told him. I could not let him go back alone into that dark and damp night. 'London is full of men looking for a refuge. Perhaps a soldier returned from the wars? They always need a place to stay and an understanding companion. Just be sure and tell them about your bad habits first.'

It was three weeks later that he brought him home. He'd followed my advice and found an ex-soldier, a doctor, with a pleasant smile, a hearty handshake and haunted eyes. He badly needed a place to stay, a task in life and someone to care for him. Although he thought he needed only one of those things.

In the first days they were there together the doctor fixed my kitchen door, the detective had sharp words with the butcher, who had been cheating me (I had suspected as much) and I made them the best meal of their lives.

They sat in their rooms and smoked and talked into the night, and I sat in the kitchen and listened to them through the air vent and there we all were. Sherlock Holmes, John Watson and Martha Hudson. Three lost souls who had found each other.